Royal
Brides

OTHER BOOKS AND AUDIO BOOKS
BY TRACI HUNTER ABRAMSON

UNDERCURRENTS SERIES

Undercurrents

Ripple Effect

The Deep End

SAINT SQUAD SERIES

Freefall

Lockdown

Crossfire

Backlash

Smoke Screen

Code Word

Lock and Key

Drop Zone

Spotlight

ROYAL SERIES

Royal Target

Royal Secrets

STAND-ALONES

Obsession

Deep Cover

Failsafe

Chances Are

Twisted Fate

Royal Brides

a novel by

TRACI HUNTER
ABRAMSON

Covenant Communications, Inc.

For Jen Leigh and Paige Edwards

Thank you for carrying me through the tough times.
Your friendship means more to me than words can express.

Acknowledgments

THANK YOU TO THE MANY people who helped me navigate so many obstacles while writing this book. My thanks to Kanani Cox and Paige Edwards for your editing advice and to my family for sharing me with the computer.

My sincere appreciation goes to the Covenant family for your continual support of my endeavors and for all of your efforts in advancing my career. A special thanks to Stephanie Lacy for your marketing efforts and to Samantha Millburn for juggling so many of life's responsibilities as we journeyed through the final editing process together.

Thanks to the CIA Publication Review Board for your continued service and support, and thank you to Tiffany Hunter for sharing your knowledge of television production. Finally, thank you to all of the readers who have asked me what happens next. I hope you enjoy this next chapter of the royal series.

Chapter 1

JEREMY STOOD SILENTLY IN THE shadows, watching, waiting. He fought against the exhaustion the long hours of preparing for this moment had piled on him. The lack of sleep and the intensive physical training were part of his job as an intelligence officer, and tonight he would have to use all the skills he had gained over the last several months.

Seconds passed, the large house to his left remaining quiet. A dog barked in a neighboring yard, and Jeremy's senses heightened. A movement to his left stirred the air, and his heartbeat picked up.

He was trained for this, he reminded himself. Nine months of learning to blend into his surroundings, where he could watch and observe. Of course, he had acquired numerous other skills as well. He now knew the basics of how to break into a house or disarm a bomb. He could hack computer systems without leaving a trace. He'd even sharpened his shooting skills, though as a farmer's son, he had come well prepared in that area. Hunting was part of his life and always had been.

He was definitely in the hunting state of mind tonight. Three targets, all armed. The house next door was their last known location; a witness had seen them there only four hours earlier. Jeremy had been standing here for more than three.

The first moved into view, but Jeremy forced himself to stay motionless, his breathing slow.

As the figure dressed in black angled past him, Jeremy counted off the pace of the man's steps. Still hidden in the depths of the shadows, Jeremy remained motionless until the man passed him. He timed his first few steps to match his target's and then rushed forward to close the distance between them.

The man in front of him turned a split second too late. By the time he recognized the threat, Jeremy was already upon him, wrapping a hand around the taller man's mouth and using a hypodermic needle to silently sedate him.

As soon as his target was down, Jeremy pulled him behind the nearby shrubbery. Once again, Jeremy settled back into the darkness and waited.

* * *

Noelle Saldera waited until the designated time before she picked up her phone and dialed. Though she had been given King Eduard's private phone number years ago, she always felt awkward using it. After all, he was the king of Meridia. She was merely the daughter of two of his servants.

The phone rang twice.

"Noelle," King Eduard greeted her. "Thank you for calling so promptly."

"Of course, Your Majesty. Your e-mail said it was important."

"Yes. I have a favor to ask of you," he said. "I know you have been working in our embassy in the United States, but I hoped you would be willing to come back to Meridia to help with Prince Stefano's wedding plans. Ultimately I would like for you to stay on and help with Prince Garrett's wedding as well."

"I would be happy to," Noelle said, even though she was torn by the thought of leaving the United States. She had enjoyed the past few months living in Washington, D.C. "When would you like me to return?"

"I have a package I need hand-delivered to Meridia tomorrow," he told her. "I realize I'm not giving you much warning, but if you are willing to courier some documents back to the U.S. in a couple weeks, we can make sure you have sufficient time to get your affairs in order before returning home permanently."

"Of course."

King Eduard went on to detail her travel plans and the timing of when she would be picked up for her flight. It wasn't until she hung up that she was struck by the oddity that the king would speak to her directly about travel plans. Why wasn't his personal secretary or another of his aides handling such details?

Regardless of the reasons, Noelle had some packing to do. In less than eighteen hours, she would be on a plane flying home to Meridia.

* * *

Two down. One to go. Jeremy had hoped the last man would come to him, but that would have been too much to ask.

A light flickered on in the house as though inviting Jeremy to come inside.

Leaving his hiding place and the two men he had sedated, Jeremy skirted the privacy fence and headed for the house. His first instinct was to approach the back door, the farthest point from where the light had come on. If he did that, though, he would leave the front entrances completely unguarded.

The vehicles in the garage concerned him the most, and he shifted his direction, opting for the side door leading into the three-car garage. He checked for alarms and booby traps before picking the lock. Fourteen seconds later, he turned the knob and slipped inside.

Even though he was accustomed to the darkness outside, he could barely make out the shape of the car closest to him. He took several tentative steps forward, realizing he would need his flashlight to navigate the path to the house door. He was reaching for his pocket when he heard the doorknob turn.

His reach instantly shifted, and his fingers closed around the handle of his pistol. His weapon was already in hand and aimed at the new arrival when the backwash of light allowed him to identify the threat.

Even though he could see the gun in the other man's hand, as well as his features, Jeremy hesitated a split second before letting his training kick in.

He fired two shots, and instantly the garage lights flipped on.

"You're still hesitating before you shoot."

Jeremy lowered his weapon. "I know."

The man Jeremy had previously considered his target now stared at him, his own gun lowered. Randall had been Jeremy's primary instructor since he had joined the CIA, and the edge to his voice made Jeremy wonder if he was going to have to undergo this final training exercise a second time.

"You chose the correct entry point to the house. Your concealment location outside was well chosen." Randall stepped closer. "But you have to learn to trust yourself. If you're in the field and a firearm is required, you have to be willing to shoot."

"Logically that makes sense, but I don't seem to be able to make myself react more quickly."

Randall slapped a hand on Jeremy's shoulder. "Trust me, when you think your life is really in danger, you'll shoot."

"Hopefully I'll never have to find out."

"That's always the hope," Randall agreed. "Come into the house. I have a delivery I need you to make."

"A delivery?" Jeremy repeated. "Is this another training exercise?"

"Not this time. This request comes from the director."

"The director?"

"Of the CIA."

"Forgive me, but how would Director Palmer even know who I am? I've only been with the agency for nine months."

"I don't know why you came to his attention, but my instructions are very specific." Randall picked up a box off the kitchen table and handed it to Jeremy, along with a paper that had been hidden beneath it. "Here are the details. You need to be in Maryland by dinnertime."

"At least I'll have time to get some sleep first." Jeremy looked down at the paper. His eyebrows shot up when he read the information contained there. Surely there must be some mistake.

He looked back at Randall, analyzing his demeanor, searching for any understanding in his expression. When he saw none, he simply nodded at Randall. He didn't know why he was being sent on this errand, but perhaps he would find some answers when he made his delivery.

Chapter 2

KING EDUARD SHIFTED ON THE couch beside his wife and prepared to hold court in his sitting room. Both of his sons sat on matching love seats across from them, each accompanied by the woman he intended to marry. Janessa Rogers, the fiery American spy, was the perfect companion for Garrett. Bright, observant, and adaptable, she continued to utilize her language and people skills well while preparing for her new role as princess. Ultimately he expected her to also play a key role in working with Meridia's intelligence service.

Alora DeSanto, Stefano's fiancée, exuded a sense of serenity and had become his eldest son's anchor in his ever-changing world. She too had a background working with the Central Intelligence Agency, her association with Janessa resulting in her introduction to Stefano. Widowed four years earlier, she and her two sons had given Stefano an instant family right after he learned he suffered from Merid's syndrome, a rare disease that had plagued the royal family for generations. The symptoms were so minor they were nearly undetectable, with one exception: infertility.

"Father, is everything all right?" Stefano asked when everyone was settled.

"Yes, but I think it's time we make some changes." Eduard saw the questions in his future daughters-in-law's eyes. "Our family has gone through a lot of challenges recently, and I feel the time has come for us to take a more proactive role in preventing future issues. Enemies of the crown have used Janessa's nationality and religion against us. Eventually someone will take note that Alora is also a member of The Church of Jesus Christ of Latter-day Saints."

Stefano shifted forward in his seat and took Alora's hand in his. "You're worried that someone will find out I have Merid's syndrome, that our citizens will protest when they find out I can't provide them with an heir."

"An heir who would be a member of the Meridian Church," Garrett added.

"That truth, or at least the result of it, will come out eventually. Given time, I believe our citizens will adapt," Eduard said. He glanced over at his wife, gathering courage before continuing. "I'm concerned about the possibility of a more immediate threat."

Awareness lit Janessa's eyes. "You're worried about my career. My past."

"Yes," Eduard said. "Your role within the CIA and Alora's former work there pose a real threat to the very fabric of our monarchy if revealed to the public."

"What is it you are asking, Father?" Garrett asked.

"It's time for Janessa to resign from the CIA and for Alora to sever ties with the agency." Eduard expected resistance from Janessa—she was often headstrong and willful—but he was relieved and somewhat surprised by her acceptance.

Janessa glanced at Garrett, a silent communication passing between them before she turned back to Eduard. "I've always known this day would come. My work overseeing security at the new U.S. naval base is winding down, and I'm already receiving my communication from the CIA through Levi Marin."

"That's another thing I wanted to speak to you about," Eduard said in regard to Janessa's coworker. "I would like to ask Levi to work in the palace until after Stefano and Alora's wedding."

"For what purpose?" Janessa asked. "His cover is well established working in security at the royal chateau."

"I want his expertise here in Calene to oversee security for the wedding. Officially he will be promoted to head of security at the palace," Eduard said.

"What about security at the naval base? The bombing at the administrative offices only happened a few weeks ago. Clearly the perceived danger that such an event might repeat itself has people there rattled."

"I spoke with Director Palmer at the CIA, and he informed me that your government has hired a private security contractor to augment the staff for the next year until the base is completed." Eduard let that information sink in before continuing. "In the meantime, any necessary communication with the CIA can go through Levi or through the embassy. If we have anything too sensitive to go through normal channels, Director Palmer assured me he can send a message through back channels."

"What back channels?" Janessa asked. "Once I'm out of the game, those options disappear."

"You're forgetting about Noelle."

"Who's Noelle?" Alora asked.

"Noelle Saldera," Janessa said. "She stood in as my double when we needed to make it look like I was leaving the country a few months ago. She's been staying with my sister since then and working at the Meridian embassy in Washington, D.C."

"If it becomes necessary, Noelle can courier information back and forth between the U.S. and Meridia," Eduard said.

"That's a great idea," Janessa said. "I would recommend chartering a plane for her, though, so sensitive material won't have to go through airport security or customs. Anything too sensitive to send via diplomatic pouch shouldn't be on a commercial airline."

Eduard nodded. "I've taken that one step further. From now on, Noelle will be flying on one of the family's private planes."

"It sounds like you've thought of everything," Janessa said.

"I hope so," he said. "There's another thing you all need to be aware of. After speaking in depth with my brother, I have agreed to protect the information that he too suffers from Merid's syndrome."

"What about Philippe? Does he know Uncle Elam isn't his biological father?" Garrett asked.

"No. No one does except those of us in this room, Elam and Victoria, and Dr. Casale, our family physician."

"I'm surprised you agreed to this, considering the way Uncle Elam betrayed us," Stefano said, referring to recent events that had nearly torn their family apart. A victim of blackmail, Elam had unwittingly found himself in the middle of a terrorist plot. "You were more than generous in allowing him to pay his debt through service rather than in a jail cell."

"He made many poor choices, but the fact that his blackmailers have been brought to justice will suffice. If Philippe's parentage eventually comes out, we will deal with it then." His voice became stern as he added,

"I want nothing more than to see all of you happily married, but let me be clear. Janessa and Alora's ties to the CIA are the number-one issue that could topple this country. After today, I don't want any mention of your former careers to anyone outside this room."

Janessa and Alora looked at one another, and both women nodded.

"We understand," Alora said.

* * *

Noelle stood beside the window of Mary's apartment and watched the cars passing by. She loved all she had learned here, experiencing the richness of the American culture in Washington, D.C., improving her English while she helped Mary with her new baby. More than anything, though, she loved her newfound religion.

When Janessa had asked her to come to the United States as a favor, Noelle had never imagined her life would be forever altered. Her ancestors had been in the service of the royal family of Meridia for generations, but they had belonged to the Church of Meridia even longer. Her time spent living with Latter-day Saints and reading a single book had changed her in a huge way. She hoped and prayed her family would accept her for the woman she had become.

Of course, one of the royals was Mormon now. Prince Garrett, Janessa's fiancé, had joined the Church this past summer, and it appeared that his family had accepted his decision.

"Are you ready to go?" Mary asked from across the room, her three-month-old daughter in her arms.

Noelle turned. "I think so."

"I wish you could stay longer. We're all going to miss you." Mary settled into the rocking chair facing the window and nodded down at her daughter. "Especially Lindsay."

"I wish I could stay longer too."

"I still can't believe the royal family is sending the king's private jet to pick you up."

Noelle didn't mention the reason for her special treatment. She didn't know why she had been chosen as a courier, but she was well versed in security as well as the procedures for protecting the royal family and the information that flowed in and out of the palace in Meridia. Her fascination with intelligence work only made her that much more intrigued with her new role.

"I also can't believe you're going to be in the middle of planning two royal weddings," Mary continued.

"In less than a year," Noelle added. She had lived her whole life at the royal chateau, the beachfront estate where the royal family spent their summers. The ten years between Prince Stefano and her had kept her firmly in the younger-sister category rather than the playmate category her older brothers had been a part of.

She thought of the opportunities that could arise from her involvement in such a momentous occasion and was annoyed with herself that she wasn't looking forward to working with the wedding planner Prince Stefano and Alora had selected. Floria was known to be difficult. Noelle enjoyed working with the details of various events, but she preferred the kind of challenge she would have today, one that went beyond caterers, music, and table decorations.

Bringing herself back to the present, she spoke to Mary once more. "At least I'll be back to visit in a couple weeks."

"You didn't tell me that."

"I thought I had. King Eduard mentioned it when he called and told me I need to bring a package home. I guess courier duties are part of my new job."

"Well, whatever the reason, it will be nice to have you back," Mary said. "Waiting to see you until Janessa's wedding next summer is too long."

"I agree. Lindsay is going to be so big by then."

A knock sounded at the door. Noelle skirted the three suitcases stacked beside her and pulled open the door. A uniformed chauffeur in his fifties stood on the doorstep. She smiled warmly, immediately thinking of her father. "My bags are right here."

"I'll take care of them." He stepped inside to retrieve the first two. He was loading them into the trunk when another vehicle pulled up behind the limousine. Noelle glanced at her watch.

She saw a man step out of the truck and retrieve a package from the front seat. This must be the package King Eduard had told her to expect. Part of her wondered if it was the importance of the package that had caused the royals to send her the private jet or if it truly was their desire to show their gratitude for her willingness to return to Meridia earlier than expected. Since the contents of the package were assuredly above her security clearance level, she doubted the answer to that question would be forthcoming.

Noelle shifted her attention from the package to the man holding it. He was just under six feet tall, his reddish-brown hair cut short. He offered a casual greeting to the chauffeur on his way to the sidewalk and continued up the steps to Mary's open front door. His inquisitive green eyes took her in as he approached.

"Is Mary here?"

"Yes, she's inside."

"Jeremy?" Mary asked, excitement in her voice. She stood and quickly crossed the room. "Jeremy! What are you doing here?"

"I have a delivery for someone named Noelle."

"That's me," Noelle said, surprised that Mary would be so excited to see a courier.

"Noelle, this is my brother Jeremy. Jeremy, this is Noelle Saldera."

Janessa's brother. Perhaps the package wasn't related to intelligence files as she had suspected but instead was a personal delivery for the soon-to-be princess.

"Good to meet you." Jeremy extended his hand.

Noelle placed her own in his, noticing the calluses on his hand and recognizing the lack on her own for the first time in months. "You too." She motioned to the box he held. "You said you have something for me?"

"Yes." He handed over the package. "Here you go."

"Thanks."

"Jeremy, can you stay for dinner?" Mary asked.

"I think I can spare a couple hours."

"Noelle, you have to stay too."

"I have a flight, remember?"

"You have a flight on a private jet," Mary replied. "Call the pilot and see if he can move back your departure time. Your driver is welcome to join us for dinner too if he wants."

Noelle wavered, not sure she should take advantage of having access to the royal family's private plane. "I don't know . . ."

"Did I mention I'm making enchiladas for dinner?"

Unable to resist, Noelle smiled. "I guess it can't hurt to make a call."

* * *

Jeremy studied the petite brunette across the table, his curiosity humming. Everything about her screamed wealth and class, from her perfect posture to her table manners.

When she had called her pilot, she'd spoken in French. The call to her father had been in Italian. When she spoke English, he could describe her accent only as European. The fact that he couldn't identify it further was surprising considering how many people he had met while serving his mission in Switzerland.

She moved like a dancer, as though she floated on air, when she went about setting the table for dinner. That was another oddity. The woman had access to a private plane, yet she clearly knew her way around a kitchen.

"How long can you stay?" Mary asked him, cutting into his thoughts.

"I'm afraid I have to head back tonight." He saw the disappointment on his sister's face and quickly added, "I did want to ask how you would feel about me staying with you for the holidays. It looks like I may be moving to the D.C. area, at least for a few months."

"That would be wonderful. You're welcome to stay as long as you want, right, Kevin?"

"Absolutely." Mary's husband nodded. "Noelle came to visit for a few days and ended up staying for three months."

Noelle didn't respond to Kevin but rather addressed her remarks to Jeremy. "I was supposed to move into an apartment near the Meridian embassy, but Kevin liked my crepes too much to let me go."

"You do make amazing crepes. And your croissants . . ."

Jeremy couldn't help but smile. "It sounds like I really should have been visiting more often."

"Noelle will be back for a visit in two weeks," Mary said. "Maybe you should see if you can get the weekend off."

Jeremy turned to Noelle, his eyes locking with hers. There was a slight rise of color in her cheeks. Intrigued, he said, "Maybe I should."

Chapter 3

JEREMY WATCHED THE TELEVISION SCREEN in the corner of the conference room, the wedding of Prince Stefano of Meridia and Alora DeSanto
unfolding for all the world to see. He didn't want to admit he was more
interested in the guests than he was in the royals. He continued to sweep
the crowd, searching for a familiar face, disappointed when he didn't
catch a glimpse of Noelle.

Their first phone conversation had happened by accident. His sister
had persuaded him to stay the night when he had delivered the package to
Noelle. When Noelle had called to let Mary know she had arrived safely
in Meridia, Jeremy had happened to be the one to pick up the phone.
Two weeks later, he had made it a point to spend the weekend at his
sister's house when Noelle would be there, more curious about Mary and
Janessa's jet-setting friend than anything else.

The contradictions in Noelle and her obvious friendship with Mary
had left him fascinated, as had the news that she was a recent convert
to the Church. By the time she'd left for Meridia at the end of that
weekend, again on a private jet, they had exchanged phone numbers.
That had been three months ago.

He thought of their last conversation more than a week before. He
still wasn't sure exactly what her role was with the royal wedding, but
Noelle had indicated that she was heavily involved with the soon-to-be
princess in preparing for the event. He was also certain Noelle would be
in attendance. So far, the television cameras hadn't given him the glimpse
he had hoped for.

Of course, with six hundred expected guests, most of whom were
famous in their own right, he could hardly expect Noelle to be one of

those the cameramen would choose to focus on. With all the hype and press coverage, he wondered if there was anyone in the world who wasn't watching. Still, he felt ridiculous sitting in a room alone, watching a wedding, of all things. Give him a soccer game and he'd be happy.

The camera zoomed in on King Eduard and Queen Marta as they emerged from the back of a limousine. Jeremy made a mental note of how the royal guards shielded the king in the same way the U.S. Secret Service protected the president. Other members of the royal family arrived at irregular intervals. He was surprised to see everyone in attendance. After several attempts had been made on the Meridian royals' lives recently, he would have expected someone to stay away from the event as a precaution.

The conference room door opened, and one of his coworkers walked in. Conrad glanced at the screen before sending Jeremy a look of disbelief. "You're seriously watching this? I thought you were doing research."

"This *is* research."

"A royal wedding is research?"

"I'm trying to determine if there is a way to attend a royal wedding while staying out of the spotlight."

"Doubtful. Why would it matter? It's not like any of us would ever get an invite to something like that," Conrad said. "Public affairs would never approve it even if we did. CIA officers are supposed to avoid cameras."

"Which is why public affairs suggested I watch the wedding today." On the screen, the bridesmaids and bride emerged from a long white limousine.

"I don't understand."

Jeremy pointed to the TV. "See the redhead? That's my sister."

As if on cue, the camera zoomed in on Janessa, the announcer giving an overview of her relationship to the royals.

Janessa Rogers, from the United States, is Alora DeSanto's maid of honor. Royal watchers are already anticipating her wedding later this year to the groom's younger brother, Prince Garrett.

Conrad shifted so he was facing Jeremy. "Your sister is marrying a prince?"

"Yep. I didn't even know she knew the guy until the media announced her engagement last year."

"She didn't tell you before it hit the news?"

"No, but I'm not sure she could have even if she wanted to. I was still in training at the farm when she got engaged."

The camera zoomed in on the bride, a petite brunette Jeremy knew to be from Italy. Beside her were her two sons, both dressed in matching black tuxedos.

The younger boy broke away from his mother and started for the church house. Janessa reached him before he could open it, leaning down to whisper something in his ear.

Apparently Jeremy wasn't the only one amused by the scene as the cameras followed the action, zooming in as Janessa straightened and took the boy's hand while she waited for the rest of the wedding party to assemble on the cobblestone sidewalk outside the historic building.

The image shifted to King Eduard, who now stood beside the bride.

"Staying away from the cameras is going to be a pain," Conrad said, "but that's pretty cool that you're going to be rubbing elbows with royalty. I mean, your own sister is about to become a princess."

"I have a hard time thinking of my sister as royalty. I grew up with her, and I bet she still hogs the bathroom."

Conrad chuckled. "That may be, but if you don't already have one, it may be time to invest in a tux."

"My sister told me the same thing." Jeremy rolled his shoulders at the thought of wearing restrictive clothing. When given a choice, he didn't even like to wear a suit jacket to church on Sundays.

"Looks like they're using local police to take care of the crowds, and there are additional guards at the entrances," Conrad said, drawing Jeremy's attention back to why the television was on in the first place.

"I have to say, I'm glad I'm not the one in charge of security for this thing."

"You and me both."

* * *

Noelle stood in the corner of the enormous church and took in the scene. Light streamed in through the tall stained-glass windows, sending beams of red, blue, and green across the marble floor and wooden pews.

The attire of the occupants of those pews added more color and an air of elegance. Every seat was filled—who would reject an invitation to a royal wedding? Royals and dignitaries occupied the front rows, followed by high-ranking government officials and friends of the royal family.

Sadly, the bride's family consisted only of her two sons, four-year-old Dante and six-year-old Giancarlo. Alora had lost her first husband and her family in a bombing four years earlier.

The romantic in Noelle appreciated the way the young widow had found a new happily ever after. Prince Stefano stood at the front of the room beside his brother, who was currently serving as his best man. Both men were dressed in formal uniforms from their previous service in Meridia's navy. In a matter of months, the two men would reverse roles for Prince Garrett's marriage to Janessa.

Noelle looked over the crowd, hoping to find the unexpected. There wasn't any reason to believe Jeremy would come to Prince Stefano's wedding, but that hadn't stopped her from wishing. She had thought perhaps his relationship with Janessa would have garnered him an invite, but she should have known that was a stretch. While Janessa was the maid of honor, Noelle doubted Jeremy had even met today's bride and groom.

Her thoughts were interrupted when she sensed movement behind her. She shifted ever so slightly until she was able to identify the new presence. Levi Marin had slipped into position a few feet inside the door. With his dark hair and average height, he had a way of blending into his surroundings. He wasn't much older than her, maybe late twenties, and Noelle was impressed that he had earned the position as chief of security at the palace at such a young age. Only a few months ago, he had been working with the security team at the royal family's summer chateau.

Noelle bit back a sigh. What would it be like, she wondered, to have such a career? Since childhood, she had been fascinated by the idea of knowing important secrets and gaining the trust of the people who mattered most in her country.

She supposed there must be women on Meridia's intelligence staff, but the old-fashioned security force still followed the centuries-old tradition: men only.

Levi nodded at the organist, and the first notes sounded. Everyone stood, their attention now on the doors leading into the vestibule. A small parade of bridesmaids entered first, followed by the bride's two sons, each carrying a pillow with a ring on it.

Noelle smiled at the memory of her last encounter with the young boys. Apparently the head gardener at the palace hadn't been pleased with their decision to bury treasure beneath his begonias.

Three young flower girls followed the boys, only one of whom remembered her duty to drop white rose petals as she walked. Another stopped, her eyes wide as she looked around the crowded room.

Janessa, the maid of honor, took the child's hand and helped her down the aisle. As soon as they reached the front of the church, the wedding march began, and all eyes turned once more to the entrance.

Alora stepped into the doorway, a vision of loveliness in her elegant, long-sleeved gown. Escorted by her soon-to-be father-in-law, King Eduard, the bride moved forward in time with the music, everyone's attention on her.

Chapter 4

LEVI LOOKED PAST ALORA, HIS gaze sweeping over the attendees. As expected, all eyes were on the bride. His job was to identify anyone whose attention might be elsewhere.

He prayed all of the security preparations over the past several months would pay off, but something wasn't sitting right with him, though he couldn't say exactly what it was.

Security cameras had been installed weeks earlier and double-checked this morning. They would allow his security team outside to monitor the crowd in case he missed something from his spot at the back of the room.

Alora reached the front of the church, and the attendees were invited to take their seats. Levi's gaze shifted slightly to the woman who stood a short distance away. He knew Noelle's file well.

Levi wondered for a moment why she had chosen to stand at the back instead of finding a seat like the rest of the guests. Then he remembered her capacity. She wasn't a guest. She was one of the many people who had helped orchestrate this momentous event.

He noticed that her gaze had fixed on a point to the left of where the princes now stood. Curious, he looked but found his view obstructed by a rather tall prince from Saudi Arabia.

Levi moved to his left until he reached Noelle, then lowered his voice. "What are you staring at?"

"I'm wondering why that woman is looking at her lap instead of watching Alora and Prince Stefano." She tipped her chin slightly in the direction of her concern and added, "Seventh row back, blue hat."

Levi leaned more to his left and saw the woman in question. He spoke quietly, knowing the miniature microphone in his communication earpiece would pick up his words. "Camera three, zoom in on the seventh row on the far end. Female, about forty, wearing a blue hat. Tell me what she's looking at."

The response came through his earpiece, and he recognized Pietro's voice. "Looks like a cell phone."

"Is it active? The dampening field should be blocking all signals."

"The screen is lit up."

"Who is she?"

"Checking." The brief silence lasted for several seconds. "Rita Sandoval. She accompanied the ambassador from Italy."

"Background concerns?"

"Nothing flagged," Pietro said. The words were barely out of his mouth when he said, "Levi, we may have a problem. It looks like there's a cord coming out of her purse, and it appears to be attached to the phone."

"How big is the purse?"

"Large. About sixteen inches by ten inches."

Big enough to conceal a bomb, Levi thought to himself.

Pietro clearly read his thoughts. "Everyone was screened coming in. You don't think she managed to get something past us, do you?"

"I don't know, but I'm not taking any chances." Levi scanned the room again. "Any other concerns sighted?"

"No. Everyone else's attention is glued on the bride and groom," he said. "What are you going to do?"

Levi considered his options. Stopping the wedding was last on the list. For all he knew, he could be overreacting. He fingered the small pouch in his pocket. If he could create a minor distraction without gaining too much attention . . .

Noelle moved beside him. "Is there anything I can do to help?"

He noticed the small purse hanging from her shoulder, and an idea snapped into place. "Come with me."

Noelle nodded, and Levi started along the back wall, pleased to see she was adept at moving unobtrusively. When they reached the opposite corner of the building, several dozen rows behind where Rita Sandoval was sitting, Levi stopped and spoke quietly to Noelle.

"I want you to walk up next to her and drop your purse."

"Then what?"

Levi retrieved the small pouch from his pocket and removed a tiny needle that contained a sedative. "I'm going to sedate the woman, and I want you to switch purses with her."

Noelle's eyes widened briefly, but again she nodded. Quickly she opened her purse and took out her cell phone and driver's license. Levi held out a hand. "I'll hold them for you."

She handed them over, and he slipped both items into his pocket. "Handle the purse carefully. We don't know what's inside."

* * *

Noelle noted the seriousness of Levi's expression, and she realized he was preparing for a worst-case scenario. Did he really think someone had managed to bring a bomb into the church?

Noelle looked at the front of the room. Prince Stefano and Alora stood at the altar, their hands joined as the minister addressed the congregation, offering words of counsel and wisdom. More than six hundred guests looked on, none of them aware that the woman in the blue hat was acting suspiciously.

Levi motioned Noelle forward, and a jumble of thoughts crowded her mind. Part of her appreciated Levi's trust in her to play a role in his plan. Another part of her wondered what they would find inside the purse.

What if there really was a bomb? What if there wasn't? How did one apologize for sedating an important guest at a royal wedding simply for staring at her phone for too long?

She reached the woman and dropped her purse as Levi had instructed, then squatted as though retrieving it, her gaze lifting to the woman beside her.

She felt Levi's presence behind her and glimpsed him casually putting his hand on the woman's shoulder. What Noelle hadn't expected was how quickly the sedative worked. Noelle barely had time to react before the woman slumped down and her purse was sliding off her lap.

Instinct caused Noelle to reach out and hold the purse and cell phone in place before they could drop to the floor. Levi held the woman up, settling her so she remained sitting. Noelle looked up to see if anyone was watching her. The man sitting beside the woman glanced over with an irritated scowl, but his focus appeared to be on Noelle rather than on the person sitting beside him.

Levi leaned over and whispered something to the man that appeared to satisfy him and then spoke quietly to the couple sitting right behind them. Noelle was surprised to see that everyone else's attention was still directed at the front of the room.

Noelle gingerly lifted the larger purse with one hand, her other hand keeping the cell phone in place on top of it. Then she straightened, leaving her empty purse on the now-unconscious woman's lap.

Levi touched her shoulder, and together they retreated to the back of the church once more. Rather than walk toward the main doors, Levi headed for an alcove in the back corner. He spoke quietly to one of the guards stationed there and then continued into a hallway that led to the church offices.

Levi passed several doors, choosing the last one on the left. He entered first, waiting for Noelle to walk through before reaching out to close the thick wooden door behind them. "Put it down, and let's see what we've got."

Noelle gently set the purse and cell phone on the antique library table. Levi squatted to peer inside, and Noelle sent a prayer heavenward that this was all a huge misunderstanding. But the expression on Levi's face sent her pulse racing and confirmed that his suspicions were well founded.

Chapter 5

It was worse than he thought possible. Levi stared at the explosive compound filling the purse, wires running from deep inside the stretched-out leather. As suspected, the cell phone was attached to the bomb, but it didn't appear to be the primary detonator. Rather, it looked like it was being used to monitor the time. Four minutes, forty-seven seconds and counting.

"How bad is it?" Noelle asked.

"Bad. It looks like the detonator is on the bottom." Levi motioned to the desk in the corner. "See if you can find some scissors."

Noelle crossed to the desk. "Aren't you going to call for help?"

"The guards aren't trained for this, and we don't have time to call in the bomb squad. I know you're not trained either, but right now all I need is someone competent who can follow directions."

She quickly pulled open one drawer and then another, rifling through them until she found the requested item. She held the scissors out. "Now what?"

"Put your hand here." Levi pointed to the top of the purse. "I need you to hold it still while I cut away the fabric."

He wasn't going to tell her that if he clipped a wire in the process, they would be among hundreds to die; nor did she need to know that this particular type of explosive was known for its wide blast radius. He shifted the scissors in his hand, clipped the seam on the bottom, and prayed they weren't going to find out the hard way exactly how wide the blast radius really was.

She kept her hand in place, holding the purse securely. Her voice was surprisingly steady when she asked, "Do we need to evacuate?"

"There isn't time." Levi looked at the timer again. Four minutes, twenty-one seconds. "Call out the time for me. Five second intervals."

He continued cutting away the stitching, pulling the two pieces of leather apart only to find the bag had been double stitched. A sense of urgency swallowed him despite having a reasonable amount of time on the clock.

Noelle called out the time as he worked. Four fifteen. Four ten. Four oh five. He forced himself to slow down when he snipped at the interior threads, gently working his fingers into the hole he had created, searching for wires. Instead he felt the cold metal of a spherical object.

"What is it?" Noelle asked.

"I think there's a grenade pressed into the side of the bomb." He continued to use the scissors to widen the hole, now working away from the grenade.

"Hand me my phone," Noelle insisted. "Three minutes, forty-five seconds."

Levi handed it over, not pausing to ask who she planned to call at a time like this. To his surprise, she used her free hand to push a button and activate a flashlight app. She aimed it into the hole he was continuing to widen.

Levi pulled the hole open as wide as he could, now nearly six inches. With the added benefit of extra lighting, he caught the reflection of a second cell phone to the left, along with several wires running from it.

"I can see the wires." He cut away the leather more aggressively until he reached the cell phone.

"Three fifteen."

Finally he managed to open the bottom seam completely. He looked at the wires, determining which would deactivate the device.

"Nine seconds!"

"What?" Levi looked at the interior cell phone, stunned to see the time was three minutes ahead of the timer they had been watching.

Scissors still in hand, he pulled at the wires, separating them and praying the bomb wasn't booby-trapped.

White wire. Black wire. Red wire. Blue wire. His mind raced, considering the options.

"Five seconds."

He pulled the green wire clear, opened the scissors wide, and cut it cleanly. For a split second, his mind registered the fact that the bomb didn't detonate, but then he focused solely on the telltale sound of a grenade pin coming loose. "Grenade!" He managed to grip it and pull it free from the purse, then he hurled it across the room, aiming for the wide-mouthed ceramic urn near the window.

Beside him, Noelle lifted the side of the table, attempting to shove it onto its side. Levi gripped the edge, helping her tip it over. They both dropped and took cover behind the table a fraction of a second before a blast shook the room and shrapnel exploded into the air.

* * *

Noelle didn't move for several seconds, her brain still trying to catch up with what had just happened. Smoke filled the room, but she didn't feel any pain other than the burning in her eyes.

"Are you okay?" Levi asked.

His voice sounded like it was underwater, but Noelle suspected it was her hearing causing the problem. "I think so. Are you?"

Levi nodded. He spoke again, but this time it wasn't to her. "Is everything okay in the chapel?" He fell silent, apparently listening to someone on his security team. "Unbelievable. We just had a grenade detonate in one of the far offices. Are you seriously telling me no one noticed?" He paused once more. "Take the woman I sedated into custody. Make it look like a medical issue. And take the king and queen out the alternate entrance. I don't want the royals all together."

Levi shifted his attention back to Noelle. "Are you sure you're okay?"

She quickly blinked several times, grateful the smoke had started to settle. "I'm fine." She stood and looked at what was left of the room. Pieces of shrapnel and shards of the ceramic urn protruded from the interior walls and from what was left of the furniture, including the table she had used for cover. A filing cabinet on the far side of the room had been knocked to the ground, several of the drawers hanging open. The brick exterior wall was blackened, and the glass from the window shattered. The seat of the office chair lay a few feet away. She wasn't sure where the rest of the chair had landed.

"Pietro said they heard something inside, but they thought it was a truck backfiring. The wedding is finishing up now."

Noelle looked at him, wide-eyed. "No one else knows what just happened?"

"No, and we're going to keep it that way. The only person who truly knows about this bomb besides us is whoever planted it."

"You told security to take her into custody."

"Yes, but she was simply the delivery method. Whoever put her up to bringing that bomb in here didn't plan on letting her live long enough to tell about it."

"What do you mean?"

"You saw yourself that there was a three-minute difference between the real timer and the one she was watching," Levi said. "Makes me think she was going to make a quiet exit a few minutes before the bomb went off."

"But whoever sent her in with it saw her as expendable."

"Exactly." Levi studied Noelle for a brief moment. "What are your assigned duties today?"

"Now that the church ceremony is over, I'll fill in wherever I'm needed," Noelle said. "I had planned to slip out at the end of the ceremony and check on the last details for the reception. Obviously that didn't happen." Noelle cringed inwardly at what Floria would say when she realized Noelle wasn't where she was supposed to be. "I imagine this will be my last job working for Floria after today, especially if I'm not allowed to tell her why I'm not where I'm supposed to be." She let out a frustrated sigh. "Now what?"

"As soon as everyone leaves the building, I'll have the bomb moved to the naval base for analysis." Levi spoke into his earpiece once more, ordering one of his men to come secure the room and wait with the bomb.

"What are we going to do?"

"I'm going to stick close to the royals and make sure there isn't a backup plan in case this one fails. As for you, you're going to go about your duties as if nothing's happened."

Noelle started to protest, but she quickly recognized the wisdom in Levi's words. Calling attention to the failed attempt would only take the focus away from the wedding and create fear for the local citizens. "In that case, I'd better freshen up before I go to the reception."

Levi gave her a curt nod. "You saved a lot of lives today. I hope you know that."

Her lips curved. "Thanks."

* * *

Adrienne Acord stood at the back of the room at the television studio and watched the dozen images on the bank of screens. During Prince Stefano and Princess Alora's wedding ceremony, all talking had ceased and the images were allowed to speak for themselves. Now that the ceremony was over, the newscasters were discussing the importance of today's royal wedding.

For this live feed, the news director was calling the shots. He dictated which camera to send live and when to switch to background. This was the domain of the beautiful and powerful people in the news world. She was the back-room person, the person who made everyone else look good.

Within the hour, her job would begin. She would take these hours of images and cut them into snippets for highlights on her own station as well as thousands of other stations around the world.

Knowing how limited her time would be once her real work began, she didn't allow herself to only focus on the feed that would stream to their viewing audience. Instead, she let her vision scan the many images.

She had noticed movement in one of the background angles a moment before, but no one was visible on the side of the church where it had occurred. She looked at that screen again, still feeling as though something wasn't quite right.

"Does something seem off on monitor nine?" Adrienne asked the director.

He gave a quick glance and shook his head. "The action is all inside now."

"I thought I saw something."

"If it wasn't a royal, it doesn't matter," he said sharply. "Stay focused on what's important."

Embarrassed for being called out in front of everyone, she clamped her mouth shut. He was right, she reminded herself. What everyone wanted today was to see the bride and groom, not a cloud of dust that had already dissipated into the breeze.

Chapter 6

KING EDUARD LISTENED TO THE detailed report, his stomach curling at the thought of how close they had come to tragedy the day before. So many precautions had been taken, yet someone had nearly managed to wipe out his entire family. Did the bomber know that a royal wedding was the only time the entire family would ever be in the same place at the same time? And what would happen when Garrett and Janessa married in a few months? Would they have to leave a family member home to protect against the possibility of someone succeeding where this attempt had failed?

"How did the bomb get past security?" Eduard asked as soon as Levi finished giving him the highlights of the day before.

"It was ingenious, really," Levi said. "Everyday items were pressed into the sides of the explosive, and an insert covered the top of the bomb so when someone looked inside, it appeared that the purse was simply overfull."

"Anything to indicate who is behind it?"

"Not yet. The woman who smuggled the bomb into the church isn't talking."

"Does she know her coconspirators tried to kill her?" Eduard asked.

"She doesn't believe it. I have Langley searching their database for any similar incidents, and they're running traces of the base materials. Unfortunately these things take time." Levi held up a paper. "I plan to meet with Janessa later today."

"There's no need to discuss this with Janessa," King Eduard said firmly. "She has enough to worry about preparing for her own wedding."

"Your Majesty, do you think it's a good idea to leave her out of the loop? She's been an integral part of the security plans at the chateau and for this wedding."

"I realize that, but it's time for her to leave the intelligence work to someone else. She will be an official member of the royal family in a matter of months, and if we aren't careful, the press will realize she isn't who they think she is."

"You don't really think anyone would be able to figure out she's with the CIA, do you?"

"Former CIA. As you know, her resignation went into effect two months ago." King Eduard stood. "However, I do think it may be time for me to ask your CIA for a replacement."

"I would appreciate that. I prefer not to remain shorthanded, especially after yesterday."

"I will call Director Palmer today," Eduard said. "Thank you for all of your service to my family."

Levi stood. "I do have one more request."

"What's that?"

"Noelle Saldera. I would like to have her assigned to work as a liaison between the household staff and security. She was instrumental in our success yesterday, and I believe she would be a useful addition to my team at the chateau. I assume you plan on transferring me back there since that's where Prince Garrett's wedding reception will take place."

"Yes, that's still my plan." He pondered for a moment. "Call Noelle in to meet with me, and we'll speak to her about making a change in her duties."

"Thank you, Your Majesty." Levi bowed his head slightly and left the room.

As soon as the door closed, Eduard picked up the phone and dialed. Director Palmer picked up on the second ring. "King Eduard, I thought I might be hearing from you today. I'm afraid I don't have any updates for you though."

"I am actually calling about another matter," Eduard began. "I understand you hope to put more agents in Bellamo."

"With the naval base nearing completion there, creating a small office in that region would be useful for us. I believe it would also benefit you and Interpol. In fact, I think you'll approve of our intended station chief."

"Who might that be?" Eduard asked.

"Levi Marin."

Eduard considered the implications of such a personnel change. Levi had arrived almost a year earlier as part of a two-man team assigned to assist his family when a bomb had detonated outside the U.S. embassy. His coworker had been Janessa. "I can't think of a better candidate, but I have to admit I'll be sad to lose him."

"Think of him as a team leader. If you're willing, I would like for him to transfer back to work with your security team at the chateau until after Prince Garrett and Janessa's wedding. I also would like to send in one more person to work with him there."

"I was going to suggest exactly that, but it won't be easy to insert another agent without raising suspicions," Eduard warned. "We put a hiring restriction on our staff several months ago to alleviate security concerns during this vulnerable time."

"I understand completely, but we have found the perfect man for the job. No one will suspect a thing." Director Palmer let silence linger for a brief moment before he added, "The agent is Jeremy Rogers, Janessa's brother."

King Eduard absorbed this bit of information. Janessa had never mentioned her brother's position with the CIA, and he hoped he could be trusted. Regardless, he didn't see any other option to bring in the help Levi requested. "In that case, when does he arrive?"

"I can have him there by tomorrow."

"Excellent. We'll have rooms prepared for him before he arrives."

"Thank you. I'll let you know as soon as we have more information on the bombing attempt."

"Any help you can provide is appreciated."

* * *

"You said your plan was foolproof. What happened?"

"I don't know. I saw Rita successfully clear security, and she was visible briefly on camera when Princess Alora walked down the aisle."

"Could she have disabled the bomb? Maybe she realized we planned to have her die along with everyone else."

"That's not possible. The secondary timer was well hidden, and if she did discover it, the grenade would have gone off if she tried to disarm it."

"Then something must have been faulty in the device itself." His mouth tightened into a thin line. "Where is Rita now?"

"She's missing. My guess is she left early and fled the country."

"Check the television cameras. One of them must have picked up something."

"I've already gone over the recordings. The focus was on the wedding ceremony the whole time."

"Look again, and don't limit yourself to what was televised. There are always more angles than what the public sees."

"How exactly do you propose I get the raw footage?"

"You're resourceful. I'm sure you'll figure something out." His eyes hardened. "Failure is not an option."

"Yes, sir."

* * *

Jeremy heard the door across the room open and close, but he kept his attention on the papers spread across his desk. With dozens of cubicles in the huge office area, people were always coming and going, and he'd learned to tune out the buzz of conversation and the constant flow of movement. In the back of his mind, he sensed the change in energy level and heard the hushed whispers that accompanied the new arrival, but it wasn't until he heard his name mentioned that he looked up.

"Jeremy's cubicle is right over there," Conrad said.

Jeremy stood, looking over the five-foot-high partitions. He wasn't sure what to think when he saw the director of Central Intelligence heading toward him.

Director Palmer closed the distance between them. "Jeremy Rogers?"

"Yes, sir." Jeremy shook the hand the director offered him. "Is there something I can do for you, Director?"

"I believe there is." He glanced around at Jeremy's coworkers, several of whom were openly watching the exchange. "Let's take this conversation somewhere a little more private."

"Our conference room is over there." Jeremy pointed to the left, and the director stepped back to let Jeremy lead the way.

As soon as they entered the conference room, Director Palmer closed the door and both men sat at the oblong table. "I understand you are interested in an overseas assignment."

"Yes, sir," Jeremy said. His mind whirled as he tried to find some reason that the director would seek him out. He knew many agency employees went through their entire careers without ever interacting with this level of management.

"Excellent. I have an opportunity for you, but you need to leave immediately. Would that be a problem?"

"No. I'm actually staying with my sister right now since I was told I would only be in this office temporarily. I didn't want to sign a lease somewhere until I knew where I would be working."

"Smart," Director Palmer said. "Your flight leaves at seven o'clock tonight."

"Tonight?" Jeremy asked, stunned.

"That's right. I want you in Meridia by tomorrow afternoon. You will be working at the royal chateau."

"Meridia? Does this assignment have anything to do with the fact that my sister is engaged to Prince Garrett?"

"It does. That's why you're the perfect choice. You speak French, and you can also socialize freely in the upper levels of society without anyone being suspicious. I would suggest you study up on Italian though. You'll need it."

"What do I tell my sister? Janessa tends to be the suspicious type."

"Our naval base in Bellamo is nearly complete. Your cover story is that you have been hired by a government contractor to consult with the base personnel. Since your degree is in electrical engineering, it shouldn't be hard to convince everyone at the chateau that you're working out of your room there. This also gives you a reason to consult with the naval base personnel if needed."

"Is there anything else I need to know?"

"Your immediate supervisor will be Levi Marin. He has been under-cover as an employee of the royal family for nearly a year. He works with their security staff and will be moving his base of operations back to the chateau to help prepare for your sister's wedding." He slid an envelope across the table, the words "Top Secret" and "Eyes Only" stamped across the front. "Here is your travel information. My phone number is also in there. Don't be afraid to use it. This assignment has the potential to be high profile, and I don't want any surprises."

Jeremy took the envelope, opening it long enough to scan the travel information. He slid the paperwork back inside and looked back at the director. "Sounds like I had better go pack."

"One more thing." Director Palmer stood. "One of the things that makes you the most valuable in this assignment is your close relationship with the royals. You need to do everything you can to integrate yourself into your sister's social circles. The more people you know before the next wedding, the better."

"Are you expecting a problem at Janessa's wedding?"

"Always expect a problem. If you're lucky, you'll be able to solve it before it arises." Director Palmer extended his hand. "Good luck."

"Thank you, sir."

Chapter 7

NOELLE WALKED THROUGH THE MAIN parlor in the palace, as awed by the ornate ceilings and elegant furnishings as she had been the first time she'd visited here at the age of eight. The view through the windows was simply breathtaking: the village of Calene spread along the shore, the Mediterranean rolling a blue-gray beneath the cloudy sky. A storm was brewing, and the lack of fishing boats on the water indicated it was going to be a bad one.

She took a deep breath, thinking of the storm of emotions she had endured over the past twenty-four hours. The reality that she and hundreds of others had almost died the day before hadn't truly sunk in until night had fallen and she had retired to her room alone. The tears had come then, racking sobs born from unreleased emotions. Within minutes, they were gone and she had forced herself to put the events in perspective, analyzing each moment over and over.

Her questions replayed through her mind now. Who would want to hurt the royal family? Why had her life been spared? What if Levi hadn't known how to disarm the bomb or she hadn't noticed the second detonator? Why had she focused on the woman in the blue hat so quickly?

The last question puzzled her more than any of the others. Logically she should have been paying attention to the bride and groom, yet her eyes had wandered long enough for her to take notice of the woman and the oddity of her behavior. A flood of warmth washed over Noelle, and she knew her actions the day before hadn't been born of logic alone. For whatever reason, the Lord had let her function as a vessel to stop the attempted attack, and because of Him, Meridia still had a royal family.

She continued through the room into the entryway and saw Levi walking down the hallway to her right.

Levi caught sight of her and motioned her forward. "I was just coming to find you. Come inside. King Eduard and I want to speak to you."

A little intimidated about being called before the king, Noelle followed Levi through the door. King Eduard stood when she entered and motioned to a seat across from his desk. "Please come in and sit down."

Noelle curtsied to him and then took the seat he offered. King Eduard lowered himself into the chair behind his desk, remaining silent until after Levi closed the door and sat beside her.

"My family is indebted to you for your service yesterday," he began.

"I was happy to help, Your Majesty."

"I understand you assisted in Prince Stefano's wedding preparations and are expected to help with Prince Garrett's."

"That's correct."

"Levi suggested we add to your duties, provided you are agreeable." He shifted his gaze to Levi.

"I want to augment the security staff at the chateau by bringing in a member of the staff to work as a liaison," Levi said.

"Why is that necessary? The security staff has full access to the rest of the staff there."

"Yes, but people tend to filter their conversations when security officers are present. I would like you to work with me, to be my eyes and ears among the staff as we prepare for Prince Garrett's wedding," Levi explained. "How would you feel about working in an intelligence capacity?"

Stunned by his words, Noelle studied the man beside her as well as the man across the desk. They were offering her a chance to step into a world that had fascinated her for years, but she wanted more. Mustering her courage, she shifted her attention to Levi once more. "That depends."

"On?"

"On whether information is going to flow both ways." Noelle clasped her hands together and forced herself to be open and honest with the men who had the power to change her future. "I've always been fascinated by intelligence work, but spying on my family and friends is hardly what I had in mind. I want to be able to make a difference. It seems to me, if I know what you know, I'll have a better understanding of how I can best help you."

King Eduard's lips curved slightly, and he spoke to Levi. "I think she may be even better suited for this job than you thought."

"I agree," Levi said before asking Noelle, "When do you return to the chateau?"

"Tomorrow."

"Meet me tomorrow afternoon in the security office there, and I'll brief you on what we have on the bombing attempt so far." Levi stood and extended his hand. "Welcome to the world of intelligence."

She stood and put her hand in his. "Thank you."

* * *

Levi approached the U.S. embassy with a combination of curiosity and irritation. He had a schedule to keep, and this early-morning summons by the U.S. ambassador didn't bode well with his plans to return to the chateau before Prince Garrett and Janessa. Admittedly, however, he found himself mentally going over the scenarios of why he had been sent for in the first place. He hoped to arrive and find that some progress had been made on the bomb discovered two days earlier at the wedding.

He bypassed the main reception area and headed upstairs toward the ambassador's office, where an aide was waiting for him. "Mr. Marin, thank you for taking time to come in this morning." The man before him was midtwenties, polished, and already quite the diplomat. He waved him forward. "Right this way."

They walked down the hall together, passing several doorways before the aide opened one on the left. "Here you are."

Levi wasn't surprised to see the ambassador, but the other man in the room heightened his curiosity and replaced his irritation with concern. "Director Palmer. I wasn't aware you were here in Meridia."

"I'm not," Director Palmer said simply.

"I see." He didn't see, but he knew the director of Central Intelligence wasn't about to share more information than what he deemed necessary.

"I will leave the two of you to talk." The ambassador stood. "Director Palmer, I will let you know if I receive any further information on the matter we discussed."

"Thank you." Director Palmer waited for the door to close before motioning for Levi to take a seat. As soon as Levi complied, he continued. "We are still waiting for the forensics to come back on the bomb found at the wedding, but some information surfaced that you need to be aware of."

"What's that?"

"King Eduard allowed one of our interrogators to conduct the interview with Rita Sandoval."

"And?"

"And we may have a bigger problem than we realized."

"A bigger problem than someone trying to blow up the entire royal family of Meridia?" Levi asked, disbelief in his voice.

"We believe this was one of several attacks intended to destabilize the area."

"For what purpose?"

"The oil trade." Director Palmer leaned back in his seat. "Like it or not, oil is money, and money is power."

"You're talking about North Africa."

"Yes. Sandoval doesn't know exactly who paid her to plant the bomb, but the million she received in her bank account was supposedly only a drop in the bucket. She was promised much more once the monarchy fell."

Levi leaned forward. "What now?"

"Now I'm creating a new field office in Bellamo and promoting you to station chief. King Eduard agreed to let you work out of the chateau until Prince Garrett and Janessa's wedding, after which we will establish offices for you in town. I'm also sending in some help."

"Who?"

"Jeremy Rogers."

"Rogers? He's not related to Janessa, is he?"

"Yes. He's her younger brother. He started with us a year ago. He's been working in the European division since finishing his training."

"With all due respect, sir, there must be some other way," Levi insisted. "Bringing in a rookie on such a high-profile case is risky at best."

"I agree, but this was the only way to do so without alerting the staff," Director Palmer insisted. "The hiring freeze by the royal family has tied our hands."

"Can you at least give me his file?"

"There isn't much point, but here it is along with his cover information." He shifted a file into Levi's hands before continuing. "Other than going through training at the farm, his only experience is working for a few months on the European desk."

"Language skills?"

"French and Portuguese."

"I guess it would have been too much to ask for you to send someone who speaks Italian."

"I realize he'll have a learning curve with the language, but many people in Meridia speak French," Director Palmer said. "Where I think you'll find his skills most useful is running deep background checks. He has quite a knack for it."

Levi let out a sigh. "When does he arrive?"

"Later today. If you hurry, you might even beat him to the chateau." He looked at his watch. "Then again, maybe not."

"It sounds like I'd better get going."

Both men stood and shook hands. "And don't forget, Levi. I was never here."

"Understood."

Chapter 8

JEREMY HAD ALWAYS THOUGHT HE would prepare for his first overseas assignment by spending weeks researching everything from the local customs to the economy and political climate. Never had he considered that he would barely have enough time to throw his clothes in a suitcase and rush to the airport.

He might have at least used the overseas flight to read about Meridia, but the only material he could find on the run was a recent news article about the Meridian oil industry. Now he was getting a firsthand look at the picturesque view as he drove past quaint villages, most of the houses built with traditional red-tiled roofs. Skyscrapers weren't anywhere to be seen, and often along his drive, he enjoyed a stunning view of the Mediterranean.

His sister had offered to send a car to pick him up at the airport, but thankfully the navy had agreed to lend him a vehicle to use during his time in the country. As he passed a thickly wooded area, he hoped he would have some free time to explore the countryside.

Jeremy slowed the car when he made the final turn, and the royal chateau came into view. Quite simply, the scene before him was breathtaking. The woods he had been driving through seemed to end abruptly at the edge of a fairy-tale setting. Towers and turrets spread out over the bluff of land overlooking an expansive stretch of beach. A fountain bubbled in the front courtyard, the drive circling it.

Jeremy rolled down the window when he reached the gate and gave his name. For a moment, he worried his sister had forgotten to leave his name with the guards, but after a check of his ID, the gates opened and he was waved through. He pulled up in front of the main entrance and was barely out of the car before he heard his sister's voice.

"Jeremy!"

Janessa was at the top of the wide steps leading to the heavy wooden doors. She hurried down them despite the heels she wore.

"You're here!" Her arms came around him the moment she reached him.

"I'm here." Jeremy held her close for a moment before leaning back so he could take a closer look at her. "You look great. Very stylish."

"Oh, stop."

"I'm serious." He gathered her close again. "It's good to see you. It's been too long since you were home for Lindsay's blessing."

"It's not like you're ever home either." She shifted and linked her arm through his. "Tell me about the new job. I can't believe you ended up here."

"I think you had a bit to do with that."

Her eyes narrowed suspiciously. "What do you mean?"

"I mean, it didn't hurt to have a place to stay when my company decided to send someone over here."

"Ah. So I'm a way for them to cut costs."

"And a way to make sure I didn't end up in the middle of a project somewhere in South America when I'm supposed to be here for your wedding."

"I guess there is that too." Janessa looked up at him. "Do you really think you'll be able to stay here that long? My wedding isn't for another five months."

"The contract is for at least six months." Jeremy hesitated. "Are you sure it's okay for me to stay here? I may be able to get quarters on base."

"Nonsense. It will be wonderful having you here, and I look forward to you getting to know Garrett better. It's hard knowing that the family hasn't had the chance to spend much time with him."

She led the way into a wide hallway, and Jeremy could only stare. The entryway was the size of Mary's living room, an enormous parlor situated off to one side. In front of him, a wide, sweeping staircase curved up to the second floor, the banister freshly polished.

A uniformed maid stood inside the door, and Janessa motioned to her. "Brenna, would you please have Jeremy's things brought in from his car and taken to his rooms?"

"Yes, signorina." Brenna curtsied.

"I can take care of that myself," Jeremy said, oddly uneasy at someone taking care of such a basic task for him.

"Let us spoil you a little bit," Janessa insisted.

"Really. I can do it."

"If you insist." Janessa motioned him forward. "Come on. I'll show you your rooms." She started up the stairs, pausing briefly until Jeremy started after her.

He caught up to her and lowered his voice. "You really live here?"

"Pretty unbelievable, huh?" Janessa turned down a wide hall and pushed open a door to her left. "This is yours. I'm in the next suite down."

He followed her inside and again stopped and stared. The living area in front of him was nearly as large as the entire apartment he had planned to rent in Virginia. Despite the cloudy sky, light filtered in through the double french doors on the far side of the room.

Janessa walked inside and motioned to a short hallway on his right. "The bathroom and bedroom are through here. Also, there is a safe located in the top drawer of the dresser. You can set the combination." She pointed to another door on her left. "There's a second bedroom there, but it's currently furnished to serve as an office."

"I feel like I'm staying in a five-star resort." Jeremy rested a hand on the back of a cream-colored settee. "Are you sure Prince Garrett is okay with this?"

"He's the one who insisted." Janessa's phone rang, and she glanced down at it. "That's him now." She hit the talk button. "Am I late?"

She took a step toward the door. "I'm on my way now."

As soon as she hung up, Jeremy motioned her toward the door. "Go do what you have to do. I'm sure I can entertain myself."

"Sorry about this. I have an appointment I can't miss, but I'll see you at dinner tonight, okay?"

"See you then."

"And feel free to look around. If you need anything, let the staff know."

"Thanks."

With a quick wave, she darted out of the room and down the hall.

Jeremy stepped toward the balcony doors and stared out at the scenery. He could understand now why his sister was so content with making a life here. The view was stunning.

Blue water stretched out in front of him, the waves rolling up on the white sand a short distance from the chateau. Gardens filled much of the space between the building and the beach, though many of the plants were dormant during these winter months. He could imagine they would be alive with color once spring arrived.

In a habitual gesture, he slipped his hand in his pocket and fingered his cell phone. His thoughts turned to Noelle, and he found himself conflicted about whether he should call to let her know he had arrived in Meridia. It was odd, he thought to himself, that he would feel a need to announce his presence, and he was uneasy at the prospect of putting a woman before his work.

He should be thinking about his duties here and figuring out exactly how he was supposed to make contact with his new boss.

Deciding that unpacking his car was a logical first step to preparing for his new duties, he turned from the balcony and headed for the door.

Chapter 9

NOELLE STOOD AT THE BASE of the front steps of the chateau and stared out at the ocean. "I've missed this."

"We've missed you." Enrico set one of Noelle's suitcases beside the limousine as Renzo, one of his assistants, approached.

"Thanks again for picking me up from the palace."

"It's the least I could do for my favorite daughter."

Noelle couldn't help but smile. "I'm your only daughter."

"So you are." He turned to Renzo and handed him the keys. "Will you please wash the car and park it in the garage?"

"Yes, sir." Renzo helped Enrico unload the remaining suitcases from the trunk and set them at the base of the stairs.

"We can take care of these." Enrico lifted two of the three suitcases as the front doors opened.

Hearing a set of footsteps approach, Noelle looked up just as a raindrop splashed on her cheek. She was stunned to see an unexpected guest. "Jeremy? What are you doing here?"

"I'm here to visit my sister." He jogged down the steps. He was three from the bottom when the heavens opened.

Enrico hurried toward the door to get her luggage inside, and Noelle turned to collect her last bag.

She started to lift it, but Jeremy took it from her. "I'll get that for you."

Together they rushed toward the door, the rain soaking them. Jeremy hurried past Enrico so he could open the door for the others. Once inside, Noelle swiped at the wet hair now plastered to her cheeks and tucked it behind her ears.

"Papa, this is Jeremy Rogers. Jeremy, this is my father, Enrico Saldera."

Her father set her bags down and turned to Jeremy. He spoke in English, though his Italian accent was apparent. "Ahh. You must be Janessa's brother."

"Yes." Jeremy extended his hand. "Good to meet you, sir."

"It's good to meet you too." Enrico picked up the two largest suitcases once more. "Noelle, I will take these to your room."

"Thank you." Noelle watched him disappear down the main hallway before she turned back to Jeremy. "I'm surprised you didn't tell me you were coming."

"I knew you were busy with Prince Stefano's wedding," Jeremy said.

Her thoughts immediately went to the moment the grenade went off. She forced that image away and instead tried to remember the reception and the joy Prince Stefano and Princess Alora had shared. "I have to say I'm glad to have that event behind me."

Footsteps sounded on the marble floor, and Noelle turned as Brenna approached. Delighted to see her childhood friend, she hurried toward her. "Brenna! It's so good to see you!"

Brenna gave her a hug, a grin on her face. "It's been too long since you've been home."

"I know." Remembering her manners, she took a step back and motioned to Jeremy. "Brenna, have you met Jeremy Rogers?"

"Yes. We met when he arrived," Brenna said. "Prince Garrett asked that I extend his invitation for both of you to join him for dinner this evening. The French ambassador and his entourage will be in attendance."

Noelle managed to hide her surprise that she was being invited to an official function. On occasion over the past few years, she had accompanied one of the princes to an event when they'd needed an uncomplicated date. That certainly wouldn't be the case tonight. It took her a moment for the possibilities to filter through her mind, and she keyed in on those who would undoubtedly be included on the guest list. "If he's trying to set me up with the ambassador's aide again, we're going to have a nice chat about interfering."

"I'll leave that discussion to the two of you." Brenna looked amused. "Dinner will be at seven."

"Thank you, Brenna. I'd better go unpack."

"Here you go." Jeremy handed her the suitcase he still held.

"Thank you." Noelle took a step toward the hallway before turning back to Jeremy. "I'll see you at dinner."

"I look forward to it."

* * *

Jeremy watched Noelle retreat down the hallway and again thought how gracefully she moved when she walked. The revelation that they would be dining with foreign dignitaries was a little unsettling, especially since he had yet to connect with Prince Garrett and had barely spoken to his sister since his arrival. He had hoped for a little more insight into how things worked here in Meridia before being thrown into the fire.

At least Noelle would be there too. He didn't know what to think about the idea that Prince Garrett was trying to play matchmaker for her. The spurt of jealousy surprised him, as did his delight in Noelle's lack of interest in the prospect.

He glanced out the window by the door. The rain pelting down outside had altered his plans to unload his car right away. He didn't mind getting wet, but he preferred not to track water through the chateau on his first day.

His cell phone vibrated in his pocket, and he retrieved it to find a brief message from a number he didn't recognize. *Meet me in the library. Main hall. Third door on the right.*

Intrigued and not entirely sure who would have his number, Jeremy started down the main hall, a space that was easily three times the width of a standard hall in the U.S. He passed several chairs and antique occasional tables, fresh flowers in a crystal vase atop the one nearest the door leading to the library.

He stepped inside to find himself alone. Book-filled shelves lined the walls, and a table dominated the center of the room. He browsed the shelf nearest him, discovering an impressive selection of French literature.

"See anything interesting?"

Jeremy turned to face the man standing behind him. He was about Jeremy's height—six feet tall—with brown hair, and his dark eyes quietly studied Jeremy as he reached behind him and closed the door.

"I'm Levi Marin, your new boss."

Jeremy accepted the hand Levi offered. "Jeremy Rogers." He paused before stating the obvious. "But you already knew that."

Levi simply held out a book. "I understand you have some experience running deep background checks."

"That's what I was doing in my last assignment."

"Good. Inside here you'll find a list of the employees for your sister's wedding as well as the preliminary guest list."

Jeremy opened the book to reveal folded pages inside a hollowed-out volume. He unfolded the first page and scanned the others, instantly overwhelmed. "There must be over five hundred names here. This will take months."

"Which is why I'm giving it to you now. Our first priority is clearing the employees since they will have access to the chateau and the wedding venues earlier than the guests will."

"I'm going to need secure access to Langley's database."

"Director Palmer already sent the necessary equipment. I will deliver it to your room when you unload your car." Levi motioned toward a chair. "There's something else we need to discuss."

"What's that?" Jeremy asked as he sat.

"There was an incident at Prince Stefano's wedding you need to be aware of." Levi put both hands on the chair across from Jeremy, but he remained standing. "Understand, only a handful of people know about this."

"Know about what?"

"There was a bomb."

"A bomb?" Jeremy's heart jumped into his throat. A bomb in the same place his sister had been? He swallowed hard. "What happened?"

Levi took a deep breath and let it out before finally sitting in his chair. "We were fortunate that the person who smuggled it inside was noticed in time. It was hidden inside a woman's purse. We drugged the woman, switched purses, and managed to remove the explosive from the chapel, ultimately disarming it in one of the offices."

"Any idea who was behind it?"

"We have the woman who smuggled the bomb in custody, but so far she hasn't been terribly helpful, and the background check on her didn't give us any more clues. Director Palmer mentioned some talk of someone trying to destabilize this region, but so far we have no idea who's behind it. All we know is that the possibility exists that someone might try a repeat performance at your sister's wedding."

"We can't let that happen."

"No, we can't," Levi agreed.

"Can you get me a copy of the initial reports on the bomb and a list of those who were in attendance at Prince Stefano's wedding? I'd also like to see the raw footage from the television crews. You never know if one of the cameramen might have picked up something without realizing it."

"I have a copy of the reports in my office. I'll bring that with your equipment," Levi said. "As for the television footage, I'll have to make some calls."

"I'd appreciate it." Jeremy stood, still struggling with the emotions Levi's revelation evoked. He hoped his voice sounded calm when he asked, "How do you want me to report to you?"

"I assume your phone can send and receive encrypted text messages."

"Yes. The agency issued it to me."

"Good. You can text me when you have any information, and I'll arrange to run into you," Levi told him. "I imagine your sister will introduce us within the next few days. When that happens, tell her we met when you arrived and were looking for the library."

Jeremy nodded, recognizing the wisdom in keeping the deception as close to the truth as possible. "Should I go unload my car now? I was going to wait for the rain to ease up."

He motioned to the book. "Go secure that in your room and wait another twenty minutes. Then start unloading. You'll need time to get ready for tonight."

"How did you know about that?"

Levi held out his hands and offered him a wry smile. "It's my job to know."

* * *

Noelle entered the enormous kitchen, her heart melting when she saw her mother standing by the stove, a spoon in her hand. Patrice Saldera had been running the chateau's kitchen for as long as Noelle could remember and had long been considered the best cook in the province.

Her mother turned, and her eyes lit up the moment she saw her. "Noelle!" Patrice dropped the spoon on the counter and hurried toward her with outstretched arms.

Noelle accepted the embrace and breathed in the familiar scents of baked bread and her mother's floral perfume.

When Patrice pulled back, she held her daughter at arm's length. "Let me look at you. It's been too long."

"Mama, I saw you at the wedding three days ago."

"Waving at me from across the cathedral hardly counts. How are you? How did you like working for Floria?"

"I learned a lot and slept very little."

"You know what I always say about getting enough sleep."

"Yes, Mama," Noelle said. Tongue in cheek, she added, "Now that I'm home, I'm sure you'll tuck me in bed every night to make sure I'm not up too late."

Patrice chuckled. "If you don't behave, that's exactly what I'll do. Don't think twenty-three is too old for me to turn you over my knee."

"Seems to me the last time you turned me over your knee, I was seven." Noelle laughed. "We both know the boys are the ones who caused all the trouble around here."

Before her mother could comment on Noelle's frequent role as instigator, Noelle changed the subject. "Do you need help with anything?"

"We're fine for now. You go get settled in."

Noelle snatched a croissant from a basket on the counter and grinned. "Thanks, Mama."

"You're as bad as Gianessa."

"If you weren't the best cook, you wouldn't have to worry about people sneaking food out of the kitchen." Noelle broke off a piece of croissant and popped it into her mouth as she sauntered out of the room. The familiar taste made her realize how much she'd missed her home.

Though she knew she should probably get unpacked, she glanced at her watch and decided to take a quick detour to Levi's office. When she arrived, she found him alone in front of a bank of security cameras displaying various views of the chateau and the grounds.

"I thought you had a staff to keep an eye on all of this," Noelle said, closing the door behind her.

"I do. I gave them some time off so they wouldn't see you up here."

"You don't want your staff to know I'm working with you?"

"Not particularly. The fewer people who know your true purpose here, the better." Levi handed her a file folder. "Here is a list of the attendees for dinner tonight. The ambassador has only been in Meridia for two years, and most of his staff turned over at that time."

"You don't expect any problems with any of the guests, do you?"

"No one has raised any red flags, but I still expect you to keep your ears open."

"Were you responsible for my invitation to the dinner tonight?"

"Actually, no. That was a fortunate event I hadn't planned on." Levi retrieved a cell phone from his pocket. "Do you have your cell phone with you?"

"Yes." She retrieved it from her purse and held it out.

Levi took it from her and hooked a cable from her phone to the one he held.

"What are you doing?"

"Setting up your new phone. It can send and receive encrypted messages. We don't want to take a chance on anyone intercepting anything between us." He completed the transfer and activated her new phone before handing it to her. "I programmed my number in already. I want you to check in with me in the morning. Of course, if you hear anything of concern, call me right away."

"The French have been our allies for centuries. I seriously doubt there will be anything to worry about tonight."

"Expect the unexpected and you'll find that everything is not always as it seems."

"I'll remember that."

Chapter 10

"Your Majesty, are you sure about this?" Janessa spoke into the phone to her future mother-in-law. "I know Floria did a wonderful job with Alora and Stefano's wedding, but I seem to have a hard time communicating with her."

"She can be a bit opinionated, but she's the best there is," Queen Marta said.

"She's also a tyrant."

"Oh, she's not that bad."

Janessa shifted her phone from one ear to the other. "She called my father and told him if he didn't buy a new tux, he couldn't come to the wedding."

"Oh, dear. That probably didn't go over well."

"Not at all."

"Janessa, I know Floria wasn't your first choice to help you plan your wedding, but the truth is, you need someone to oversee the details. A royal wedding has a lot of complexities, and your temple ceremony only adds to them."

"I know. You're right."

"If she gives you too much trouble, give me a call, and I'll talk to her. I think once she gets to the chateau and you start putting those final details in place, everyone's stress will ease."

"I hope so."

* * *

Jeremy stepped out of his room, grateful that Janessa had told him his suit and tie would be acceptable at tonight's dinner. He supposed he was going to have to invest in a tuxedo before too much time passed, but he was grateful he didn't need one tonight. He hated bowties.

His sister emerged into the hall. Her hair was swept up into some kind of complicated twist, and her blue gown shimmered as she moved. Jeremy let out a low whistle. "Look at you."

Janessa tucked her purse beneath her arm and closed the distance between them. "Are you ready for your first state dinner?"

"No."

Janessa laughed. "I see honesty still sits easily on you."

"I don't know about that. I do feel a bit out of my league though."

"You'll be fine. You even speak the language." Janessa tucked her arm through his. "Come on. The food alone will make up for any boring conversation."

Jeremy escorted her downstairs and into the enormous living room. French doors led to a terrace on the far side of the room. The fading sunlight filtered through tall windows along one wall, and the furniture was arranged to encourage intimate conversations. Jeremy wondered how such a large space could feel like home.

A distinguished-looking man who appeared to be in his early fifties stood near the entrance and nodded a greeting to Janessa as they approached.

"Martino, have you met my brother?" Janessa asked in English.

"I haven't had the pleasure," Martino said, his voice carrying a slight hum of disdain as though speaking English in Meridia was beneath him.

"Jeremy, Martino manages the chateau," Janessa said.

"It's good to meet you." Jeremy extended his hand.

"You as well." Martino's formal air melted away when someone called his name from across the room.

They all turned. Noelle was walking toward them dressed in yellow and looking like a vision. Her dark hair flowed over one shoulder, the flirty hemline skimming past her knees. When she reached them, she stood on her toes and kissed Martino on the cheek. "Martino, you look wonderful. How is it that you never age?"

He didn't answer her question, but warmth filled his voice. "It's good to have you back, Noelle. You have been missed." Martino turned his attention to the door when the first guests arrived. "If you'll excuse me, I believe it's time to get this evening started."

"In that case, I'd better go find Garrett," Janessa said.

Jeremy sensed his sister leave them, but his eyes stayed on Noelle. "You look stunning."

Warmth colored her cheeks. "Thank you. You look rather handsome yourself."

As Martino showed the first guests inside, Jeremy glanced over at the new arrivals. "I'm starting to think I may need to invest in a few more suits while I'm living here."

"Living here? I thought you were only here for a visit."

"No. My company transferred me to the naval base here in Bellamo. I'll actually be doing a lot of my work from here at the chateau."

Her surprise was replaced by delight. "I had no idea."

"Maybe if you're not too busy, I can convince you to show me around tomorrow."

"I'm happy to, but I wonder if I can ask you a favor."

"Anything."

As voices filled the front hall, Noelle tucked her hand into his arm and nudged him into the parlor. "Do you see the man over there? Late twenties, blue tie."

"Yeah. What about him?"

"Can you hang out with me tonight and make sure he doesn't corner me?"

"Standing in as your date isn't a favor. That's an honor."

"That's sweet of you to say."

"I gather that's the ambassador's aide you mentioned earlier?"

"Yes. My impression is that he's the type who would like to have a girl in every port, so to speak. I'm not interested in fulfilling that role in Meridia."

"I don't blame you." They continued farther into the room, and she lowered her voice. "Come on. You can stand watch while I rearrange the place cards on the table."

"We have assigned seats?"

She didn't answer, apparently already focused on her objective, as she led the way to a doorway across the room.

Jeremy stood in awe as they entered the next room. An enormous table stretched down the center of the massive dining hall. Three chandeliers were evenly spaced overhead, and the place settings confirmed that tonight was very much a formal dinner. He hoped he could figure out which fork to use when.

Noelle quickly circled the table, picking up one place card and carrying it with her until she found what she was looking for. She switched two cards, and then two more. Once she was satisfied with the new seating arrangement, she hurried back to the door, a look of mischief and humor on her face.

"All done?"

She nodded. "I had to make sure I didn't put Michel too close to your sister either. She and Garrett aren't terribly fond of him."

"Then why would Garrett try to set you up with him?"

"He isn't really. He just knows that by having me here, Michel won't be as likely to cause trouble. I believe there was a little incident between him and your sister when they were both living in Paris."

"What kind of incident?"

"The kind where he tried putting moves on her and she broke his nose."

Laughter burst from him, and he struggled to stifle it. "Are you serious?"

"Very." She slipped her hand back into the crook of his arm and motioned with her other hand toward the guests. "Shall we?"

"I guess we shall."

* * *

Noelle had expected to translate for Jeremy, or at the very least thought he would suffer disapproval when he expected the guests to converse with him in English, so she was delighted to learn he not only spoke French but also did so fluently.

Ambassador Fitzroy was among the first to make Jeremy's acquaintance, and the older man didn't waste any time trying to ferret out new information. "Tell me, Monsieur Rogers, how do you feel about your sister marrying into royalty?"

Jeremy looked across the room where his sister and Prince Garrett were chatting with another couple. "They seem to be a good match."

"Surely it must be of some concern to know that your sister has to give up her American citizenship to become Meridia's next princess."

"My sister's happiness is more important to me than what country issues her driver's license. I have no doubt she will thrive wherever she chooses to live."

Michel stepped between the ambassador and Noelle. "Noelle, you are even more beautiful than I remembered."

"Thank you, Michel." Noelle shifted slightly to put a little more distance between them. With this man, every inch counted. "May I introduce you to my date, Jeremy Rogers."

"Your date?" His eyebrows drew together slightly, forming a wrinkle of disappointment. "I wasn't aware you were seeing anyone."

Jeremy spoke before Noelle could respond. "Ambassador Fitzroy, will you excuse us? Noelle promised me a look at the gardens before dinner."

"Of course." Ambassador Fitzroy nodded stiffly.

Jeremy offered his hand. "Noelle?"

"We'll see you both at dinner," Noelle said as a farewell. She slipped her hand into his and let him lead her toward the terrace doors.

"Do you have a wrap?" he asked in a lowered voice.

"Not with me," she whispered back.

He unbuttoned his suit jacket and shrugged out of it, putting it around her shoulders before he opened the door.

"You're going to freeze."

"I'll be fine." He nudged her out the door and closed it behind him before adding, "Besides, we both needed a quick escape."

Noelle pulled his jacket more firmly around her shoulders to ward off the chill and looked out at the Mediterranean. The last of the sun's rays shimmered on the water, the earlier storm clouds barely visible in the distance. "Did you really want to see the gardens?"

"Might as well. You did promise to show me around."

"I'm afraid we don't have enough time to explore everything before dinner." She started down the wide steps, grateful she had his arm to hold on to—heels and stairs weren't always the best combination for her.

"In that case, show me your favorite part."

Noelle thought for a moment. She had never considered favoring one part of the grounds over another. A smile spread slowly over her face as one memory warmed her.

She motioned to their right and started down a winding path that led to a section of the seawall. "When I was ten, Queen Marta decided to throw a surprise party for Prince Garrett's sixteenth birthday. The invitation was stamped 'Top Secret.' I carried that invitation around with me for weeks, pretending I knew secrets no one else was privy to."

They passed by trailing vines and a glossy lemon tree. When they emerged at the thick stone wall, Noelle motioned toward the water. "I used to sit on this wall and stare out at the boats coming and going, pretending I was keeping track of everyone and everything."

"So you wanted to be a spy when you were little?"

Her laughter rang out, amused both by the reality of his words and the irony that, in a small way, she was fulfilling that childhood ambition. "I know that isn't a typical career choice for a child, but growing up around so much security, it was fun to see how much we could get away with without the guards noticing."

Jeremy chuckled. "And to think you look so innocent."

"According to my mother, looks can be deceiving."

Jeremy looked out at the ocean, and an odd expression came over him. "Isn't that the truth." He fell silent before turning back to her. "I suppose we should head back in."

Noelle fell in step with him, not sure what to think of his sudden change of mood. "I hope you don't mind me calling you my date."

"Not at all. In fact, I think it's time we go out on a real date. That is, if you're willing."

Noelle looked up at him, her stomach fluttering unexpectedly. "I'd like that."

"Do you have plans tomorrow?"

"I was going to go riding in the morning, but after that, I'm free as far as I know."

"Can I take you to dinner tomorrow night, then?"

"I'd like that."

"Great. Then it's a date."

Chapter 11

NOELLE LED HER HORSE OUT of the barn, anxious for some time alone with her thoughts. Dinner the night before had been a pleasant surprise, and she was already looking forward to her date with Jeremy.

She also couldn't help but wonder if she had revealed too much of herself when she had spoken of her childhood dreams. The last thing she needed was for Jeremy to become suspicious of her as she tried to adapt to her new role in the spy world. Not that she was really a spy.

The dinner conversations had been tedious at best. Even though she and Jeremy had sat together during the meal, the ambassador's continued pleas with Prince Garrett about increasing oil exports to France dominated the evening. Maybe she should have rearranged their seats to be at the opposite end of the table when she'd had the chance.

She had met with Levi briefly and shared a summary of those conversations, but now she was ready to get out and enjoy the unseasonably warm weather and the freedom of riding on the wide stretch of beach between the chateau and the naval base a few miles away.

"Hey there."

Startled, she turned to see Jeremy standing behind her. He was dressed casually in jeans and a sweatshirt. "Good morning. I didn't expect to find you up and around so early."

"I have a feeling it will take me a few days to adjust to this time zone." He approached her horse and ran a hand along the gelding's neck. "He's a beauty."

"Do you ride?"

"I grew up on a farm. I think I learned to ride before I could walk."

Her lips curved up. "Would you like to join me? We can start on that tour I promised you."

"Are you sure you don't mind? I don't want to intrude."

Though she had been looking forward to riding alone, she found she didn't mind adjusting her plans to include Jeremy. "I don't mind at all." She looped her horse's reins around a hitching post near the barn entrance and motioned inside the huge structure. "Come on. Let's find you a mount."

Ten minutes later, they were both enjoying the beach on horseback.

"I didn't realize until last night that you spoke French. Where did you learn to speak it so well?"

"I served my mission in Geneva."

"I can't imagine that was an easy mission. Europeans aren't always the most open to new religions."

"I'm sure every mission has its challenges." He glanced over at her. "You were obviously open to learning about the gospel."

"Yes, but after seeing all of the corruption in the Meridian Church, I was ready for a change."

"What about your family? How do they feel about you becoming Mormon?"

"Excellent question."

Jeremy urged his horse to quicken its pace, waiting until he could see her face before he asked, "And the answer is?"

"I don't know." Embarrassed by the truth, she worried he wouldn't understand, but she'd already said too much. "I haven't told them yet."

"Why not?"

"At first it was because I didn't want to try to explain it to them over the phone," she said, trying to find a way to put her feelings into words. "Then, when I got home, I was only here for two days before I moved to the palace to help with Prince Stefano's wedding. I didn't want to ruin what little time I had with them by bringing up such a difficult subject."

"I gather you expect your family to be upset over your decision."

"Honestly I'm not sure. I'll have to talk to them about it soon though. Sunday is only a few days away, and this will be the first time I attend church here."

"Perhaps you can drive there with me."

"I'd like that."

"Have you been by the new temple site yet?"

"No. It's supposed to open early this summer, and I heard there's going to be an open house. I'm really hoping I can go to it."

"Me too." Jeremy shifted his attention to the half dozen sailboats dotting the deep-blue water. "Are there always this many boats on the water?"

"Not usually this time of year. I think people are just taking advantage of the nice weather. During the summer, though, the numbers increase."

"I would have thought these waters would be restricted because of the vessels going in and out of the naval base."

"Those boats are about as close as they're allowed to come." Noelle waved toward the beach behind them. "There's a harbor on the other side of those rocks where a lot of locals launch from."

"Do you sail?"

"Growing up here, I didn't have a choice but to learn," she said. "What about you?"

"I'm afraid there aren't a lot of places to sail in Iowa."

"Do you want to learn?"

"I'd love to," Jeremy admitted, "but I'm not sure I'll have much time with this new job starting up."

"What exactly will you be doing?"

"I'll be consulting on the new facilities being built at the naval base."

"You're an engineer, right?"

"Yeah. Electrical engineer." He looked out at the water and then shifted his gaze to the chateau as they rode by. "This place is amazing. I can't believe my sister lives here."

"You live here too now."

"Yes, but that's temporary. This is her home."

"How long do you expect to stay?"

"Six months or so. The great thing is that I will be here through my sister's wedding."

"Just pray you don't get roped into helping with the wedding."

"I'm already praying. After hearing how crazy your life was before Prince Stefano's wedding, I'm planning to keep a low profile around here."

"Good luck with that. The wedding planner, Floria, arrives Monday. I imagine she'll have this place turned upside down before she even unpacks." Noelle leaned down and patted her horse's neck. "Come on. Let's give these horses a good run."

She leaned forward and tapped her heels against the horse's sides. Her mount responded, trotting for two steps and then moving into a canter. As soon as she saw Jeremy come up beside her, she grinned at him. "Race?"

He grinned back. "You're on."

In unison, they pushed for more speed, and Noelle found the freedom she had been craving since returning to Meridia.

* * *

Jeremy knew he probably shouldn't have indulged in such a long ride with Noelle, but Director Palmer had told him to socialize with the upper levels of Meridian society. He didn't have a clue if Noelle was related to the royal family somehow or if she was simply part of their social circle, but he imagined it would take him some time to figure out how everyone was connected.

He didn't mind having an excuse to spend some time with Noelle, royal or not, regardless. He had already spent far too much time thinking about her, and that had been before he'd known they were going to be living in the same country.

He also appreciated the opportunity to get a better lay of the land. Literally. Together they had ridden to where a jut of land interrupted the beach, the far side of which was home to the naval base.

From the information Director Palmer had given him, the new U.S. naval base was being built on what used to be part of the Meridian naval base. Once completed, the two would coexist side by side.

After getting a glimpse of a destroyer coming into port, he could now see how the boating lanes were shared between the recreational and fishing vessels and the naval vessels traveling to and from the base.

From the beach, Noelle had led him down a trail that circled through the woods surrounding the chateau. Finally they emerged in the clearing where the barn and open pastures were located.

A man in his seventies stood beside a mare that appeared to be ready to foal. He rubbed the horse's belly, speaking softly to her in Italian. When he heard them approaching, he stood and turned toward them.

"Noelle!" He then rattled off a string of Italian Jeremy couldn't understand.

Noelle dismounted and was quickly scooped up in the older man's arms. The man might have been elderly, but he moved with an agility that rivaled someone half his age.

Jeremy dismounted and watched the animated conversation between the two.

Finally Noelle turned to him. "Jeremy, this is my grandfather, Paolo Saldera." She then spoke in Italian, and Jeremy was able to pick out enough to recognize that she was completing the introduction.

Jeremy offered his hand. "It's good to meet you, sir."

Paolo said something to Noelle, and she laughed. "My grandfather said I need to give you Italian lessons if you plan to stay for long."

"I think he's right. If you're offering, I would seriously take you up on it."

"I'm sure we can arrange something."

Jeremy tied his horse to a hitching post and leaned down to uncinch the saddle. Paolo said something to Noelle, who in turn translated. "He said that he will take care of the horses for us."

"Are you sure?" Jeremy asked.

Noelle nodded.

"Let me at least take the saddle inside for him." He pulled it off and carried it into the tack room. After the saddle and pad were properly stored, he emerged outside where Noelle waited for him.

"*Grazie*," Jeremy said, nodding toward Paolo.

"*Di nada.*"

"See, we have you speaking Italian already."

"I think I may need to learn a few more words than that."

"Maybe a few."

Chapter 12

JEREMY TAPPED ON THE COMPUTER keys, inputting names in various search engines as he started his background checks. He would have to talk to Levi about getting a printer and a locked filing cabinet. He processed information so much better when he could look at it in black and white instead of on a screen.

A knock sounded at his door, and he quickly closed his web browser. "Come in."

Janessa pushed the door open. "There you are. I was wondering where you were hiding."

"I'm hardly hiding."

"Close enough. You should come downstairs and have lunch with me and Garrett."

"Sounds good." Jeremy closed his computer and opened the drawer where his safe was located. After securing his computer, he followed his sister into the hall and down the stairs, then through the main-level hallway. "Is anyone else eating with us?"

"No. It's just us today." Her eyebrows lifted. "Was there someone you were hoping would be eating with us? Noelle, perhaps?"

"Just wondering."

Garrett approached from the other direction. "Just wondering what?"

"If Noelle was eating with us." Janessa reached up and kissed Garrett's cheek. "I think my brother is smitten."

Garrett slapped Jeremy's back good-naturedly. "You have good taste."

Garrett pushed open a wide door and led the way into a restaurant-style kitchen. The woman standing at the counter was slightly round and held a large butcher's knife in her hand.

Janessa spoke in French when the woman turned. "Patrice, this is my brother Jeremy. Jeremy, Patrice does the cooking here at the chateau."

"Were you the one responsible for dinner last night?" Jeremy asked, also opting to speak in French.

Patrice nodded.

Jeremy turned to Janessa and sent her an apologetic look. "Sorry, sis. Now that I'm here, I may never leave."

Patrice chuckled. "Don't worry, Gianessa. If he stays too long, I'll put him on dish duty."

"She did that to me often enough growing up," Garrett said under his breath.

"Usually after he broke something." She waved toward the far side of the room. "Go sit down. Lunch will be ready in a minute."

Janessa led the way across the room and through the door leading to a breakfast room of sorts. Eight chairs surrounded the square table, and a hutch dominated the far wall. The table was already set for three, complete with a pitcher of water and another of juice in the center.

"What did you think of the company last night?" Garrett asked as they all sat.

"It was interesting. I didn't expect the French ambassador to be so blatantly single-minded."

"He was that," Garrett agreed. He filled his water glass and proceeded to fill Janessa's and Jeremy's as well. "I wanted to thank you for helping divert Michel's attention last night. It's never easy to refuse his request to have Noelle dine with us, but I appreciated knowing she wouldn't have to deal with his advances."

"I was happy to help."

Patrice entered the room balancing two plates on one arm and carrying a third in her other hand. "Here you are. Let me know if you need anything else."

"This looks wonderful," Janessa said.

Four-inch-high club sandwiches, side Caesar salads, and french fries that appeared to have just come off the stove. Jeremy was sure he had died and gone to heaven. He lowered his voice. "Do you eat like this all the time?"

"Now you know why I make a point of going for a run every day."

After Janessa offered a blessing on the food, Jeremy bit into his sandwich and rolled his eyes in appreciation. "This may be the best sandwich I've ever had."

"You certainly won't go hungry while you're here," Garrett said. He set his sandwich down and looked at Jeremy. "So, what's the deal with you and Noelle?"

"I met her at Mary's house a few months ago, and we've talked a few times. No big deal."

"She's a great girl. We grew up together."

"Is this you telling me to watch my step because she's like a younger sister to you?"

Garrett chuckled. "Something like that. Although I should warn you that she does have two older brothers who would probably get to you before I could."

"Good to know." Jeremy took another bite and considered using Garrett's friendship to his advantage. "Since you know her so well, maybe you can suggest where I might take her to dinner tonight?"

Garrett fell silent for a moment. Then he seemed to accept the situation and nodded. "I have a few ideas."

* * *

Noelle knocked on Prince Garrett's office door, her earlier conversation with Jeremy replaying in her head.

Garrett called from behind the closed door. "Come in."

She pushed the door open and peeked inside. "I'm sorry to bother you, but do you have a minute?"

"For you, of course." He stood and waved her inside. "Is everything okay?"

"I hope so, but I need your advice."

Humor danced in his eyes. "Is this about your date with Jeremy?"

"How did you know about that?"

"We had lunch together today."

"He's only been here a day and you're already questioning him?"

"Someone has to do it. Stefano is on his honeymoon, and Archer and Saul aren't around." He motioned for her to sit and reclaimed the chair behind his desk. "What's going on? Are you nervous about your date?"

"Maybe a little, but that's not why I'm here. I need your advice on something that happened while I was living in the U.S."

"You got a tattoo?" he asked playfully.

"No, I got baptized."

"Baptized?"

"I'm Mormon."

Garrett fell silent as surprise melted into acceptance. "That's wonderful, Noelle. I'm happy for you. When did this happen? And how did I not know about it?"

"You had a lot going on here while I was living in the U.S."

"Your parents don't know yet, do they?"

"No. That's what I was hoping to talk to you about. You obviously went through this. How did you tell your parents when you converted?"

"It wasn't easy," Garrett admitted. "I tried telling them a few times, but national security kept taking precedence. Ultimately I sat down with all of my family and explained to them that this was something I needed to be happy. It took some time, but eventually they accepted my decision."

"I keep playing possible conversations with them over and over in my mind, but I honestly have no idea what to expect."

"Surprise at first. Maybe even some hurt that you've abandoned your culture." Garrett rested his forearms against his desk and leaned forward. "My advice is to remember that beneath it all, they love you and want you to be happy. Let them vent their feelings, and be patient with them. They haven't had the opportunity to work through the possibilities the way you have."

"You're right." Noelle stood. "Thanks for the advice."

"You're welcome." Garrett stood as well. "Janessa and I normally leave for church around eight thirty on Sunday mornings. You're welcome to drive over with us. I'm sure we'll be giving Jeremy a ride too."

"Thanks."

"And let me know if you need someone to talk to after you break the news to your parents. Like you said, I've been through this before."

Noelle crossed to the door. "I'll see you later."

She left his office, her thoughts filled with the possible reactions from her family. Hurt was inevitable. Even if they were accepting of her decision, they would be hurt because she had waited so long to confide in them. And, of course, there was the concern that they would struggle with the idea of her having left the Meridian Church.

Thinking of her upcoming date with Jeremy, she made a decision. She would wait to talk to her parents until tomorrow. After all, what was one more day?

* * *

Jeremy straightened his tie and pulled his keys from his pocket. He thought of the background checks he needed to start on and the new equipment in his room he should be setting up in his office.

The news of a bombing attempt at the last royal wedding weighed heavily on his mind, an attempt that could have cost his sister's life. He needed to get to work, but tonight he wanted to remember what life was all about away from work. For months he had entertained the idea of spending time with Noelle socially, time to get to know who she was when she wasn't surrounded by his family and distracted by his niece.

Tonight he was going to give himself that gift. Tomorrow he would dig in and make sure everything was done to protect Janessa and those she cared about.

He walked outside and crossed to the twelve-car garage. Twelve cars. The need for such a large structure was yet another symbol of how different life was here than from where he grew up.

Sure, they had plenty of vehicles on his family's farm in Iowa. Work trucks, tractors, and the SUV his mother drove. Only his mother's car had ever rated high enough to score a spot in the garage. And he certainly hadn't ever seen a limousine in his drive back home, except for the weekend Garrett and Janessa had come for a visit. No, it was nothing like this.

The thought crossed his mind that this life was normal for Noelle. He still wasn't quite sure how her family fit in with the ruling class. From what his sister had told him, the chateau belonged to Garrett, yet it appeared Noelle had not only grown up here, but her parents and grandfather also still resided here. He didn't understand how they could be well-off enough to provide Noelle with a private plane but didn't live in their own home.

Jeremy walked into the garage, surprised to find Enrico inside.

"*Buona sera*," Enrico offered before switching to his heavily accented English. "I understand you and my daughter are going into town together."

"Yes. I hope that's okay with you."

He gave a curt nod. "May I ask where you are taking her?"

"Bonvivante."

Now his thick eyebrows lifted. "Did you know that's her favorite restaurant?"

"Prince Garrett mentioned it," Jeremy said. Not sure how he would feel if their roles were reversed, he opted for full disclosure. "Even though

I've known Noelle for a few months, this is our first real date. Do you have any ideas for where I might take her after dinner?"

He fell silent for a moment, as though debating whether to help or hinder Jeremy's evening plans with his daughter. After a moment, he asked, "Have you been dating many other women since meeting my Noelle?"

"No, sir. Since I met your daughter, I've lost interest in dating anyone else," Jeremy said, hoping his answer would meet with Enrico's approval. The older man's posture relaxed slightly, and Jeremy felt like he had won a small victory.

"One can never go wrong with a walk on the beach. There's one place she's particularly fond of." Enrico pulled a map off the counter that stretched along the width of the garage and gave him directions.

"Thank you, Mr. Saldera. I appreciate your help."

"Call me Enrico. When my boys come home to visit, there are too many Signore Salderas to keep us straight."

"Where are your sons?"

"My youngest is away at sea. He is in the navy. My oldest is in his last year of medical school."

"I hope I get the chance to meet them while I'm here."

"You will. They will both be at Prince Garrett's wedding." He glanced at his watch. "You'd better get going. You don't want to keep my daughter waiting."

Jeremy nodded and held up the map. "Thanks again for your help."

"Have fun tonight."

"We will."

Chapter 13

NOELLE TRIED ON EVERYTHING IN her closet. Twice. Jeremy had mentioned having dinner together, but she had no idea where he was taking her and worried he might expect her to make a suggestion.

Her favorite restaurant in Bellamo was so expensive she didn't feel comfortable suggesting it, but she preferred not to eat at one of the family-style diners in town. While the food was wonderful at many of them, she had little doubt that they would run into any number of her friends and acquaintances. She wanted a chance to get to know Jeremy better, not catch up with everyone she had known since childhood.

She glanced at her watch and realized her time for debating had run out.

She sorted through her jewelry box and found a simple pair of pearl earrings, a gift from her mother, and the pearl necklace she had inherited from her grandmother. After putting them on, she dug out a pair of shoes that matched the black dress she now wore.

Annoyed at herself because she was running late, she grabbed her coat and hurried out of her room. When she arrived in the main entryway, Jeremy was walking through the front door.

"I'm sorry I'm late." Her heels clicked on the tile as she entered.

"You're right on time." He moved toward her. "You look stunning."

Her smile bloomed, and she could feel a blush rising in her cheeks. "Thank you."

"Let me help you with your coat." He took it from her and helped her slip it on.

When he took her hand in his, little butterflies erupted inside her, and she wondered how she would be able to eat anything at dinner with her stomach already so full of nerves.

When they reached his car, he released her hand and opened the door for her, waiting for her to get settled before closing it and circling to the driver's side.

To her relief, he didn't ask for dining suggestions. Instead, he asked about her day, and they fell into easy conversation. It wasn't until they pulled up in front of the restaurant that she realized where he was taking her. Curious, she looked over at him. "This is my favorite restaurant. How did you know about this place?"

"I might have asked Prince Garrett for some suggestions."

"That was very thoughtful. Thank you."

"You're welcome." He climbed out and helped her from the car.

When they walked inside, the ambiance was everything Noelle remembered. Classical music played softly, and the scent of freshly baked bread and spices wafted through the air. The lights were low, and candles flickered atop linen-draped tables.

Jeremy spoke to the maître d' in French. "Reservation for Rogers."

The older man checked his book and motioned for them to follow. He led them to a table by a window overlooking the water. Once they were seated with their menus in hand, the maître d' said, "Your waiter will be with you shortly."

"Thank you."

Jeremy left his menu unopened as he enjoyed the view outside. Noelle let her gaze wander to the waves crashing in beneath the darkening sky, the white foam rolling onto the sand before dissipating when the water rushed back into the sea.

"I've always loved this view," Noelle said.

"It's definitely nothing like the view from Mary's window."

"Very true, but I enjoyed living so close to the city. D.C. has some amazing sights. I felt like everywhere I turned there was another treasure to be discovered."

"One of these days I need to take some time to play tourist there."

"I gather you didn't see many of the sights while you were staying with Mary?"

"I'm afraid I spent most of my time either working or driving to and from work."

"You won't have to worry much about that here. The naval base is only a five-minute drive, and that includes passing through security."

His eyes narrowed slightly. "I wouldn't have thought you'd spent any time there."

"I don't usually, but one of my brothers was stationed there for training when he first joined the navy. I used to visit him a lot, usually delivering some of my mother's cooking."

"He must have loved that."

"Definitely. My mother is an amazing cook."

"So are you. I've had your crepes, remember?" Jeremy opened his menu. "Do you have any recommendations?"

"I've never had anything I didn't like here, but the duck is amazing."

They chatted about the various dishes and local cuisine. By the time their appetizers were served, Noelle's nerves had subsided. As they ate, she was reminded of how much she enjoyed Jeremy's company and found herself grateful that he would be in Bellamo for the foreseeable future.

* * *

Jeremy couldn't have asked for a better evening. A beautiful, interesting companion, wonderful food, and the kind of ambiance he rarely experienced outside of watching it on a television screen.

"I have to say you have excellent taste in restaurants," he said as they walked out into the cool night air. "The food was better than I expected."

"I'm glad you liked it." Moonlight danced over her skin, and he wondered what it was about her that had prompted him to keep in touch with her over the past few months even though he had never anticipated living in the same country, much less the same residence.

He supposed her easy way with his family had intrigued him at first, making him feel like he was missing out on something by being away. Now he realized her openness and honesty also tugged at him. Could it be that his job working in intelligence made him crave honesty in others when he couldn't always offer it himself? He pushed that thought aside and focused once more on Noelle. "Thank you for coming with me tonight."

"I'm glad you asked. This has been really nice."

"Are you up for a walk on the beach? Maybe we can work up an appetite for some dessert later."

"I don't know that I can eat another bite, but a walk sounds nice." She started toward a path that led to the water on the far side of the restaurant, but Jeremy took her hand and directed her toward the car instead.

"The beach is that way."

"I heard there's a nice spot on the edge of town." He helped her into the car, pleased when she didn't question their destination. A few minutes later, he pulled into a parking space across from a house that had been converted into a restaurant. "If you aren't hungry enough for dessert, we can always get something to take home."

"How did you know about this place?"

"Your father."

Both elegant eyebrows lifted. "Have you been talking to everyone about me?"

"Not everyone." They got out of the car and started toward the beach, walking hand in hand.

"So do you do this often?" she asked.

"Do what?"

"Spy on people."

He banked down the surge of guilt. Remembering his CIA instructor's advice to stick as close to the truth as possible, he said, "Only on people who matter."

"Should I be flattered?"

"Definitely."

* * *

Noelle felt like she was walking on air as she made her way through the servants' quarters and into her room. Her date had been perfect in every way. She was touched by the effort Jeremy had made in soliciting advice from those who knew her best. After their walk on the beach, they had shared a piece of the caramel torte she was so fond of and then taken a leisurely drive through town.

She heard the whisper of voices as she passed by Regina's quarters. She slowed her steps, concerned that Regina was up at such a late hour. Her housekeeping duties typically began at six o'clock each morning, and she rarely stayed up past ten.

Noelle glanced at her watch. Eleven forty-five. She stopped by the door and listened. It took only a moment to realize Regina was talking on the phone rather than to someone in the room.

"I know I promised, but the royal family isn't hiring right now." She paused, clearly listening to the other person's response. "What do you expect me to do? Security isn't approving any new hires." Another pause. "The only thing I can think of is to try Floria. She'll be arriving within the week. I have to think she'll need some help for the wedding. Yes, I'll let you know if I hear of anything."

The conversation was ending, so Noelle continued down the hall to her room. She pulled out her cell phone and sent a message to Levi, outlining the call she overheard. She doubted it was anything of concern, but Levi had repeatedly said to let him know about anything out of the ordinary.

Pushing aside thoughts of Regina and whatever friend was angling for a job, Noelle replayed her night with Jeremy and wondered when she would see him again.

* * *

Adrienne Acord spent her days surrounded by swans. Day in and day out, she edited the images that would make up the nightly news. The men and women in front of the cameras always looked so polished, so perfect. Adrienne knew they had a makeup artist committed to making sure they appeared flawless on camera, but the more she watched their images, the more she felt like the ugly duckling who didn't belong.

The talent and producers had already headed home after the last news broadcast, but Adrienne remained, making sure the highlights from today would be easily accessible tomorrow.

She shut down her editing equipment and headed down the hall toward the back entrance. The overhead lights shone brightly, as though they could somehow convince her it wasn't well past midnight.

After retrieving her car keys from her oversized purse, she pushed open the door and walked across the nearly empty parking lot toward her car.

A blue sedan sat two spaces down from her hatchback, and she wondered if the security guard had a new car. Typically his pickup was the only vehicle still in the lot when she left each night, and she couldn't see it in its usual spot.

Looking forward to going home and collapsing in bed, she dropped her purse onto the passenger seat and shoved the key into the ignition.

Instead of the engine starting when she turned the key, she heard only a series of clicks.

"You've got to be kidding me," she mumbled under her breath. She tried again and then a third time, each attempt yielding the same result.

Her mind whirled with possibilities, not of what had caused the car trouble but of who she could call in the middle of the night for help. She lived alone, and she didn't have any family nearby.

She climbed out of the car with the intent of asking the night guard for help but noticed his pickup parked beside the news van on the far side of the lot just as she heard footsteps approaching.

She whirled around and caught sight of a man walking toward her. In the dark, she couldn't tell much about him, but her racing heart helped exaggerate his size and stature.

When he angled toward the blue sedan and unlocked it, she relaxed slightly. He started to climb in and then looked over at her as though noticing her for the first time. "Is everything okay? It's awfully late to be out in a dark parking lot."

Not quite ready to reveal her troubles, she asked a question of her own. "Who are you? And what are you doing here this time of night?"

"Oh, sorry. I was just bringing some dinner to my brother. He works security here." He offered his hand.

She stared at it a moment, not sure what to do. She was alone with a man she had never seen before, her car wouldn't start, and it was the middle of the night. Manners won out, and she put her hand in his.

"Hey, aren't you Adrienne?"

Now she took an uneasy step back. "How do you know my name?"

"My brother told me about you. Described you to a tee: the hard-working beauty who is always the last to leave. I guess I'd better get going." He opened his car door but again hesitated. "Are you sure you're okay?"

Had he really just called her a beauty? Her thoughts jumbled at the unexpected compliment, and a thread of trust was formed. "Actually, my car won't start."

"I can take a look if you want." He closed his door once more and stepped toward her.

"That would be great, if you don't mind." She stepped aside while he opened the hood to take a look, using the flashlight app on his phone to compensate for the darkness. He then dug some jumper cables out of his trunk to make sure it wasn't the battery.

After ten minutes of looking and fiddling, he finally closed the trunk. "It looks like it's the alternator, which means we'll have to wait until tomorrow. Can I give you a ride somewhere?"

Wavering, she once again considered her options. Though limited, she couldn't bring herself to trust a stranger enough to get into a car with him. She looked across the lot again, and a new idea formed. "Thanks for the offer, but I can go borrow the keys for the news van."

"Are you sure you'll be okay?"

"I'll be fine. Worst case, I'll put in some unplanned overtime."

"Okay. If you're sure."

She retrieved her purse from her car and turned to thank him for his help only to see a blur of movement. Something connected with her head, and the last thing she heard was her keys dropping to the ground.

Chapter 14

JEREMY SHIFTED THE DESK IN his office so he could enjoy the view out the window while also having easy access to the door. He had awoken early and set up the equipment Levi had delivered to his room and was now arranging the paperwork that would accompany his first task.

When he had taken computer classes in college, he had never anticipated using his skills to circumvent and hack into other people's systems, but more often than not, that was exactly how he spent his days.

A knock sounded on his door, and he moved out of his office and crossed his living room to open it. He was surprised to find Levi standing in the hall. "Is everything okay?"

"Can I come in?"

"Yeah, sure." Jeremy stepped aside, closing the door as soon as Levi entered. "Is something wrong?"

"We just got the preliminary report on the bomb planted at the wedding."

"And?"

"The analysts at Langley believe the bomb maker was Ivan Byrd."

"I'm new at this. Who is Ivan Byrd?"

"He's a mercenary type, someone who will contract out to anyone able to pay a high enough price."

"Then there's no way to be sure who was behind it."

"Not yet anyway. The finance folks are trying to track any payments to him, but I doubt they'll find anything. Byrd has been doing this for a while. He's too smart to leave a paper trail."

Jeremy studied the man across from him. While his demeanor was businesslike, the fact remained that something about this news must have been pressing for Levi to risk coming to his room. "What aren't you telling me?"

Levi crossed the room and lowered himself into a chair. He waited for Jeremy to sit across from him before speaking. "Even though Byrd freelances, his clients typically come from the same circle."

"What circle is that?"

"People whose main objective is to gain profit and power. These aren't your typical terrorists trying to make a point or striking at a perceived enemy. These people only focus on targets that are a means to an end."

"You think they'll try again, that they'll strike at Janessa's wedding."

"That's exactly what I think they'll do." Levi nodded. "Or at least they'll try."

"Why Meridia? What would someone like that have to gain by targeting the royal family?"

"The royal family and a significant number of dignitaries and leaders from all over the world."

"I realize the wedding will be a target-rich environment, but again, why here? There are any number of peace talks and trade summits they could go for, several of which would include the king of Meridia."

"I've been going over threat assessments for hours, and I've come up with three logical reasons."

Jeremy waited silently.

"First, we've heard chatter that someone may be trying to destabilize this region, likely to disrupt the oil trade here." He shifted forward in his chair. "Though small, Meridia is the leading oil exporter in Europe, except for Russia."

"If someone were to knock out the royal family, who would take control of the government here?"

"Theoretically the ruling council. That brings me to the second possibility. Someone could be trying to clear the path to take the throne."

"That should be easy to figure out. Who was the highest ranking royal family member not at the wedding?"

"That's just it. Everyone was there, including the majority of the ruling council. Only four council members weren't in attendance."

"If you give me their names, I'll run backgrounds on all of them."

Levi pulled a piece of paper from his pants pocket and handed it to him. "There's one more name on there I want you to run too."

"Who's that?"

"Gustave Nardini. It's probably nothing, but he was talking to one of the maids late the other night, asking for help in finding a job here."

"I'll check him out." Jeremy scanned the names briefly, none of them looking familiar. "You said you had three logical reasons Meridia could be a target. What's the third?"

"The third would be to target one of the guests at the wedding, someone whose security is so tight that this would provide more access than normal."

"It sounds like I have my work cut out for me."

"And then some." Levi stood. "I suggest you get your office set up soon. Five months may seem like a long time, but your sister's wedding will be here before we know it."

"I was working on that before you got here," Jeremy told him. "I did want to ask you something though. My cover is that I'm working as a contractor for the naval base. Is there any way I can get access over there to maintain appearances?"

"The new administration building is still under construction, so there isn't any office space for you at the moment, but I can get you credentials so you can make some visits and create the illusion that you're working there."

"I'd appreciate it. Thanks."

Levi stood. "Let me know if you find anything."

"You know I will." Jeremy watched him leave and headed back to his office. Like it or not, it was time to get to work.

* * *

Noelle sprinkled flour onto a cutting board and began rolling out a piecrust. Her mother stood beside her, mixing the ingredients for the crepes she planned to make for dinner. With only a few days until Floria would arrive to begin working on Janessa's wedding, Noelle had hoped to find a quiet moment to talk to her parents about her newfound religion. Unfortunately her father had left the chateau early that morning to drive Garrett somewhere and her time with her mother had included a constant stream of staff members coming and going.

While she wasn't happy with the constant interruptions, she knew Levi appreciated the updates she was able to provide him about the staff and their lives away from work. Ronaldo had gotten himself into hot water with his latest love interests, both of whom had thought of themselves as his only girlfriend. Lilia had missed more work than usual because her daughter was recovering from pneumonia.

The text messages to Levi often resulted in a brief meeting as she was passing through the halls. The door opened, and Noelle glanced over at Jeremy, who was walking in. A look of confusion appeared on his face when he saw her.

"Hi, Jeremy." Noelle turned to face him. "I assume you've met my mother."

"Your mother?" Again confusion flickered across his face. "We've met, but I didn't realize you were related."

Patrice wiped her hands on her apron. "Jeremy, would you like some lunch? I have some ham and cheese in the refrigerator."

"That sounds perfect. Thank you." When Patrice moved to get the food for him, he held up a hand. "I can get it. You have your hands full."

"There are rolls and croissants in the basket on the table."

Noelle was surprised when her mother didn't argue. It wasn't often she let people make themselves so comfortable in her kitchen.

Jeremy proceeded to line up ingredients on the far counter, using a croissant for his bread. Silence hung uncomfortably in the room as they all went about their various tasks.

Had she done something to upset him? Everything had seemed so perfect the night before. She searched for a way to break the ice, but words eluded her.

A few minutes later, Jeremy put everything back into the refrigerator, wiped down the counter, and picked up his sandwich and a napkin.

"Thank you."

"You're welcome," Patrice said. "Don't work too late today. Dinner is at seven."

"I'll be there," Jeremy promised and promptly left the room.

Noelle stared after him, a sinking feeling in her stomach. What had changed between them, and what could she do to change it back?

* * *

Jeremy didn't know what to think. The last thing he had expected when he'd walked into the kitchen in search of food was to discover that Noelle was actually the daughter of the chateau's cook.

How could that be? He had seen her and her father arrive here in a limo, the driver clearly treating Enrico as though he was in charge. Everything about Noelle screamed wealth and class, and her transportation between Meridia and the U.S. had definitely been several steps above coach.

"Hey, Jeremy," Janessa called out to him from down the hall.

"How's it going?"

"Besides having to deal with the wedding planner from hell? Just fine."

"Uh-oh. What happened?"

Janessa motioned for him to follow her into her room. As soon as she closed the door, she let out a frustrated sigh. "I assume you heard about my wedding planner telling Dad he had to buy a certain type of tuxedo, right?"

"She didn't," Jeremy said in disbelief.

"She did . . . right before she informed me that the blue I chose to be one of my wedding colors wouldn't photograph well if it's a cloudy day. She then proceeded to tell me what color I am going to use instead."

Jeremy leaned against the back of the couch, his untouched sandwich still in his hand. "I thought those kinds of decisions were supposed to be the bride's."

"So did I."

"You still have five months until the wedding. Maybe you should fire her and find someone else." His stomach grumbled, and he took a bite of his food. He offered a bite to Janessa, but she shook her head and paced across the room before turning back to face him.

"I talked to Queen Marta on the phone yesterday, planning to suggest exactly that."

"And?"

"When I hinted at replacing Floria, the queen insisted that she is the best and promised it will all settle down once she gets here."

"When is that supposed to happen?"

"Monday."

"And how long will she be staying?"

"Until the wedding."

Jeremy paused in the act of taking another bite. "Maybe you should have another chat with the queen. This isn't like you to get stressed out. Your wedding day is supposed to be one of the happiest days of your life, not an obligation you can't wait to have behind you."

"You're right." She let out a sigh. "I guess I'll see how things go when she gets here. If they're still tense after a week, I'll insist we find someone else."

"That a girl."

"How is everything going for you? When do you start working?"

"Actually, I started today. I got my office all set up in the spare room. I guess office space is limited at the base because of the bombing there."

Janessa tensed briefly before nodding. "I understand the construction of the new admin building will take close to a year to complete."

"Can I ask you something?"

"Sure."

"What's the deal with Noelle and her family?"

"What do you mean?"

"Just wondering about them. What can you tell me?"

Janessa sat in one of the chairs in her sitting area, waiting for Jeremy to sit as well before speaking. "Not much to tell. Her father, Enrico, is the head chauffeur here at the chateau, and her mother is the cook."

"She's the daughter of servants here." Everything began falling into place. "That's why she grew up here."

"Yeah. I thought you knew that."

"How would I know that? When I met her, she was flying back and forth to the U.S. in a private plane. My first night here, she attended a formal dinner. And she arrived here in a limo."

Janessa's eyes narrowed. "Do you have a problem with her being a servant?"

"No, of course not. I just don't understand why she would mislead me like that."

"I doubt it was intentional. She probably assumed you were aware of her family situation."

"Are you sure? How well do you know her?"

"Not that well. She's been in the U.S. most of the time I've been in Meridia. Mary knows her better than I do, and, of course, Alora and Stefano know her well. She spent the past three months helping them plan their wedding."

"Is that what she does? Plan weddings?"

"She worked as one of Floria's assistants. After dealing with the woman myself for the past week, I think Noelle probably deserves a medal for surviving the job."

"So she's here to work for What's-Her-Name again in preparation for your wedding."

"Exactly."

Jeremy stood, mentally sifting through the new information. "I'd better get back to work. Hang in there."

"Thanks."

As soon as Jeremy left, he went back to his office and sat at his computer, preparing to run more background checks. His curiosity about Noelle prompted him to flip to the second page of service personnel, where Noelle's name was listed, and type in her name.

He didn't have to dig deep to confirm what Janessa had already told him. Noelle and her brothers had grown up associating with the royal family. When he ran her family background, he discovered that the Salderas had been in service of the royals for generations.

If she came from such a proud tradition, why had she misled him? Was she ashamed of her family and where she'd come from, or had she really assumed he already knew who she was?

Still trying to reconcile reality with his previous perceptions, he reached for Levi's list of suspects and got down to work.

Chapter 15

NOELLE KEPT HOPING THEIR PATHS would cross, but she hadn't seen as much as a glimpse of Jeremy since lunch on Friday. She heard through the grapevine that he had been present at dinner Friday night, but she had been recruited to help in the kitchen and had never made it into the dining room.

Her mother had taken some food up to his room Saturday morning, apparently concerned when Janessa mentioned he was working hard trying to get up to speed on his new job.

As time passed, the lead in her stomach sank deeper and deeper, and she wished she could find a way to make everything go back to the way it had been when Jeremy had first arrived. She had so looked forward to spending time with him over the next few months, especially knowing they shared the same standards and beliefs.

Several times over the past two days, she had looked for an opening to discuss those beliefs with her family, but her father's duties had kept him away from home most of the weekend. The only time she knew she would have both parents in the same place at the same time would be Sunday supper.

Resolved that she had to tell them of her baptism, she decided their reaction couldn't be any worse than the constant imaginary conversations going through her head.

Dressed for church, she walked into the entryway, her heels clicking on the tile floor. Her steps slowed when she saw Jeremy descending the stairs.

Her heart squeezed painfully in her chest when she noticed the hitch in his step when he saw her.

"Hey there." He continued to the landing. "I gather you're riding over with Prince Garrett and Janessa too."

"Yes. I hope you don't mind."

"Why would I mind?"

She could play it off that his inattention the past two days hadn't bothered her, but subtlety wasn't her strong suit. "I don't know. I thought maybe you were avoiding me."

"I've just had a lot on my mind. And I've been spending a lot of time at the naval base."

She wanted to accept his pat answer, but the way he looked at the floor after saying the words caused her to press on. "Did I do something to upset you? I thought everything went so well on our date, and now you seem like you don't want to be around me."

"I guess I'm still trying to figure things out." He seemed to gather his thoughts, and his shoulders lifted. "I hadn't realized your parents worked here."

Confusion came first. Slowly she replayed her various interactions with Jeremy, trying to see herself through his eyes. "You thought I was rich."

"Well, yeah. The first time I met you, you rescheduled a private plane so you could change your dinner plans."

"And now you're disappointed to find I'm from the working class."

"No. I'm concerned that you would be embarrassed by that fact. I don't understand why you never mentioned it."

"I am not embarrassed by my family, nor did I realize you weren't aware of our social status." Her shoulders straightened, and she made a point of looking him in the eye. "Honestly I'm disappointed that you would care about such things."

"I care about you," Jeremy said, deflating her anger. He closed the distance between them and took her hand. "It was a shock to realize how little I really know about you."

She fell silent for a moment. "You really don't care that my mother is a cook and my father is a chauffeur?"

"Of course not. They're both wonderful people, and I think you're lucky to have them."

"I agree." Nothing he could have said to her could have been more endearing. She heard footsteps approaching and lowered her voice. "Is this our first fight?"

"I don't know. Was it a fight?" Jeremy asked.

"You two are already fighting?" Janessa asked when she reached them. She looked up at Garrett and grinned. "This could be serious."

"It could be," Garrett said. "Are you ready to go?"

"We are." Jeremy moved to the door and opened it.

Noelle had the sudden concern that her father might be driving them and that she would have to explain where she was going. She was greatly relieved when Garrett collected the keys to one of the cars he often drove himself.

When Jeremy opened the car door for her, she was grateful to see the tension between them now gone. She hoped her conversation with her parents later would have a similar outcome.

* * *

Jeremy hadn't attended such a small branch since his mission. The church building was large enough to house a ward, but only about fifty people were in attendance.

Janessa took her place as the pianist, and Jeremy couldn't help but wonder if the branch members ever got tired of singing the same ten songs over and over again. He was well acquainted with his sister's musical talent and her lack of desire to practice.

When the sacrament was passed, he kept his hymnal open, reading through several familiar songs and trying to reconcile the Italian words with those he understood in English and French. He really was going to have to take Noelle up on her offer to teach him Italian. During the prayer, he had only understood about every third word.

When the first speaker stood, Noelle leaned closer and whispered, "Do you want me to translate?"

He shook his head. "No. I'll see what I can understand on my own."

"Let me know if you change your mind."

It didn't take long for him to change his mind. Throughout the meeting, he whispered questions about various words. It took him until the third speaker to figure out enough of the theme to gain some understanding.

By the time he reached priesthood opening exercises, he decided he needed to spend more time around the native speakers. Lessons in Italian would most certainly help, but immersion had helped him learn French, and he hoped the same tactic would work again. Or perhaps he would be able to use a combination of the two learning styles. When he thought of the potential threats at his sister's wedding, he found a new resolve to gain the skills necessary to do his job well.

"Jeremy, how much were you able to understand?" Janessa asked on their drive home.

"Not as much as I had hoped," he admitted. "I was just thinking I need to immerse myself in the language. So far everyone I've met speaks either English or French, at least enough for me to communicate."

"Not everyone," Noelle said. At his look of confusion, she added, "My grandfather."

"Paolo would be a great person to talk to," Janessa agreed.

"I'm sure if you're willing to help feed horses or muck out stalls, he'll be happy to talk to you all you want."

"I gather he's in charge of the stables?"

"Yes, and he doesn't speak a word of English or French."

"It sounds like your grandfather and I are about to become well acquainted," Jeremy told Noelle. "Maybe you and I could go riding tomorrow morning and you can ask him if he's okay with me hanging around."

"I'd love to, but Floria is supposed to be arriving tomorrow."

"She isn't due to arrive until ten," Janessa said. "You could go out early."

"Do you mind an early ride?"

"That sounds great."

Garrett and Janessa chatted with him as they drove, but Noelle seemed to draw into herself as they got closer to home.

"Are you okay?" Jeremy asked.

"Just nervous. I'm planning on telling my parents about my baptism at dinner tonight." A sigh escaped her. "I just hope they don't kick me out."

"They can't kick you out," Garrett reminded her. "It's my house."

"Sometimes I think my mother forgets that fact," Noelle said wryly.

"Do you need some reinforcement?" Jeremy asked. "I'm happy to be with you when you talk to them."

"I don't know." She hesitated, clearly considering. "I'm not sure how they would feel if they realized you know about it and they don't."

Garrett glanced at them in the rearview mirror. "That's true, but your mother may be more likely to listen to what you're saying if someone else is there."

"You may be right."

"We could all have dinner together," Janessa suggested. "We don't have to say we already knew about your decision. You can act like you're telling all of us at the same time."

"I wouldn't want to intrude on your time together," Noelle said.

"It's not an intrusion. We have Sunday dinner with your family a lot. It's the one time during the week that we banish your mother from the kitchen."

"I'm surprised she lets you."

"She wasn't going to at first, but when we explained that we didn't want anyone to have to work on Sundays, she was more agreeable."

"If you don't mind, that would actually be great."

"Tell your family we're eating at five. That will give us plenty of time to talk."

"Thank you. And if you want to send any prayers my way between now and tonight, those are welcome too."

Jeremy took her hand in his. "You got it."

She looked over at him and asked hesitantly, "Is this something I could get a blessing for?"

"Of course." Pleased that she would think of such a thing, Jeremy said, "I'd be happy to give you one when we get home. Or Prince Garrett can, if you'd prefer."

"Absolutely," Garrett agreed. "Although, Jeremy, you can drop the title when it's just us. We are about to be related."

"Done."

Chapter 16

THOUGH HER FAMILY TYPICALLY ATE at the table in the kitchen, Noelle used Janessa's and Garrett's presence as an excuse to have their meal in the breakfast room. Even though the staff was now given Sundays off, that didn't mean someone wouldn't come into the kitchen searching for something to eat, and she wanted to ensure some privacy.

The roast her mother had prepared the day before was already on the table, and Janessa filled their water glasses. People moved in and out of the kitchen like a well-orchestrated dance until everyone finally sat down to eat and the blessing was said on the food.

Noelle thought her heart was going to explode in her chest.

Jeremy must have sensed her anxiety because he reached over and gave her hand a squeeze before passing her the bowl of potatoes. She scooped some onto her plate and passed it on.

Their conversation came in a mix of languages, mostly French and Italian.

Hoping to distract herself, she spoke to her grandfather. "*Nonno*, Jeremy is trying to learn Italian. I thought you might let him help you with the horses and teach him."

"I'm always happy to have help around the stables." He wiggled his eyebrows. "You like this one."

Laughter erupted, and Jeremy looked at her, confused. "What did I miss?"

"Nothing. I was asking my grandfather if he would help you learn Italian, and he's teasing me."

Jeremy leaned closer and whispered in her ear. "He knows I have my eye on you, doesn't he?"

"Something like that," she whispered back. She wasn't sure what pleased her more: Jeremy admitting that he was interested in her or the fact that he had a sense of humor. "He did say you can help out anytime though."

"That's good. Maybe I can spare some time after we ride tomorrow."

Noelle translated for him and was surprised when an impromptu Italian lesson began. Both her father and grandfather held up various items on the table, naming each one. Forks, knives, glasses, the table itself. Jeremy was a good sport, repeating each item in an attempt to commit the words to memory.

Noelle waited until dessert was served before she finally mustered her courage. Drawing a deep breath, she spoke in Italian. "There's something I need to tell all of you."

"Is everything okay?" her father asked.

"Yes, everything is fine. It's just that I made a decision while I was in America, and I don't know how you will feel about it."

"What decision?"

"I joined the Mormon church."

Silence.

Her father laid his hand over her mother's, undoubtedly an attempt to calm the storm brewing inside her.

"I know this must come as a shock," Noelle said. "I've been wanting to tell you, but I started working in Calene, and I didn't want to say anything until I could tell you together."

More silence.

In all of her imaginary conversations, someone had always responded. This was beyond her wildest nightmare.

"Please say something."

Her mother shifted her seat back. "What is there to say? You're a grown adult. You can choose as you please." She stood. "It's your business if you decide to keep secrets from your family, waiting months to tell us something that is so obviously important to you."

"I'm sorry. I didn't know how to tell you. I was afraid you would be disappointed in me, that you wouldn't understand."

"That I wouldn't understand what?"

Noelle stood and circled the table to stand beside her mother. "The truth I found, the peace I found when I learned of the restored gospel. I felt like I discovered who I really am, and part of that discovery was knowing how important all of you are to me." She took her mother's hand. "I was afraid I would lose you by leaving the Meridian Church."

"You will always be my daughter, and I will always love you," her mother announced, her rigid stance relaxing slightly. "I am disappointed that you would ever question that."

"Mama, I'm so sorry. Can you forgive me?" Noelle asked. "Please?"

"I need to start on these dishes." Patrice took a step away, picked up her plate, and headed for the door.

Her heart heavy, Noelle turned and saw the disappointment on her father's face. He too stood. "Give her time."

Noelle managed to nod, tears threatening. Her father followed her mother into the kitchen, and Noelle forced herself to face her grandfather.

To her surprise, he lifted his empty dessert plate. "Is there any more cherry pie?"

Noelle laughed through her tears. She couldn't help it. "Yes, Grandpa. There is more cherry pie."

"I'll get it," Janessa said.

Jeremy shifted in his seat. "Noelle, come eat something. You hardly touched your dinner."

"Maybe I should go after them."

"Like your father said, give them time," Garrett said. "Once they've talked, it will be easier for them to figure out what they're feeling."

"What they're feeling is disappointment," Noelle said.

"Yes, but they're good people, and I have to think that eventually they'll accept your decision," Garrett said.

"I hope you're right."

He winked at her. "I try to make a habit of it."

* * *

Jeremy was pulling on his boots when a knock sounded at his door. Surprised that anyone would be at his door at seven thirty in the morning, he stood and strode quickly across the room.

"Levi, what are you doing here?" Jeremy waved him inside and shut the door. "I thought you planned to keep our contact minimal."

"Don't worry. Janessa is the only person living in this wing besides you right now, and she's already downstairs getting ready for her meeting with Floria."

"I thought the wedding planner wasn't getting here until ten."

"She's not." Levi shrugged. "I stopped asking about this kind of stuff months ago."

"Did you ever get that video feed for me from the wedding?"

"I did. That's one of the reasons I stopped by." He pulled a flash drive from his pocket and handed it to Jeremy. "It's all on there. I also saw something on the news that may be of concern."

"What's that?"

"One of the editors at the station that had the television rights for Prince Stefano's wedding has disappeared."

"When?"

"Thursday night. Apparently she usually works late, but her producer said she was still at work when he left the studio shortly before midnight. No one has seen her since."

"Are you worried her disappearance has something to do with the bombing attempt?"

"I'm not sure, but something feels off about it. Her car was still in the parking lot when her coworkers arrived on Friday morning. The police checked it out and said the alternator was bad." Levi crossed his arms. "The thing that concerns me is that there was a security guard on duty there. I would think if she couldn't get her car started in the middle of the night, she would have asked him for help, or she would have called someone."

"Let me guess. Her phone didn't show any outgoing calls, and the security guard didn't see a thing."

"Got it on the first try."

Jeremy considered for a minute. "You said she's one of the editors at the TV station?"

"Yeah. Why?"

"Is there any way you can get me access to the studio's editing suite?"

"I think I can make that happen. What are you hoping to find?"

"I spent a summer during college working at the local station. If someone wanted to gain access to any of the film there, all they had to do was access the editing suite." Jeremy held up the flash drive. "When was this copied for us?"

"Sometime on Thursday. I didn't get it until now because I wanted to wait for an agency courier to bring it instead of sending it through regular channels."

"That's great. That means I can compare it to what's at the studio and make sure nothing is missing. Maybe someone wanted to make sure they weren't seen on camera when they were waiting for that bomb to go off."

"I'll let you know when I can get you access to the studio."

"Thanks." Jeremy glanced at his watch. "I'd better run. I'm supposed to be meeting Noelle to go riding."

"You do realize you're supposed to be working here, right?"

"Believe me, I'll put in the hours. I wanted to take advantage of Paolo's willingness to help me with my Italian."

"I'm sure spending time with Noelle isn't a hardship either."

"There is that too." Jeremy led the way to the door and looked back at Levi. "You really do know everything, don't you?"

"I certainly try."

Chapter 17

NOELLE HAD BARELY SLEPT, TOSSING and turning throughout the night, her mother's disappointment echoing through her mind. The simple truth was that she had been wrong not to talk to her parents when she'd first decided to get baptized. She had let fear dictate her actions, and now she had to live with the hurt her deception had caused.

She debated hitting her alarm and rolling over to get some more sleep, but she needed to get out of her room and away from the memories of the night before.

Her mood improved when she reached the barn and found her grandfather and Jeremy attempting to communicate in broken Italian. "Starting your lesson early?" she asked.

"Something like that." He studied her for a moment. "Did you get any sleep last night?"

"Not much." She started toward the stables. "Did you and my grandpa figure out which horses need to be exercised today?"

"I think he was trying to con me into taking out the stallion in the second stall." Jeremy looked at her warily. "He's not trying to get me thrown, is he?"

"Take it as a compliment. He doesn't let just anyone ride Midnight. That's one of Stefano's horses."

"I still think I'd prefer a leisurely ride this early in the morning."

"I'm sure that can be arranged." Noelle spoke to her grandfather briefly, deciding on their mounts. A few minutes later, she and Jeremy headed for the beach, walking their horses side by side.

"My sister was telling me about Floria. Is she really as hard to work with as Janessa let on?"

"Let's just say she knows how to get things done."

"When we talked on the phone, you always sounded busy with work, but I don't remember you complaining about her."

"Floria is very good at what she does, and what she does best is order people around. As long as you do what you're told and don't argue, she's easy to work for. People who want to put in their opinions tend to have trouble with her."

"Um, how well do you know my sister?"

"Well enough to know she isn't anything like Alora."

"What do you mean?"

"Prince Stefano and Alora were more interested in protecting their family and their privacy than they were about wedding details," Noelle explained. "Your sister can be easygoing about a lot of things, but she doesn't seem like the type who appreciates being told what to do."

"You've got that right." A seagull took flight and startled Jeremy's mount. He reined in until the horse settled and fell back in step beside Noelle's.

"I think Queen Marta is hoping I can keep the peace between them."

"It doesn't sound like that's going to be easy."

"Probably not, but that's the job I've been given."

"How did you end up working for Floria?" Jeremy asked. "I would have thought with all of your family working here at the chateau, you would have ended up working here too."

"I've helped plan a lot of events over the years. Floria needed some assistants, and she had to draw from people who had already been cleared by security. I was a logical choice."

"I watched Prince Stefano's wedding on TV. It was impressive," Jeremy said. "I can't imagine the number of hours that went into planning it."

"You won't have to imagine it," Noelle reminded him. "You're about to see a royal wedding come together right before your eyes."

"Now you're scaring me."

"You haven't seen anything yet."

* * *

He paced across the living room, the news playing on the television. Anxiety hummed through him as he waited impatiently. When the door opened, he pounced. "Did you have to kill the woman? It's all over the news."

"No one knows she's dead. They only know she's missing."

"You never said anything about killing her."

"Have you forgotten that it was less than two weeks ago that we tried to blow up more than six hundred people?"

"Yes, but that would have served a purpose. The investigation into the missing woman could compromise our plans."

"We have a bigger problem than Adrienne Acord. Someone is running a background check on me."

"How can you be so sure?"

"I have a tracker on all of my accounts. Several of them flagged earlier today."

"We knew this might happen. Obviously the royal family will take every precaution before the wedding."

"Yes, but no one went this deep before Prince Stefano's wedding." He hesitated before voicing the heart of his concern. "What if the bomb was discovered and the royal family knows about our attempt?"

"How could they? You said yourself that the bomb was foolproof. If they tried to disarm it, the grenade would have exploded."

"Maybe it did." He held out his tablet to reveal a recording. "This is from one of the angles that wasn't televised. Watch this window right here."

He tapped on the upper corner of the image and hit play. Several seconds in, a flash of light appeared, followed by dust spewing from beneath the windowsill and glass shattering on the ground. "Those walls are over a foot thick. It's possible someone took the bomb out of the chapel and tried to disarm it in one of the offices."

"With the thick walls, it could have gone off and everyone would have remained oblivious to the threat," he finished for him. "The bomb would have leveled the building, but the grenade would have only taken out the people nearby."

He considered the possibilities before continuing. "If that is what happened, someone must have at least been injured in the blast. Check out the local hospitals as well as the obituaries. Let's see who they treated that day."

"What does it matter who was injured? That doesn't change the fact that our attempt didn't work and the royals could know about it."

"Yes, but if the bomb wasn't faulty, we can use the same ploy again, only this time we'll send in a backup."

"Security isn't going to fall for the same trick twice."

"Which is why our next bombs will look completely different." His confidence didn't waver when he added, "This *is* going to work."

"I'll talk to Ivan and see what he can come up with."

"And start working on who else we can insert into the guest list."

"I don't know that getting in that way will work twice. We may have to be more creative this time."

"Find a way to make it happen. We won't get another chance at this."

"I know."

* * *

Janessa gripped her hands beneath the table, reminding herself that her temper would not serve her well. She was supposed to be learning how to be diplomatic, after all.

Maybe she was improving in that area. Floria didn't seem to notice that Janessa had become increasingly silent as her presentation continued.

Only a week ago, Janessa had spoken to Floria on the phone and outlined exactly what she wanted for her wedding and the reception that would follow. She hadn't thought at the time that her request for simple elegance was unreasonable. The food, flower, and entertainment suggestions had already been well researched. Janessa had sent Floria photos of the wedding cakes she liked, and she had already started working with the queen's personal designer on her wedding dress.

Now Janessa sat in stony silence while she listened to Floria describe a lavish event with a ridiculous number of bridesmaids and groomsmen. The number of musicians at the reception made her head spin, and she didn't want to think of the security issues in clearing them all. She might not officially work for the CIA anymore, but that didn't discount her sensitivity to their workload.

Noelle sat across from her, diligently taking notes. Several times she looked at Janessa with concern on her face.

"I have appointments set up later this week with two more dress designers," Floria continued. "We'll have at least one backup made in case the design leaks to the press."

Needing a break from the ridiculous, Janessa spoke to Brenna, who was standing at the edge of the doorway. "Brenna, would you please tell Patrice we are ready for her samples?"

"Yes, signoria." Brenna ducked out of the room as Floria straightened in her chair.

"Samples? What samples?"

"For the reception. Since it will be held here, it only makes sense to have Patrice oversee the food."

"We'll hire caterers for that," Floria insisted. "You can't expect to use a household cook to prepare the food for an event like this."

"A household cook?" Noelle repeated the words, and Janessa recognized the stab of insult hanging in the air. "Our cook is widely recognized as being the best in the province."

"And the caterers I'm bringing in are from outside the province," Floria announced haughtily. "They served us well for Prince Stefano's wedding."

"Yes, but they had access to their own facilities in Calene," Noelle reminded her.

Brenna arrived with a tray of artistically arranged hors d'oeuvres. She set it on the table between Floria and Janessa.

Noelle spoke to Brenna now. "Brenna, do you think it's plausible to have caterers working out of the kitchen here for the wedding?"

Clearly unprepared to enter into the discussion, Brenna tensed briefly. A silent message seemed to pass between her and Noelle, and she slowly shook her head. "It would be difficult."

Floria waved a hand through the air. "She is nothing but a servant. What does her opinion matter?"

"It matters because she's right," Noelle insisted. "We will have a significant number of guests staying here. My mother can't meet their needs if she loses her kitchen to a bunch of caterers."

Before Noelle could continue, Floria interrupted her. "You have made your point."

Surprise reflected on Noelle's face, followed by a sense of relief. That expression had barely appeared before Floria continued. "I believe it would serve us both if you find other employment. I will not tolerate such insubordination, and in front of a client, no less."

Noelle absorbed the words, and Janessa felt rage burning inside her. She watched Noelle push back from the table, her head held high.

"I appreciate the opportunity to work with you, Floria." She turned to Janessa. "I wish you the best of luck with your wedding." Noelle left the room without looking back.

Floria turned to Janessa. "I apologize for my former assistant's behavior. Now, about the caterers—"

Janessa straightened her own shoulders. "I think I'm going to have to agree with Noelle on this."

"I beg your pardon?"

"Thank you for your time, Floria, but your services are no longer needed." Janessa stood. "Brenna, would you please show our guest out? I have some other things I need to attend to."

Brenna barely managed to fight back a smile. "Yes, signoria."

Chapter 18

Jeremy approached the kitchen with trepidation. He hadn't seen Patrice since she had left the dinner table last night, and he wasn't sure what kind of reception he would receive when she saw him next.

He noticed Garrett approaching from the other direction, a similar expression on his face.

"You know her better than I do. Is this going to be awkward?" Jeremy asked.

"There's only one way to find out." Garrett reached for the door and pushed it open. "You go first."

"Thanks a lot," Jeremy muttered under his breath.

Patrice didn't look up, her hands covered in flour as she kneaded dough on the counter. "Breakfast is on the table."

Both men passed through the kitchen without a word. They entered the breakfast room to find a basket of croissants, a plate of toast, and a pitcher of water.

"Is this Patrice's version of bread and water?"

"Yep." Garrett took a seat and reached for the jam.

Jeremy sat beside him. "I've had worse punishments."

"You and me both. We still don't talk about baseballs and broken windows in front of Patrice."

"Thanks for the warning."

The kitchen door creaked open, followed by determined footsteps. Jeremy looked up when Janessa stormed into the room. She keyed in on Garrett. "Has your mother called yet?"

"Nooo." Garrett drew the word out, clearly confused. "Is there a reason I should expect a call from my mother?"

Janessa gripped the back of the chair beside him. "I fired Floria."

"You what?" Garrett stopped in the middle of smearing jam on his toast. "Janessa, you can't expect to plan this wedding alone, and she's the only one qualified to handle an event of this scale."

"Which your mother pointed out to me a few days ago." She huffed out a breath. "Garrett, I'm sorry. I tried, but I can't work with that woman."

"Tell me what happened."

Janessa described how Floria had blatantly ignored all of the requests she had given her and then went on to replay how she'd refused to let Patrice oversee the food for the reception. "And to top it all off, she fired Noelle."

"She did what?" Jeremy asked.

"Noelle insisted her mother couldn't function if caterers were working out of her kitchen. She's right, by the way." Janessa held up a hand as she made her point. "Then she insulted Brenna, acting like her opinion didn't matter because she was a servant. Things went downhill from there."

Movement sounded at the door, followed by Patrice's voice. "My Noelle lost her job because she defended my cooking?"

"Noelle lost her job because she stood up for you and everyone else who lives here," Janessa corrected. "You should be proud of her."

Tears shimmered in Patrice's eyes. Her gaze swept over all of them, finally landing on Jeremy. "Noelle likes to walk in the garden when she's upset. Will you take her a jacket? It's still hanging on the hook by the back door."

"I'd be happy to." Jeremy picked up his croissant to take with him.

Garrett's phone rang, and he let out a sigh before answering it. Jeremy stood listening to Garrett's side of the conversation, expecting to hear a debate over the former wedding planner's release. To Jeremy's surprise, Garrett offered Janessa an apologetic look when he said into the phone, "I understand. We'll figure out a way to make it work."

When he hung up, Janessa pounced. "You didn't just agree to rehire Floria, did you?"

"No. Worse."

"I'm not sure what could be worse than that," Janessa said.

"Oh, something," Garrett said. "Philippe and Elaina are coming to visit. They're arriving tomorrow afternoon so they can attend the opening of the new play in Bellamo."

"Who are Philippe and Elaina?" Jeremy asked.

"My cousin and his wife."

"And how long are they staying?" Janessa asked skeptically.

"That's the loaded question." Garrett sent a look of apology to Patrice. "It looks like we'll need to arrange for a dinner on Wednesday night."

"How many should I plan for?" Patrice asked.

"Let's plan for twenty-five. I don't want to be cornered by Philippe, and the more people we have here, the better."

"I gather you aren't fond of your cousin," Jeremy commented.

"You'll see why soon enough," Garrett said. "Though, if you repeat any of this, I'll deny it."

"I didn't hear a thing. Where do they live?"

"A little too close for comfort sometimes. Their primary residence is one of the family properties in a village about twenty minutes from here."

"Then why would they need to stay with you?"

"That's another loaded question for which I've never received an adequate answer. I believe the simplest explanation is that our home is bigger than theirs." Garrett looked up at Patrice and added, "And we have the best cook."

"Flattery isn't going to work on me," Patrice said, although she couldn't quite hide the smile trying to form.

"It was worth a try." Garrett glanced over at Janessa. "With my cousin's impending arrival, this really isn't a good time to be without a wedding planner. Patrice can only do so much."

"I know," Janessa said.

"Don't you worry," Patrice said and patted Janessa's arm. "Everything will work out."

"I hope so."

"Good luck." Jeremy moved toward the door. "I'd better go see how Noelle is doing."

"Hey, Jeremy," Janessa called after him.

"Yeah?"

"You're welcome to bring a date to dinner Wednesday night. Like Garrett said, the more the merrier."

"Thanks," Jeremy said, fully aware that everyone present knew who he was interested in. "I'll see what I can do."

* * *

What was she going to do now? In less than twenty-four hours Noelle had managed to completely disappoint her family and get fired from her job. Not exactly her best day.

She leaned on the seawall and stared out at the water, the waves crashing up over the sand in the timeless battle between land and sea. She watched a sloop pass by, its sail full. Maybe she should take some time out on the water. After all, she didn't have anything better to do.

She blinked hard against the tears that threatened. What was she going to do? Without a reason to work at the chateau, she would no longer be of any use to Levi and the royal family in an intelligence capacity, and she couldn't stay without a reason, not with how her family looked at her now. Tears threatened, and she tried to blink them back.

"Hey there." Jeremy approached, draping a jacket over her shoulders. "Your mom asked me to bring this to you."

Noelle looked up at him, annoyed at herself when a tear spilled over. "She did?"

"She did." He reached out and wiped her tear away. "She was very touched by the way you stood up for her today."

Noelle didn't ask how her mother had found out. Rumors in the chateau had only one place to go: in circles. "I stood up for my mother and got fired in the process."

"You weren't the only one who got fired."

"What?"

"Floria won't be causing you and Janessa any more stress. My sister wasn't happy with the way Floria was treating people and decided she'd rather plan her own wedding than deal with that woman for the next five months."

"I don't know whether to celebrate or offer your sister my condolences. I know Floria is a pain, but she knows what needs to be done, and she has the connections to make things happen," Noelle said. "I don't think your sister has any idea what she just signed up for."

"What she signed up for was to marry the man she loves. Everything else will fall into place." He held his hands out. "Or it won't. As long as she and Garrett are married at the end of the day, the wedding will be a success."

"That's a simplistic way of looking at it."

"Sometimes simple is best."

"I think that's exactly what Janessa was trying to tell Floria. I don't think Floria speaks simple."

"Probably not, but I bet you can," Jeremy said, clearly considering. "If someone as experienced as Floria needed an assistant to plan Janessa's wedding, I imagine my sister could use one as well. I think you should volunteer for the job."

"I'm the reason she ended up in this mess. Besides, I only assisted Floria for a few months. She has been doing this for years," Noelle said. "I'm not qualified."

"Forget about Floria's résumé. If you can do the job, you're qualified. I think you can do the job."

"I don't know . . ."

"At least try. If nothing else, you can help Janessa find a replacement. Until then you can keep her from getting overwhelmed with the details."

"I guess I can ask her if she wants some help." She turned back toward the chateau. "I thought you would be working by now."

"I can spare a few minutes before I head over to the naval base." He took her hand. "Are you still worried about your parents?"

She let out a sigh. "I should have trusted them. I should have told them the truth right away."

"We all make mistakes, Noelle. They know that."

"I hate feeling like there's this big void between us." Tears threatened once more.

"Come here." He tugged on her hand, pulling her toward him. Her arms came around his waist as he embraced her. "It's all going to work out. I promise."

"I hope so."

They stood together, a minute stretching into two as her tears faded away. When she finally felt like she had her emotions under control, she pulled back enough to look up at him. "Thanks for not making me feel like an idiot. I hate it when I cry."

"You've had a crazy couple of days." He kept his hands firmly around her waist, his eyes meeting hers.

Her heartbeat quickened when his gaze lowered to her lips and he leaned toward her.

"Noelle?" Brenna's voice called out a moment before she emerged from a nearby path. Her cheeks reddened when she saw Noelle still caught in Jeremy's arms. "Oh, sorry."

Jeremy stepped back, and Noelle turned to face her friend. "It's okay."

"Janessa asked me to find you. She said she wanted to meet with you in her office."

"Can you tell her I'll be right in?"

Brenna nodded, eager to disappear the way she had come.

As soon as they were left alone, Jeremy said, "That reminds me. I wanted to know if you would be my date for dinner Wednesday night."

"I'd like that." She thought over the upcoming schedule. "What's happening Wednesday night?"

"Prince Philippe and Princess Elaina are gracing us with their presence."

"Maybe I should reconsider my answer."

"My sister had a similar reaction, which is why she and Garrett are inviting several others to join us."

"Smart. Very smart." Noelle took a step back. "I guess I'd better go see what your sister wants."

"I guess so." Jeremy took her hand in his once more. "There's just one more thing."

"What's that?"

He edged closer and lowered his lips to hers. The gesture was so natural that she leaned into it as though he had kissed her a thousand times. The cold air evaporated, the sound of the waves crashing and the seagulls in the distance drowned out by the beating of her heart.

He pulled back, confusion illuminating his face for a brief moment. Then he spoke, his voice low. "Whether you decide to work for my sister or not, I hope you know my vote is for you to stay here at the chateau one way or another."

Her lips curved up. "That's my vote too."

Chapter 19

FACING THE IMPENDING ARRIVAL OF Garrett's cousin, a man who could be the poster child for the word *arrogance*, Janessa decided it was time to put her affairs in order.

After asking Brenna to find Noelle, she sent a text to Levi. Now she picked up her phone and called her future mother-in-law.

"I see your plan to give Floria a chance didn't last as long as expected," Queen Marta said dryly.

"I'm sorry, Your Majesty. I tried, but the woman is impossible. Besides ignoring everything Garrett and I asked for, she insulted the staff here and has no regard for security concerns."

"I'll admit we did have some run-ins with her over security when planning Stefano's wedding." Marta's sigh sounded through the phone. "Now that you got your wish, how do you want to proceed? You and Garrett have a full social calendar between now and your wedding, and I'm sure you're aware of how long it takes to run full background checks on prospective replacements."

"I'm sure there are many people who could do the job, but I would like to handle the details in-house."

"The chateau's staff is wonderful, but this is an enormous undertaking. You need someone to oversee everything, and I simply don't think you can do that alone."

"I agree. I would need to hire someone to take the lead. I have someone in mind, but I would appreciate your opinion."

"Who is that?" Marta asked.

"Noelle Saldera."

"Noelle?"

"Yes. She was heavily involved in planning Alora and Stefano's wedding, and she knows the staff and their capabilities." Janessa paced across her office. "Not to mention, Floria fired her for trying to stand up for my wishes."

"She's young and doesn't have a lot of experience, but the most important thing is whether the two of you can work well together."

"I believe we can."

"Then I support your decision," Marta said. "Good luck."

"Thanks. I have a feeling I'll need it."

"I have faith in you."

Janessa hung up and looked over at Levi standing in her office doorway.

"You asked to see me?" Levi asked.

"Yes. Please come in and close the door."

Levi complied, lowering his voice as he walked farther into the room. "This isn't a good idea, the two of us meeting alone."

"Relax. It may be driving me crazy that I'm out of the loop, but I want to talk to you about something else." She motioned to the seat across from her. "As you've probably already heard, Floria and I have had a parting of ways."

"I am aware."

Janessa wondered briefly if there was anyone in the chateau who hadn't already heard of how abruptly that particular relationship had dissolved. "I just got off the phone with Queen Marta regarding a replacement."

"Janessa, I don't have to tell you what a risk it is to bring in someone we haven't already vetted. Trying to push through background checks is how things get missed."

"I know." She was interrupted by a knock at her door. "Come in."

The door opened, and Noelle entered. Janessa saw the moment Noelle saw Levi, and she recognized the flash of concern in the other woman's expression. Not sure what to make of it, she motioned for Noelle to come in.

"Please come in and sit down. I assume you already know Levi."

"Yes." She settled into the chair beside Levi. "We worked together when I was helping with Prince Stefano's wedding."

"Excellent. I hope you won't mind working with him again." Janessa rested her forearms on her desk. "As I was just telling Levi, I need to replace Floria. With the heightened security within the royal family, my options are somewhat limited, and I prefer to work with someone I know. Noelle, would you be willing to take the job?"

"Me?" She swallowed. "I was going to offer to assist you . . ."

"You would be assisting me, and unlike your predecessor, I believe you will actually hear what I have to say."

Noelle's eyes lit with amusement. "I think every bride should have the wedding of her dreams."

"Then you'll do it?"

"Yes." She nodded. "Just tell me where you want me to start."

"You can start by moving into your new office." She motioned to the outer office reserved for her assistant. "With the current hiring freeze, I won't be hiring a new assistant until after the wedding. Let's meet over lunch, and we'll see if we can get these plans in motion."

Noelle stood. "Would you like me to have something sent up from the kitchen?"

"Please." Janessa thought of the scene between Noelle and Patrice the night before. "If you want, I can call your mom and order lunch."

"No, that's okay. I need to face her eventually." She took a step back. "Is there anything else you need?"

"That'll do for now. Thank you." Janessa stood and followed Noelle to the door. As soon as Noelle passed through the outer office and disappeared into the hallway, Janessa closed the door and turned to face Levi. "You recruited Noelle?"

"What are you talking about?"

She circled to the front of her desk, folding her arms as she leaned against it. "She hasn't learned to hide her surprise yet."

"I think you're imagining things." Levi stood and took a step back. He lowered his voice when he added, "And don't forget you're out of the spy business now."

"So you keep telling me."

* * *

Levi was five feet from his office door when his cell phone vibrated in his pocket and he heard the accompanying chime that indicated he'd received a text message. He pulled his phone free and read the text from Jeremy.

He changed directions and headed down the hall toward the guest quarters. Jeremy must have been waiting for him by the door because he opened it before Levi had a chance to knock.

Ducking into the room, he closed the door behind him. "What's so important?"

"A couple of things." He held out several sheets of paper. "I worked through the background checks for the four council members who weren't at the wedding."

"And?"

"Vick Dubeau was in the hospital recovering from knee-replacement surgery, and Angelo Fallasi was in Paris for a family emergency. Apparently his father was in a serious car accident."

"I remember hearing about that," Levi said. "What about the other two?"

"I have no idea. Bernardo Campesi is the president of the ruling council. I wondered if perhaps he was deliberately absent in case of an emergency."

"It's possible. I can check that out with King Eduard." Levi looked down at the papers Jeremy had given him, scanning through the information. "So we have no idea why Marcel Beaumont missed the wedding."

"None. He was only appointed to the council last August. Is it possible he wasn't on the guest list?"

"Maybe. I'll check it out and get back to you."

"There is one more thing."

"What's that?"

"I've completed the initial background checks on about fifty of the guests for my sister's wedding."

"And?"

"Eight of them came back with alarms on."

"What do you mean?"

"I mean these people have alerts set to let them know if anyone is running their names. The list is in what I gave you."

Levi read through the list, noting that three of the four council members were on it. "This could just mean these people are cautious."

"It could," Jeremy agreed. "Or it could mean they have something to hide."

"Stay on it. Let me know if you find anything else."

"I will."

Levi left Jeremy's room and looked down at the list of names once more. There was no doubt about it. Security for Janessa's wedding was going to be a nightmare.

* * *

"Mama, can we talk?" Noelle asked. She couldn't stand the tension lingering between them, and she desperately wanted to find a way to repair their relationship.

Patrice put down the dish she had been drying and turned to face her. "I heard what happened today with that wedding planner."

"You heard I was fired."

"I heard she insulted my cooking."

Noelle couldn't help but smile. "That wasn't exactly what happened. She most definitely didn't give you the credit you deserve."

"Brenna said as much." She set her dish towel aside and opened her arms in invitation.

Relieved beyond words, Noelle stepped into the hug, holding her mother tightly. "I'm really sorry, Mama. I never meant to hurt you."

"I know you didn't." She held on for a minute, the tension melting away. When she stepped back, she added, "Just promise you won't keep any more secrets from me. You know you can trust me with anything."

Noelle thought of her work with Levi, of the king's request for her service. She chose her words carefully when she said simply, "I know, Mama."

"What are you going to do for a job now?"

"I've been promoted, so to speak."

"Promoted?"

"Janessa asked me to take Floria's place."

Surprise came first, followed by a look of pride. "You will do a wonderful job."

"I'm glad you think so because the first thing I need to do is enlist your help with the food."

She smiled fully. "Janessa and I have discussed a few ideas."

"Exactly. For right now though, I need to fix us some lunch. Janessa wants to start going over ideas while we eat."

"You go get started." Patrice shooed her toward the door. "I'll bring something up."

"Thanks, Mama."

"You're welcome."

Feeling like several weights had been lifted from her shoulders, Noelle kissed her mother's cheek. "I love you, you know."

"I know. I love you too."

Chapter 20

JEREMY SIGNED IN AT THE front desk of the television studio, and the receptionist gave him directions to the editing suite in Italian. He decided his time spent with Paolo was paying off when he only had to ask for her to repeat herself once. He moved forward, hoping he had understood her correctly. Once past the main desk, no one seemed to care who he was or where he was going. If he was right, he probably could have accessed any number of areas without anyone's being the wiser.

Security cameras were few and far between. He took special note of their placement when he reached his destination. Other than one located thirty feet from the editing suite door, none was visible.

An editor showed him the equipment and how to access the video footage for various shows and news programs. Jeremy didn't tell him he could have figured it out on his own; he just watched to see how easy it would be to bypass any passwords or security protocols. The answer was a little unsettling. Anyone who could get through the door could copy anything they wanted.

Jeremy took a seat and started his search for any material accessed the night Adrienne Acord disappeared. The local news and various clips from the stories covered were the most prominent, the last of which had been closed down at 1:12 in the morning. The next entry was made at 1:47, a complete download of the royal wedding footage.

Concerned, Jeremy asked, "Can I get a download of everything from Prince Stefano's wedding day?"

"Yeah, but I thought we already sent that over."

"You did, but I think my file may have been corrupted." Jeremy lowered his voice. "I'd appreciate it if you'd keep that to yourself. I really don't want my boss to know I had to come back to get another copy."

"No problem." He looked at Jeremy with understanding. "Let me get that for you."

A few minutes later, with a new flash drive in hand, Jeremy explored the building further. Numerous hallways and doors led outside, most of them without any surveillance, and anyone could have come in and slipped past security. His grip tightened on the flash drive. The question was whether they were looking for something specific or trying to cover something up.

* * *

Philippe and Elaina's belongings arrived long before they did. When Jeremy heard a vehicle pull up outside, he looked out expecting to find Garrett's cousin. He instead discovered a van parked at the front entrance, the driver unloading a ridiculous number of suitcases.

So much for their visitors staying only a few days.

Remembering his sister's earlier comment about them trying to move into the chateau last summer, he secured his work and went in search of Janessa. He discovered her in the main entry with Martino and the pile of suitcases.

"I can't believe this," Janessa said, pacing across the room and waving a hand at the luggage. "They can't just move in without asking first." She turned back to Martino. "Can they?"

"I'm afraid it wouldn't be the first time Prince Philippe has made such an attempt."

Jeremy glanced out the front window at the departing van. Looking at the baggage up close, he wondered how it had all fit into the back of the regular sized van. "This doesn't look good."

"No joke." Janessa huffed out a breath.

Ignoring his sister's frustration, Jeremy keyed in on Martino's words. "If it isn't the first time they've tried moving in, how did you get rid of them before?"

"Renovations."

"Renovations?"

"The guest wing does look fantastic, don't you think?" Martino asked.

"I do." Jeremy agreed. "I gather the renovations were recent."

"Eighteen months ago."

"I can't deal with this. Philippe and Elaina expect to be entertained all the time, and Patrice will organize a revolt if she has to deal with them. And that's not even taking into consideration the fact that we're in the middle of planning a wedding."

"Why doesn't Patrice like them?"

"Because they're spoiled, pompous brats." Janessa looked around to make sure they were still alone. "Did I just say that out loud?"

"Yeah. You might want to censor those thoughts when they're standing in the room," Jeremy suggested.

"Good call." She lifted her hands and let them fall back to her sides. "I'm at a loss. Any suggestions?"

"Philippe and Elaina like to be pampered, huh?"

"They don't like it. They demand it."

"And all of the guest rooms are in the same wing?" Jeremy asked, an idea forming.

"That's right."

Martino motioned to the stairs. "The guest suites are all in one wing upstairs, and the family quarters are in another. There are also separate living quarters where several staff members reside."

"How many rooms are empty in the servants' quarters right now?"

"Four, but they're all single rooms and rather small."

"Perfect." Jeremy turned to his sister. "How would you feel about roughing it for a few days?"

"What do you mean?"

"If you tell me when you're ready for the pampered prince and princess to leave, we can have an electrical problem in the guest wing. A couple of days of no heat, lights, or hot water, and I think they'll reconsider wanting to stay here."

Martino caught on to his logic. "We could, of course, offer them alternative lodging in the servants' quarters . . ."

"Which they would see as an insult," Janessa finished for him. "It's a great idea, but what's to keep them from trying to invade the family quarters? Garrett is the only one living there right now."

"Perhaps we could convince Queen Marta to visit for a day or two," Martino said. "Even though Prince Stefano and Princess Alora are on their honeymoon, their boys would probably enjoy a visit for the weekend."

"That's a great idea. If they were here when we had our little mishap, the family quarters would be completely full." She focused on Jeremy once more. "Do you think you can figure out how to get the utilities to shut down in only that one area of the chateau?"

"Leave it to me." Jeremy nodded. "You just figure out how to fill the rest of the available rooms."

"I'll call the queen right now." Janessa pulled out her phone. "And Jeremy?"

"Yeah?"

"I'm really glad you're here."

"Me too." He watched her dial a number and continue on into the parlor, where she could have a little privacy. Jeremy turned back to Martino. "You'll give me warning if she decides to get rid of me, won't you?"

"Of course," Martino said in his typically formal tone. "I suspect, however, that Janessa would be the first to tell you if it became an issue."

"You're probably right," Jeremy admitted. He patted a hand on the nearest suitcase. "Too bad she can't be blunt with the other side of the family."

"It is indeed."

* * *

Levi looked at Jeremy's latest background reports, concerned by the one on top. Gustave Nardini, the man who had spoken on the phone to Regina several nights before, had spent the two months prior to Stefano's wedding traveling. Turkey, North Africa, France, Ireland. In a couple of places, he had left one country only to disappear for a week or more before appearing hundreds or even thousands of miles away.

The most disconcerting stop on Nardini's agenda had been Northern Ireland, the last known location of Ivan Byrd, the suspected bomb maker.

The source of the man's travel funds had been another red flag. According to the background check, his bank accounts were insufficient to support him on such an extended vacation, and his credit card activity during his trip had been noticeably absent. Not once had he made a charge.

He must have been using cash, the source of which was unknown.

Levi took out his phone and called Director Palmer. "Sorry to bother you, sir, but we may have identified a problem."

"What've you got?"

Levi proceeded to outline the information Jeremy had uncovered as well as the conversation Noelle had heard.

"I'll put him on our watch list and see what our analysts here at head-quarters can dig up," Director Palmer said. "Does your analysis indicate any motivation for this guy?"

"Nothing of significance. He's a Meridian citizen and hasn't shown any strong political ties that we know of."

"Sounds like more of a hired hand than a mastermind."

"Exactly. That's what worries me," Levi said.

"I'll let you know if we find anything. Do you have any other leads?"

"I was able to confirm with King Eduard that Bernardo Campesi deliberately didn't attend Stefano's wedding for security reasons. Marcel Beaumont wasn't on the guest list because he wasn't acquainted with the couple," Levi said. "Jeremy is still running background checks on the other guests."

"Keep me in the loop."

"Yes, sir." Levi thought of the unexpected value Noelle had provided as well as the developing relationship between Jeremy and her. "Also, I'd like to bring Jeremy into the loop about my informant here. I think we can get a lot more accomplished if the three of us are working together instead of always having me as the middle man."

"I realize that would make it easier on you, but we can't risk the potential security concerns that would create," Director Palmer said. "We haven't fully vetted Noelle, and maintaining Jeremy's cover is paramount." "Things could get complicated around here with so many moving parts not knowing about the others," Levi said, pressing the issue. "It's hard enough that Janessa's no longer in the loop."

"I'm sorry, but I can't authorize compromising Jeremy's cover. I'll put a rush on the analysis of Gustave Nardini and get back to you as soon as I can."

"Thank you, sir." Levi hung up. He knew when he joined the CIA that his job would include keeping secrets, but this was becoming ridiculous.

Chapter 21

Noelle dressed for her date with Jeremy, doubts plaguing her. When she had accepted his invitation, she hadn't thought things through.

Dinner with Prince Philippe and Princess Elaina would be a stiffly formal affair, at best. She didn't want to entertain worst-case scenarios. Needless to say, they would be less than pleased if they realized one of the other dinner guests was the hired help.

She heard a knock at her door and opened it to find Jeremy standing in the hall, a crystal vase filled with flowers in his hands.

"Are you sure Prince Garrett is okay with me coming tonight?" Noelle blurted out.

"Hello to you too." He held out the flowers. "Prince Garrett is well aware that you are my date, and he is expecting you to be there."

"I'm sorry. I'm just nervous. Prince Philippe and his wife are not the types who socialize with the hired help."

"Then I doubt they'll have much to say to either of us."

"Yes, but your sister is marrying Prince Garrett."

"My sister is a commoner from the United States. Trust me, if these people are as snobby as everyone says, our only challenge will be saving Garrett from getting cornered by them all night."

"I guess I never thought of it that way." She took the flowers from him and inhaled deeply. "Thank you for these. They're beautiful."

"So are you." He leaned on the doorjamb while she set the vase on the small table beside her door. "Are you ready?"

"As ready as I'll ever be." She followed him into the hall and lowered her voice. "Has your sister said anything about how long Prince Philippe intends to stay?"

"Yes, but I guarantee it won't be as long as he thinks."

* * *

Jeremy led Noelle into the parlor, instantly identifying Prince Philippe and Princess Elaina from across the room. Philippe didn't look anything like his cousin, the man's high forehead, heavy brow, and pointy chin contrasting with Garrett's chiseled features. Philippe was also several inches shorter than Garrett and didn't share his athletic build.

Elaina stood beside Philippe, her fitted red gown leaving her shoulders bare.

It took only a moment before Jeremy noticed the stiffness in the room. "Prince Philippe and Princess Elaina aren't speaking to anyone," he whispered to Noelle.

"I'm not surprised," she whispered back. "They aren't known for being the friendliest couple. In fact, quite the opposite."

Jeremy's gaze swept the room, and he managed to identify several of the faces from the background checks he had been conducting. Councilman Aubin stood beside his wife and twenty-four-year-old daughter, Gemma. Chatting with them was the French ambassador and Michel.

"I didn't realize your friend was coming tonight," Jeremy said.

Noelle wrinkled her nose. "Neither did I."

Michel leaned closer to Gemma, who smiled at something he said.

"It looks like he has moved on," Jeremy said.

"Thank goodness."

Janessa noticed Jeremy and Noelle from across the room and headed their way.

"Every time I see my sister dressed up like this, I feel like I've entered an alternate universe."

"I gather she wasn't the type to dress up and play princess when she was little?"

"More like the type who was always on the back of a horse."

Janessa reached them and put a hand on Jeremy's arm. "I'm glad you made it. You both look great."

"Thanks," Jeremy answered for both of them. "If these dinners are common occurrences, though, I really do need to buy a couple more suits and find the nearest dry cleaner."

"The dry cleaning is easy. It's just like in a hotel. If you put it in the dry cleaning bag hanging in your closet, the maids will have it sent out for you," Janessa said. "As for new suits, I think I may need to have my new assistant show you to the tailor's shop in town."

Jeremy considered the concept that the money he was saving by not paying rent was likely to go out the window on clothes over the next month or two.

"I'd be happy to. I was planning to meet with the florist tomorrow morning. If you want, I could drop you off at the tailor's while I'm there."

"That's not a bad idea if you don't mind me tagging along." Jeremy looked across the room once more, noticing Garrett playing host as he chatted with his cousin. "I have a feeling I won't want to be around the chateau tomorrow anyway."

"Maybe I should come with you too," Janessa said, her voice low. She took a deep breath. "I guess I'd better go give Garrett some support. It looks like he needs it."

"How can you tell?"

"He's standing next to Philippe. That's all the sign I need." She straightened her shoulders and seemed to muster her courage. "Do me a favor and interrupt us in five minutes if we don't escape by then. I'll want to introduce you around anyway."

"You've got it," Jeremy agreed.

* * *

Noelle had secretly hoped to avoid meeting Prince Philippe. Though she had seen him many times over the years, the only encounter that had included a conversation had been at the stables when he had been irritated to find out she had been exercising the horse reserved for his use at the chateau. That irritation had exploded into outrage when he'd ignored her grandfather's guidance to take some time to settle his high-strung stallion down before mounting it and had been thrown off before he'd even made it out of the stable yard.

When five minutes passed and Garrett and Janessa remained trapped by their manners, Jeremy took Noelle's hand. "I guess we'd better save them."

"You're right." Noelle straightened her shoulders as Janessa had done only a few minutes before. "Lead the way."

They crossed the room together, and Noelle drew strength from Jeremy's presence beside her. The moment they stepped beside Janessa, Garrett shifted his attention to them.

"Philippe, I don't believe you've met Janessa's brother," he began in English, shifting his gaze to Jeremy. "Prince Philippe and Princess Elaina, may I present Jeremy Rogers and his date, Noelle Saldera."

Philippe didn't move for several seconds, and Noelle wondered if he was testing Jeremy, waiting to see if he would extend his hand prematurely, something that would be a breach of etiquette. Thankfully, Jeremy waited for Prince Philippe to extend his hand first.

"It's a pleasure to meet you," Philippe said stiffly.

"You as well," Jeremy replied. "I understand you will be staying here at the chateau for a few days."

"Our plans are not yet finalized," he said, his words deliberately vague.

"If you'll excuse us," Janessa said. "I'd like to introduce Jeremy and Noelle to some of our guests."

"Garrett, I had hoped to speak with you privately for a moment," Philippe said before they could make a clean escape.

"I prefer not to neglect our other guests. I'm sure we can find a time to chat tomorrow." Garrett took Janessa's hand in his and made an authoritative exit. "Excuse us."

Noelle gratefully let Jeremy escort her away from Philippe and Elaina. They crossed to a nearby couple and made introductions. For the next twenty minutes, Noelle mingled with several of the most powerful men in her country, men she typically only saw on television or from the other side of a serving tray. Bernardo Campesi, Zerbino Aubin, Marcel Beaumont, and Vick Dubeau, all from the ruling council. Several members from the economic committee were present, as well as Dr. Casale, the royal family's longtime physician.

She stood beside Jeremy now, listening to him discuss safety procedures for oil refineries with Vick Dubeau. The French ambassador joined in on the discussion, the topic shifting to oil-production levels.

When Princess Elaina stepped beside her, Noelle was more than ready to talk about something besides oil.

"I meant to ask earlier, are you and Jeremy staying here at the chateau?"

She was fishing for information, and Noelle felt her protective instincts kick in. "We are."

"I hadn't realized Garrett was entertaining other guests when we made our plans to come."

"I wasn't aware you were coming to visit until a few days ago," Noelle said, choosing her words carefully. "I was honestly surprised to hear of your arrival since Prince Garrett and Janessa have such a full schedule as they prepare for their wedding."

"That's one of the reasons I'm here."

"I don't understand."

Elaina didn't reply, turning instead to greet Bernardo Campesi of the ruling council. "Bernardo, it's so good to see you again. Did you enjoy the play last night?"

Realizing she had been dismissed, Noelle turned her attention back to Jeremy's conversation and prayed dinner would be served soon.

Chapter 22

AFTER THE STIFF FORMALITY OF the night before, Jeremy was happy to dive back into work on Thursday morning. He didn't know how his sister dealt with all of the protocol, not to mention her snobby future in-laws. He hoped the rest of the royal family was more like Garrett than Philippe.

He knocked on the door to the security office, waiting for Levi to open it before he entered. As had been the case for several previous meetings, Levi was the only person present so they could speak privately.

"What's the latest?" Levi asked after he closed the door.

"I ran the news feed from the TV station against what they originally sent us," Jeremy said. "Nothing was missing, but someone did copy the same files."

"To what end?"

"I don't know. I gather the missing editor is still missing?"

"Yes. There's an ongoing search, but her cell phone was in her car, which was parked at the station. Without any electronic signatures to track, the police don't have anything to go on until someone comes forward with new information."

"You said her cell phone was in her car. What about her wallet and keys?"

"Neither was found."

"I have to think that with the timing of when the wedding footage was downloaded that someone either convinced her to let them into the editing suite or they used her keys to access it without her."

"You realize that once this guy got what he wanted, he wouldn't have any reason to keep her alive."

"I know." Jeremy drew a deep breath, trying to look at the situation without letting his emotions interfere with logic. "We can't do anything for her at the moment beyond what the police are doing. The real concern is why someone cared so much about accessing the information in the first place."

"Best guess, he was looking for something."

"Something like where Rita Sandoval went," Jeremy said. "Whoever put her up to bringing in the bomb doesn't know you detained her."

"Or this guy could be using the footage to analyze our security for Prince Stefano's wedding so he can figure out how to get around it the next time."

"I watched the wedding on TV. Security was incredibly tight."

"It will be even tighter for your sister's wedding," Levi said. "Since the reception will be held here at the chateau, we'll have complete control over who has access. The challenge will be at the church ceremony."

"Why are they having a church ceremony if they're getting married in the temple?"

"It's the law here. Even if they marry in the temple, they have to go through a civil ceremony for their marriage to be legal."

"Does it have to be in a church?"

"I'm not sure. I thought so."

"I wonder how the royal family would feel about having the civil ceremony here at the chateau instead of at the Meridian Church. That would eliminate our biggest risks."

"I'll talk to King Eduard about it. If that is feasible, I'll have him broach the subject with Prince Garrett."

"I'll keep my fingers crossed that we can avoid having the extra venue."

"Believe me, I would be thrilled if that could happen."

* * *

Noelle listened to the chatter at breakfast, the focus today on Pascal's new girlfriend.

"She's gorgeous," Pascal said. He pulled out his cell phone and retrieved a photo. He held it out to show Ronaldo. "See?"

"She is beautiful," Ronaldo agreed. With humor in his voice, he asked, "What is she doing going out with you?"

"She has good taste," Pascal insisted over the laughter that followed.

"How did you meet?" Noelle asked, inserting herself into the conversation for the first time.

"I met her at the diner where I usually eat on my night off."

"I haven't seen her around before," Patrice commented when the photo passed by her.

"She just moved here. She's working for the bakery in town."

Noelle processed the conversation, her radar now tuning in to potential problems. While Pascal's new girlfriend's arrival might not be an issue, Noelle knew Levi would want to hear about it. The conversation continued, and she made mental notes of the details Pascal provided as well as committing the woman's image to memory.

Once breakfast was concluded, she sent a quick text to Levi. If he followed his usual routine, she suspected she would see him before the morning was through.

* * *

Levi intercepted Noelle as she passed by his office on her way out of her own. Since she had her purse over her shoulder, he guessed she was headed into town. "Do you have a minute?"

Noelle nodded and followed him into the empty security office. "Where is everyone?"

"I sent them out on rounds since we have visitors," Levi said. "What do you have for me?"

Noelle related the information she had overheard at breakfast. "It might be nothing, but I thought it odd that the bakery had hired someone new, especially since the new girlfriend met Pascal in a place he always goes."

"I'll definitely check her out. This is exactly the kind of breach we have to avoid."

"Let me know if anything turns up."

"I will."

Noelle opened the door and slipped into the hall. Levi watched her go and considered the latest intel. Though bringing her on board had been an impulse, he was starting to think she could make a future working with the CIA.

* * *

Janessa looked up from her desk when she heard movement in her outer office, her stomach grumbling as she realized it was lunchtime. Hoping

Noelle had thought to pick something up for her in the kitchen after getting back from town, she sniffed the air. Nothing.

Disappointment turned to dismay when she saw it wasn't Noelle but Elaina standing in her doorway.

"I hoped I might talk to you for a minute," Elaina said.

Janessa grasped for any excuse to deny her request, but Elaina took her hesitation as a yes. She walked farther into the office and took a seat.

"What is it you need?" Janessa asked, not sure she really wanted to know the answer.

"It's what you need that I want to talk to you about."

"I beg your pardon?"

"I heard about your falling out with Floria," Elaina began. "I mentioned a few months ago that I would be happy to help you with your wedding plans."

Janessa remembered the conversation well—Elaina's attempt to use her offer for help as a ploy to move into the chateau. At the time, Janessa had just hired Alora as her assistant, and Garrett had been immensely grateful Janessa had effectively put up an invisible barrier to keep Philippe and Elaina from encroaching on his home. It wasn't until Alora had gotten engaged to Prince Stefano that Janessa had consented to using a professional wedding planner.

"Elaina, that's kind of you to offer, but I already hired a replacement."

"Oh, I hadn't heard." She crossed one leg over the other. "May I ask who?"

"Noelle Saldera. You met her last night." At the confusion on Elaina's face, Janessa added, "She came to dinner with my brother."

"Oh, yes." Elaina remained poised, apparently not deterred from her initial objective. "I'm sure you're aware that planning a royal wedding involves hundreds of details. I would be happy to supervise Noelle. After all, I have firsthand experience from my own wedding."

"Thank you, Elaina, but that won't be necessary," Janessa said firmly. "Noelle worked on Prince Stefano's wedding, and she requires no additional supervision." She heard her outer door open once more, this time the sound accompanied by the scent of fresh bread and grilled meat. Noelle appeared in her doorway, freezing when she saw Elaina. "Elaina, thank you for stopping by, but Noelle and I have some work to attend to." Janessa stood. "Noelle, please put lunch on the table and get Martino on the phone for me."

"Of course." Noelle set the food down and returned to her office.

Elaina hesitated briefly before standing. "Let me know when you change your mind."

Janessa simply nodded, grateful when her phone buzzed. She waited until Elaina exited before she picked up the call.

"Martino, sorry. I just needed an excuse to get Elaina out of my office."

"I was about to call you," he replied. "I'm afraid your new arrivals are making themselves more at home than we expected."

"How is that possible? It already looks like they've moved in."

"Prince Philippe is planning a fox hunt in two weeks. He informed the staff that he has three couples who will need to stay in the guest quarters, and Princess Elaina has tasked Patrice with preparing meals for a number of formal events."

"Unbelievable." Janessa's mind whirled. "In that case, I need you to set up a meeting as soon as possible."

* * *

Jeremy had enjoyed every minute he had spent in town with Noelle. Well, every minute that had been outside the tailor's shop. There was something unsettling about an old guy coming at him with a tape measure. At least he wouldn't have to go through this again anytime soon. By the time he had left, the tailor had his order for two new suits and a tuxedo for Janessa's wedding.

He had planned to make up for lost time when he returned to the chateau, but he had barely arrived home when Martino called to inform him that his sister required his presence. The fact that the request was phrased more like a royal command irritated him on principle.

It was his stubborn streak, the one that hated being told what to do, that caused him to deliberately take his time in responding. When he walked into his sister's office ten minutes late, he saw Prince Garrett sitting inside and realized that perhaps Janessa's request *had* been a royal command. He looked around the worktable where everyone had gathered, surprised that Levi, Martino, and Noelle were also present.

"Sorry I'm late. I lost track of the time."

Janessa's eyebrows lifted, a sign that she knew exactly why he was late. Thankfully she didn't comment.

"Have a seat," Garrett said. "We were just discussing your idea."

"My idea about what?" Jeremy closed the door, suspecting that this meeting warranted privacy.

"How to reclaim my home."

Understanding dawned, and he sat in the empty chair between Martino and Noelle. "I thought we weren't putting those plans in play for another day or two."

"I'm very fond of the old saying 'There's no time like the present.'" The air of authority surrounding Garrett seemed out of character to Jeremy. Except for when chatting with his cousin the night before, Jeremy had found Janessa's fiancé to be friendly and welcoming. He didn't look welcoming now.

"I took a look at the electrical box," Jeremy said. "I would recommend upgrading it anyway, but it will be a simple matter to flip the correct breakers to turn off power to the guest quarters."

"What if Prince Philippe goes down to check it out himself?" Janessa asked.

"I highly doubt he would," Garrett said.

"I agree," Martino put in. "The electrical box is in the cellar. I don't think Prince Philippe has ever been down there, nor would he know how to access it."

"Even if he tried, he'd have to get past my mother since the cellar door is off the kitchen," Noelle said.

"We'll need to put a backup power source on the security cameras in that part of the chateau," Levi said. "I don't want this deception to compromise security."

"I assume you don't have all the security systems on the same circuit," Jeremy said.

"No, we don't."

"I think a battery backup system will be our best bet," Jeremy said. "Hopefully it won't take long to get your squatters to move on to greener pastures."

"How long will it take to get everything ready?"

"An hour or two." Jeremy glanced over at his sister. "The heating system is natural gas. We can shut that off now without affecting anything else."

Garrett turned toward Janessa. "I don't like the idea of you being without heat. This could take a week or more to get them to leave."

"Don't worry. Patrice offered to let Jeremy and me stay in her sons' rooms until everything is 'fixed.'" She motioned to Jeremy. "You may want to move into another space to work though."

"You can use my brother's office," Garrett offered. "He isn't expected to visit the chateau for several weeks."

"That would be great. Thanks."

"Where are Prince Philippe and Princess Elaina right now?" Noelle asked.

"They went into town to do some shopping," Martino said. "Why?"

"I was just thinking it's rather cold out today. Now might be a good time to have the staff air out Prince Philippe's room."

Garrett chuckled. "Noelle, I forgot how devious you can be."

"I'm not being devious. I'm simply stating an observation."

"It's a good one. Talk to Brenna, and have her take care of it. She's good at keeping secrets."

"I will."

"And I'll stand watch," Martino offered.

"Thank you, everyone." Garrett stood. "I assume I don't have to tell you this plan is need-to-know."

"Top-secret stuff. Got it." Jeremy rubbed his hands together and stood as well. "Let's go have some fun."

Chapter 23

"WHAT DO YOU MEAN THERE'S no electricity in our rooms?" Prince Philippe demanded at full volume.

It stirred Noelle's sympathies to watch Martino weather the assault. "I'm sorry, sir. The electrical panel has needed replacing for some time. Jeremy is trying to fix it, but he said it will be at least a few days before the new parts arrive."

"Why is Jeremy fixing the electrical panel? Surely there is a capable electrician in town who can deal with this."

"Jeremy is an electrical engineer," Noelle said, stepping forward to align herself with Martino.

"I'm afraid the electrician we typically use here at the chateau retired a few months ago. We haven't cleared a replacement," Martino said.

"This is absurd." Philippe huffed.

"Obviously we'll have to move into the family quarters." Elaina waved a hand toward the stairwell. "Have the staff move our things immediately."

"I'm afraid that won't be possible," Martino said. "The family quarters are all currently occupied."

"By whom? Stefano and Alora are still on their honeymoon, and Eduard has diplomatic meetings all week."

"King Eduard is otherwise occupied, but Queen Marta will be arriving shortly. Giancarlo and Dante will accompany her. They will be staying in their parents' quarters."

"Where are we supposed to sleep?" Elaina asked, her voice shrill.

"We do have one room available in the servants' quarters."

"I am not staying in servants' quarters," Philippe blustered. He motioned to the bags behind him, the result of their shopping spree in town. "Have our things brought to our rooms."

"I'll take care of it," Noelle said. She pulled out her phone and called Brenna. "Prince Philippe and Princess Elaina have some packages they need brought to their rooms."

Noelle waited until Philippe and Elaina were out of earshot before she said to Martino, "I don't know how you manage to stay so cool when you have people yelling at you."

"I've had a lot of practice." Martino's gaze swept upward. "How long do you think they can survive the cold?"

"I don't know, but let's hope spring doesn't arrive too early."

They both looked up to see Brenna hurrying toward them.

"Did you get the doors and windows closed before they got to their room?" Noelle asked.

"Yes, and I checked the thermostat before I came down here. It was down to fifty-eight degrees." She grinned mischievously. "I may have also accidently put the summer bedding on when I changed their sheets today."

"Well done," Martino said with sincerity. "Once we get them to leave, I think we need to tell the guards never to let them back in."

"Wouldn't that be a gift," Noelle said.

* * *

Two dark-haired bullets raced through the door, a nearly grown golden retriever chasing behind them. They were halfway to the stairs when they noticed Jeremy.

He fought back a smile when both boys skidded to a stop and bowed to him. The dog's manners weren't nearly as developed. Clearly eager to continue their play, the dog nudged at the younger boy's hands, yipping excitedly.

"Are you a prince?" the youngest asked in Italian.

Jeremy shook his head, pleased that he was able to understand the question.

"I'm afraid I'm not a prince, but my sister is marrying one."

"Who's your sister?" the older one answered, his voice more timid than his younger brother's.

"Janessa." Jeremy stepped closer and offered his hand to the boy closest to him. He was rewarded with a handshake from the boy and excited doggie kisses from the retriever. He ruffled the dog's fur. Forcing himself to use his expanding skills in Italian, he continued. "I'm Jeremy Rogers. What are your names?"

"I'm Giancarlo," the oldest responded. "He's Dante."

"And this is Roscoe," Dante said.

"It's good to meet you. My sister has told me a lot about you."

"Do you like to ride horses?" Dante asked.

"I do like to ride horses."

"Want to ride with us?"

Jeremy thought of the many reasons he should get back to work, but the appeal of getting outside and away from Prince Arrogant and Princess Annoying overshadowed them all. Philippe and Elaina had been all too vocal about their frustrations regarding their living quarters and had sent everyone running for cover. "I would love to go riding with you."

He sensed someone at the front door and looked up at an elegant woman around his mother's age. Her dark hair was pulled back at the nape of her neck, and she exuded an air of dignity. It took him a moment to realize he was staring at the queen.

"You must be Janessa's brother." She offered a warm smile and extended her hand.

"Yes, Your Majesty. I'm Jeremy Rogers."

"So good to meet you." The dog started toward her, apparently eager to offer his own greeting. Queen Marta put up one hand, and the dog plopped his bum down obediently. Without breaking stride, the queen returned her attention to Jeremy. "I met your parents briefly when they visited last fall. I found them to be delightful."

"I heard wonderful things about their visit here. They were very enamored of your country."

"That's always good to hear." She looked down at the two boys. "Did I hear someone say you were going riding?"

"Jeremy said he would come with us."

"Please don't feel obligated to take them. Paolo can oversee their ride if you can't spare the time."

"I think some time in the fresh air will do me good."

Her eyes twinkled. "That is often the case." She put a hand on each of the boys' shoulders. "You boys be good."

"We will." The moment Marta released them, they swarmed Jeremy, each one taking him by the hand. "Let's go."

"Okay, I'm coming." Eager to escape the confines of the chateau and the protocol demanded within its walls, Jeremy bowed to the queen and let himself get pulled outside.

* * *

Noelle pulled on a jacket and walked out onto the terrace. She hadn't seen Jeremy since their impromptu meeting regarding "Operation Make Prince Philippe Go Away." Obviously he had succeeded in turning off the heat and electricity to the guest quarters, but she wasn't sure where he had gone after that. She had peeked into Prince Stefano's offices, expecting him to be settling in there, but she had found them empty.

Restless and happy to avoid any possible run-ins with Philippe and Elaina, she started toward the steps leading to the gardens. Two grounds-keepers were working nearby, preparing flowerbeds for the spring planting in the next few weeks.

She glanced out at the water, stopping her forward progress when she saw four horses on the beach. She identified the trail rider as her grandfather. A smile bloomed when she also recognized Jeremy leading the way, with Dante and Giancarlo on either side of him. Roscoe, the boys' eight-month-old golden retriever, trotted along beside them.

She thought of how much she loved this spot, of the many opportunities she had grown up with because of her family's service to the royal family. Yet, as much as she loved it here, part of her yearned to see what lay beyond the horizon. She had hoped her time in the U.S. would have satisfied her desire to travel, but it had done the opposite. She wanted more.

She focused on Jeremy. She could admit to herself that his presence had greatly influenced her desire to stay here at the chateau until the wedding, but the seed of what would come next had already been planted. What would she do after the wedding? Jeremy would finish his job here around the same time. Then what?

A door opened behind her, and she turned, relieved when it was the prince she liked.

"I was wondering where those two were hiding. I thought it was too quiet inside."

"They are such cute kids."

"They are. Stefano is lucky to have them."

"From what I've seen, they adore him." Her smile widened when she saw Dante wave animatedly as he spoke.

"It sure didn't take long for them to latch on to Jeremy." Garrett fell silent for a moment. "I wanted to thank you for helping Janessa with our wedding plans. You've made a huge difference."

"I haven't done much yet, other than make a few phone calls and run some errands in town."

"You've been a sounding board for Janessa, and you're willing to listen to what she wants," Garrett said. "That's a significant improvement over what she had before."

"I'm happy to help," she said. "And I'm glad working for Janessa will keep me here a while longer. Being here has helped ease the tension between me and my parents."

"Are they okay with you being Mormon?"

"They're getting used to the idea. I still can't believe how cool my grandpa was with it though. He's the one I thought would have the biggest issue."

"I think when people reach a certain age, they gain a better perspective of what's really important." He looked down at her. "What's important to you these days? I see you're still spending a lot of time with Jeremy."

Her eyebrows lifted. "Are you trying to play big brother?"

"I've seen the way he looks at you." He nudged her with his shoulder. "Not to mention he's the same religion as you, he comes from a good family, he's educated, and we now know he's good with kids. What do you think, Noelle? Is he a keeper?"

"Don't you think you should let me go on a few more dates before I start making decisions about the rest of eternity?"

"Maybe, but just so you know, I'd consider myself lucky to have you as my sister-in-law." He lowered his voice. "You might want to wait a few more minutes to come back inside. Elaina just found out they don't have any hot water."

"Thanks for the warning."

"Your boyfriend is good at his job," Garrett said, taking a step back. "You never know. Maybe he'll decide he wants to stay in Meridia and work here."

Noelle mulled that possibility over in her mind. Could she find contentment staying here if Jeremy stayed too? She shook that thought out of her head. They had been on only a few dates. Besides, she couldn't afford to let herself get distracted from her jobs, both the one with Janessa and the one with Levi. The last thing she wanted was to find herself in a room with another bomb.

Chapter 24

JEREMY HAD THOUGHT THE FIRST cold night would chase Prince Philippe and Princess Elaina away, but he had been sadly disappointed. Though their complaints had been loud and constant for the past three days, they had overtasked the staff to make up for the lack of heat and electricity.

Two of the maids had been forced to run hot water upstairs from the kitchen for them to bathe, and firewood had been brought upstairs to help ward off the night chill.

Determined to help prod them along, Jeremy decided to throw another challenge at them. Only this time he was recruiting help that would make sure he succeeded in his quest.

He entered the kitchen and found Noelle standing beside Patrice. It didn't take a genius to figure out that Patrice was not happy and Noelle was trying to calm her down.

Guessing at the cause, Jeremy approached them and lowered his voice. He spoke in French so both women would understand him. "When is that fox hunt supposed to be again?"

"A week from Saturday," Noelle said. "Why?"

"I think it's time to rub a little salt in the wound." He put a hand on Patrice's shoulder. "Have Philippe and Elaina come down to eat breakfast yet?"

"They're in the breakfast room now."

"Perfect. Patrice, could you bring me something to eat in there? I want to talk to you where they can hear."

"Why?"

"Just play along and trust me." He saw the trust he'd asked for and continued to the breakfast room.

"Good morning," Jeremy said brightly. He picked up a glass and poured himself some orange juice.

"It's hard to have a good morning when one can't even take a hot shower," Philippe insisted. "When are the repairs going to be complete?"

"I'll start on the rewiring Monday. It should only take a few weeks to complete."

"A few weeks?" Elaina squeaked. "What happened to a few days?"

"Oh, that was to get the parts, not to finish the work."

Patrice entered holding a plate of french toast. She set it on the table in front of Jeremy.

"Thank you, Patrice. This looks wonderful."

"You're welcome."

"Also, I forgot to tell you—to get ready for the wedding, I will need to rewire the entire kitchen. I'm afraid that means we'll need to shut you down for a few weeks."

"But how will I prepare meals?" Patrice asked, and Jeremy suspected she wasn't sure if he was serious or not.

"I'm afraid it will be cold cereal and sandwiches for a while. I can keep the refrigerator plugged in, but the stove and oven will be out of commission."

"When is this supposed to happen?"

"I have a technician coming on Tuesday. We'll have you up and running by the first of next month."

"Wait a minute," Philippe said. "We have guests coming next weekend for the hunt."

"That's nice."

"It's not nice at all. How can Patrice prepare meals for all of them if you tear apart her kitchen?"

"There are several great restaurants in town. I went to one just last week that was fabulous. I'd be happy to give you the name."

"This is completely unacceptable." Philippe scraped his chair back. "This is the royal chateau, not a fixer-upper for you Yanks to tear apart."

"Prince Garrett and Janessa approved the renovations."

"Prince Garrett isn't the one who invited a dozen people to join him on a hunt." Philippe spat out the words.

"I suspected as much." Queen Marta stood in the doorway. "Patrice, the french toast looks quite appetizing this morning. Could I trouble you to fix me a plate?"

"I would be happy to, Your Majesty." Patrice curtseyed and left the room.

Everyone rose at Marta's entrance, and she looked at Jeremy. "Jeremy, I want to thank you for all of the work you have done here at the chateau to help prepare for your sister's wedding. As you've seen for yourself, our electrical systems have been in need of upgrading for some time."

"I'm honored to help, Your Majesty," Jeremy said.

"I've discussed the situation with my husband, and we have decided to close down the guest quarters for the foreseeable future. I'm sure all of our current guests will be happy to return to their homes in light of the work that needs to be done here."

"But what about the hunt?" Philippe whined.

"As you said, you are the one hosting this hunt, not Prince Garrett. I am sure you can find another venue."

"Not without a great deal of expense."

"Well, that is one of the challenges of hosting such an event." Queen Marta motioned for everyone to take their seats.

Patrice delivered her food and quietly retreated back to the kitchen.

"Let me be clear," Queen Marta said. "The royal chateau is Garrett's home. From this point forward, you are not to schedule any events here without my son's permission, and you are not welcome to stay without an invitation. Do you understand?"

"Yes, Your Majesty," Philippe said despite the fury burning in his eyes.

"Good. Now, I suggest you finish your breakfast, because you have some packing to do. I expect you both to be gone by lunchtime."

Enjoying himself immensely, Jeremy reached for the glass container beside him and extended it to Queen Marta. "Syrup?"

Clearly fighting a smile, the queen accepted the offering, drizzled some over her french toast, and took a bite.

* * *

The news that Philippe and Elaina were leaving spread through the chateau like wildfire. Staff members eagerly offered assistance to help the couple pack, and Enrico and Renzo pulled the appropriate vehicles up in front of the main entrance.

Noelle thought offering them the limousine was overkill, but she suspected her father wanted to make sure they had room for anything that didn't fit into the van Renzo would drive for them.

She was heading to Janessa's office to let her know their guests had departed when she received a text message from her mother asking for help.

She diverted to the kitchen and found her mother, Brenna, and two other staff members in full swing, an enormous amount of food arranged on serving platters lined up on the counters.

"What's going on?"

"We need help getting all of this into the dining room."

"I didn't know we had an event today."

"It wasn't planned." Patrice motioned to the counter on her left. "You can start with those."

"Okay." Confused at what might have prompted such an extensive meal, she picked up two platters and started for the dining room. Regina was already inside filling water glasses. "Do you know what's going on?"

She shook her head. "I only know your mom called us all in after breakfast and we've been working like crazy since then."

"I guess we'll find out soon enough." Noelle headed back to the kitchen for the next load. Ten minutes later, the table was set, and Martino called all of the staff to the dining room.

Everyone lined up around the table, confused whispers continuing until Prince Garrett arrived with Queen Marta. Joining them were Giancarlo, Dante, Janessa, and Jeremy.

At their entrance, everyone quieted and stood at attention.

"As all of you are probably aware by now, Prince Philippe and Princess Elaina left a few minutes ago," Queen Marta began. "I know many of you went above and beyond the call of duty to serve their needs, and for that I want to thank you. The professionalism of everyone here is to be commended." She took a step forward. "Over the next few months, we will have the added stress of preparing for my youngest son's wedding. Each of you will be involved in the process in one way or another. This luncheon is a thank-you for all the hard work you do for the royal family and for the work that awaits each of us in the months to come."

Garrett moved to the queen and pulled out the chair at the head of the table for her. After she sat down, he repeated the process for Janessa. As soon as they were both seated, Marta gracefully waved a hand toward the table. "Please sit, everyone."

Surprised and delighted, the staff complied. Jeremy waved for Noelle to sit beside him, and she could feel a blush rise to her cheeks, fully aware that many of her friends noticed the gesture.

She grinned when both Dante and Giancarlo folded their arms in anticipation of blessing the food.

Garrett remained standing and folded his arms as well. "If you all will indulge me, I'd like to offer thanks for the food that has been prepared for us."

Everyone bowed their heads. After the prayer, Garrett took his seat and motioned to the food. "Please enjoy."

Platters were passed around the table, a seemingly endless variety of pasta, meat, vegetables, and rolls. When everyone's plates were filled, Noelle leaned over and whispered to Jeremy. "I see your plan worked."

"Not exactly," Jeremy whispered back.

"What do you mean?"

"Queen Marta is a rock star. She booted them out and made sure they won't be coming back."

"She had incredible timing this morning," Noelle said. She noticed the way Jeremy's eyebrows lifted briefly before his expression became surprisingly neutral. "You knew, didn't you?"

"Knew what?"

"Did you set that whole scene up?" Her voice was incredulous as the pieces of the puzzle fell into place. "The queen walked in right then on purpose."

Now surprise lit his face. With a shrug, he whispered, "I may have offered a suggestion for some intervention."

"You are incredible."

"Not really. I thought the lack of heat would send them packing after one night. I had no idea their fireplace would heat the room so well."

She put her hand on his arm. "Well done."

"Why, thank you. Just don't spread any of this around."

"Your secret is safe with me."

Chapter 25

JEREMY DIDN'T EXPECT TO MEET King Eduard until the wedding, but when he walked into the library in search of his sister, he found himself facing the curious stare of an older, broader version of Garrett. Queen Marta occupied the seat beside the man at the large table in the center of the room. Across from them sat Janessa, Garrett, and Noelle.

"I'm sorry. I didn't mean to interrupt."

"Jeremy, come in," Janessa said. "King Eduard, this is my brother, Jeremy."

King Eduard stood and extended his hand. "It's good to meet you. I understand you have been quite helpful here during your stay."

"With your wife's help," Jeremy said, unsure if the man before him knew of his true reason for being in Meridia.

"Please join us." King Eduard motioned to an empty chair. As soon as Jeremy complied, the king continued. "We were just discussing some of the wedding details."

Jeremy looked over at Noelle and thought he saw her suppress a grin. He remained silent as the discussion picked up around him.

"Let me make sure I understand this," Janessa said. "We would be able to have our wedding ceremony here at the chateau instead of in the Meridian Church?"

"A civil wedding is permitted to replace the church ceremony," King Eduard responded.

"I'm confused. Why do you have to get married after the temple ceremony?" Jeremy asked, not letting on that moving the second ceremony out of the church had been his suggestion.

"Your temple marriages aren't recognized under our current law," King Eduard said. "I expect that will change, but the ruling council is not pleased with Garrett's conversion to your church, so I imagine it will take some time before it happens."

"Could one of our bishops perform our ceremony?" Janessa asked.

"As long as he fills out the proper paperwork to conduct civil marriages, I believe it can be arranged."

Garrett looked over at Janessa. "What do you think?"

"Security would be a lot easier to control if we don't have the extra venue," she said. "Will it bother you to not have a ceremony in the Meridian Church?"

"I don't have a problem with that." Garrett shifted his attention to his father. "What about political ramifications? Will it cause increased religious tensions if we have everything here?"

"We will undoubtedly experience some backlash, but I think it's worth it when considering the possible alternatives."

Janessa's eyes sharpened. "Is there something you aren't telling us?"

King Eduard glanced over at Noelle briefly before responding. "With royal weddings being the only event in which the whole family is in attendance, I want to take every precaution, even if that means ruffling a few feathers."

"I guess it's settled, then," Garrett said. "I'll talk with our branch president on Sunday to see if he or one of the bishops in Calene has the proper authority here in Meridia."

"Let me know what you find out. If you can't find someone, we can make arrangements for someone else to conduct the ceremony," King Eduard said. "On another note, I received a call from my brother last night."

"How is he?" Garrett asked.

"He is about to become a grandfather. Elaina is pregnant."

"Pregnant? How far along is she?" Janessa asked. "She didn't mention anything when she was here."

"According to Elam, she is nearly four months along. Apparently they were keeping it quiet, but now that she is starting to show, they are preparing to make a statement to the press."

"It appears we were fortunate to move them out of the chateau when we did," Queen Marta commented.

"I'm so glad you stepped in when you did," Janessa told her.

"My wife can be quite firm when she wants to be," King Eduard said with a hint of pride. "Now, if you will excuse me, I am going to take the boys for a ride." He glanced over at Garrett and Jeremy. "Garrett, Jeremy, would you like to join us?"

"Or you can stay and help us work on more wedding plans," Janessa said.

"A ride sounds fabulous, Your Majesty." Jeremy stood and noticed Garrett taking the lifeline his father had thrown him as well.

Unified in purpose, the three men escaped the impending conversation about decorations and went in search of their young rescuers.

* * *

Noelle walked outside onto the empty terrace. She was there only a moment when Levi approached from the gardens.

"You wanted to see me?" Noelle asked when he reached her.

"We finished running our background on Pascal's girlfriend."

"And?"

"You were right to be suspicious of her, but it doesn't appear that she has anything to do with the bombing attempt at Stefano's wedding."

"I don't understand."

"She's a con artist. She was attempting to steal Pascal's identity. We found three credit card applications for him, all using an address that wasn't his."

"Are you serious?"

"The police have already arrested her for fraud. I suspect Pascal won't be too happy when he finds out, but at least we know she isn't an immediate threat."

"That's good to know."

"Do you have anything else for me?"

Noelle pulled a folded piece of paper from her pocket. She shifted her body so the cameras wouldn't catch her handing it to Levi. "This is a list of staff members who have made large purchases lately or who are talking about doing so soon," Noelle said. "Honestly, I didn't see anything that seemed out of anyone's salary range."

"I'd rather have too much information than too little." He tucked the paper into his pocket. "I'll see you later. Keep your ears open."

"I will." Deciding she should take advantage of a few minutes to herself, she headed toward the stables to see her grandfather. She heard men's voices as she approached, and her curiosity heightened when she realized they were speaking in Italian and that Jeremy was participating in the conversation. She emerged from the path to find King Eduard and Prince Garrett chatting with her grandfather and Jeremy. A short distance away, Giancarlo and Dante stood on the bottom plank of the split-rail fence, where they were petting one of the new foals.

The conversation about bloodlines and breeding continued as she approached, and she was amazed at how much Jeremy's language skills had improved. He made an error in how he phrased something, and her grandfather corrected him. Jeremy repeated his comment again, this time without error.

"I see your time with my grandfather is paying off," Noelle said, also choosing to speak in Italian.

"As long as we're talking about horses," Jeremy said and earned a chuckle out of Paolo.

"We're expanding his vocabulary a little at a time," Paolo said.

"What are you doing out here?" Garrett asked. "I thought you were working on wedding plans with Janessa."

"Your mother had to take a phone call, so Janessa said it was a good time to take a break." Noelle's phone rang, and she looked down to see it was the florist. "Looks like it's time for me to get back to work."

"Good luck," Jeremy said.

"Thanks." Noelle hit the talk button and headed back the way she had come.

* * *

"We have to find a way to gain access to the chateau. Everything hinges on it."

"I know. I've done everything I can think of to get someone in there, but the security is ridiculous. No new employees and restricted access for contractors. Our sources indicate that motion sensors are laid out along the perimeter of the estate." He let out a frustrated sigh. "Every time I come up with a new plan, I find a dozen reasons why it won't work."

"Let me be clear. You will find a way to make this work. I don't care what it costs. I want our targets eliminated."

"I understand what you want. I'm telling you it isn't as easy as you make it sound." He held up his hands and let them drop. "Maybe when it gets closer to the wedding, we'll find more access."

"It's time to open up some possibilities." He retrieved a listening device the size of a pea from his pocket and held it out. "If we plant a few of these at various vendors the royal family might use, we can identify where we can best explore the opportunities to gain entrance."

He took the device from his hand. "Where do you want me to start?"

"The bakery, the caterers, and the florist. I'll try to find out who the new royal couple is using for their music and photography."

"I'll get started first thing tomorrow."

"And don't forget. Failure is not an option."

"So you've told me."

* * *

Jeremy felt like he had barely taken time to breathe by the time the weekend rolled around. Work dominated his days from sunup until sundown, his only break coming when it was time to eat.

Thankfully, between Noelle and Janessa, someone usually saved him from missing his meals, even though he'd taken many of those meals in his room while he worked.

As much to keep up appearances as to make an improvement to the chateau, Jeremy followed through with his suggestion to replace the main electrical panel. In the process, he consulted with Levi on enhancing the emergency backup systems to the surveillance equipment, which included several motion detectors. Those had apparently been installed the summer before to alert them to any intruders who might attempt to make their way onto the grounds from the ocean or through the nearby woods.

With the hands-on work dominating so much of his time, he had been forced to put in extra hours in the evenings to continue the background checks. He and Levi had met earlier that week and prioritized the list, but he was anxious to get past this tedious task and start focusing on who might be behind the bombing attempt at Prince Stefano's wedding.

Exhausted, he stood and rolled his shoulders to work out some of the kinks. The dishes from his dinner sat on his desk, the evidence of another night of his being too involved with work to venture out of his room.

Ready for a change of scenery, he crossed into his living area and opened the balcony doors. Cool air spilled in, but the weather had warmed considerably over the past week. Spring was on its way, and

Jeremy decided it was time to remind himself what it felt like to take a break.

He retrieved his cell phone and called Noelle. Just the sound of her voice lifted his spirits. "Hi there. Any chance you're up for a walk on the beach?"

"I would love to get outside for a while," she said, sounding every bit as frazzled as he felt.

"Great. I'll meet you in the parlor in a few minutes." Jeremy secured his room and went downstairs. He had to admit he much preferred his living space now that he had working electricity and heat again.

Noelle arrived only moments after he did. Her hair was pulled back in a ponytail, and she wore a long sweater with a pair of faded jeans. "I'm glad you called. I've been staring at possible place settings for the past two hours. I don't think I could have taken much more of it."

"Why would it take two hours to look at place settings?"

"It might seem simple, but when you have to put together the different possibilities of china, flatware, glass- and stemware, linens—"

"Never mind." Jeremy held up his hand. "I don't want to know."

She chuckled. "I don't blame you."

"Come on. Let's see if the world still exists. It sounds like you haven't been outside much lately either." Jeremy led her to the terrace doors and pulled one open.

"Everyone has been pretty swamped this week. Between the interruptions in electricity and catching up from having Prince Philippe and Princess Elaina staying here, the staff has had their hands full."

"Sorry about the electrical problems." Jeremy took her hand in his.

"It sounded like the chateau was due for an overhaul. Everyone understood." Noelle's eyes lit up. "And we all know it was one of the things that helped us rid ourselves of our unwelcome guests."

"So a little inconvenience was acceptable after the challenge of having too many princes in the castle, so to speak."

"Exactly."

They made their way into the gardens, and Jeremy glanced over at Noelle. "I feel like I've hardly seen you this week."

"That's probably because you've hardly seen me this week."

"I guess that's true," Jeremy admitted, lost in his thoughts. Other than a few mealtimes when their paths had crossed, he and Noelle really hadn't seen each other since the luncheon Queen Marta had arranged for the staff. A few random text messages had been the extent of their communication, except for the words they'd exchanged at the dinner table.

Now, with Noelle's hand warm in his, he decided he didn't want to let so much time pass between their seeing each other again. He noticed some delicate white flowers blooming along the path and leaned down to pick one. He offered it to Noelle and was rewarded with a smile.

They walked down a path to the left, past the swimming pool and to the break in the seawall, where a set of stairs led down to the beach. The moon hung low in the sky, its light spilling over the water. Jeremy headed toward the rocks in the distance.

"It really is a shame we have the beach right here and we haven't had time to take advantage of it."

"I've always loved it here," Noelle said, her voice a little wistful. "When I was little, I would sneak down here and sit on the beach and pretend I could see what was on the other side of the water."

"Do you like to travel?"

"I've always wanted to travel, but I never had the chance before I went to the U.S."

"Where did you learn to speak English so well?"

"I studied in school, but most of what I learned was from listening to Garrett and Stefano," she said. "When they came here on vacations, Queen Marta insisted they still study their languages."

"I wouldn't have thought you would study with them since you're so much younger than they are."

"I didn't exactly study *with* them."

Jeremy noticed her amusement. "Let me guess. You learned English so you could spy on them."

"They always insisted on speaking English to keep me from knowing what they were up to."

"I never realized you were so devious." He thought of the secrets he was keeping from her and pushed aside a little tug of guilt.

"If they hadn't tried to hide things from me, I wouldn't have needed to be devious," she said. She changed the subject. "How is your work going? Will it settle down now that the electrical work is done at the chateau?" She looked at him warily. "You aren't really going to rewire the kitchen, are you?"

"And mess with your mom's home cooking? Not a chance."

"Does that mean you'll start having normal hours again?"

"I hope so. Starting on Monday, I'll have to check in at the naval base each week, but the rest of the time I should be able to work from my office here." Not wanting to dwell on the work he had waiting for him in his office, he said, "I think we need to make time for this."

"Time for what? Walks on the beach?"

"Time together." He stopped and turned to face her. "I've missed you."

"I've missed you too."

He thought of the first time he'd kissed her, the week before, of how natural she had felt in his arms. His throat instantly went dry. Surely it couldn't be that way again.

Testing his theory, he leaned down and brushed his lips against hers. His heart bounced hard and high in his chest, and he couldn't help but pull her closer. The breeze fluttered over them, bringing the scent of the sea.

His hands came up to frame her face, his thumbs brushing against the softness of her cheeks. When he gathered her close, she trembled against him, and he felt himself sinking into somewhere unknown. He pulled back to see her eyes dark, her lids heavy. "If we're not careful, this could become a habit." Before she could respond, he kissed her again, losing himself in the moment.

Chapter 26

"Has the CIA had any luck tracking down Ivan Byrd?" Jeremy asked.

"None. He was last seen in Northern Ireland, but it looks like he cleared out of there and hasn't been seen since. And no one has made any progress on the missing editor either." Levi raked his fingers through his hair. "There's a threat out there. I can feel it, but I have no idea how to figure out where it's coming from."

"I did a deep background check on that guy who asked Regina to help him find a job," Jeremy said. "When I did my initial research, he looked okay, but when I started digging, his information looked a little too neat. I think it's possible he's using an alias."

"That would make sense. Director Palmer called me this afternoon. Apparently they did track his movements into Africa."

"Where?"

"Algeria and Libya. It appears he may have some ties to Caspian Oil," Levi said. "We had trouble with them a few months ago. The president of the company had to step down after being put on Interpol's watch list for his involvement with some bombings here in Meridia."

"What was his motivation?"

"King Eduard had just denied the company's request for offshore drilling. He was trying to take out the ruling family and put someone else in power who could overturn the decision."

"Maybe someone else there is planning the same thing."

"It's possible," Levi said. "See if you can find any connection between any of our council members and either Caspian Oil or Gustave Nardini. I want to know if any of them were in the same country at the same time."

"I haven't found anything so far, but I'll look again."

"I also think we may need to take a more proactive role in identifying whoever is behind this."

"How so?"

"I think we should hire Nardini and see if he'll lead us to our culprits."

"I don't know . . ." Jeremy said, every instinct in him balking at the idea. "Can we risk bringing in someone who might be involved? We might as well give him permission to plant a bomb right under our noses."

"I hope he tries."

"Are you insane?"

"No. Logical." Levi paced across the room while Jeremy stared at him, bewildered. "We'll put a bug on his phone and track his movements. If we're lucky, he'll lead us to whoever he is working with long before Janessa's wedding. Worst case, we catch him in the act and pressure him to turn informant on his colleagues."

"No, worst case is he succeeds in planting the bomb and someone gets killed."

"I know it sounds crazy, but I think this is our best bet," Levi insisted. "But I do think we need to add another level of security to make sure your worst-case scenario never has a chance to happen."

"What level is that?"

"I have a friend working in London. His bomb-sniffing dog is the best I've ever worked with," Levi told him. "I'll run this idea by Director Palmer and King Eduard. If they approve, I'll ask for Alan to be transferred here until after the wedding."

"Assuming this crazy plan does get the go-ahead, do we tell Regina what we think her friend is up to?"

"No."

"What about anyone else on the staff? I have to say I'm not crazy about the idea of this guy living down the hall from Noelle."

"I'll task Martino to keep an eye on him, and we can install extra security cameras in the servants' quarters hallway."

"I think we should plant surveillance equipment in this guy's room too."

"That's not a bad idea. I'll run all of this by the powers that be and let you know what they say. In the meantime, see if you can trace Nardini and Caspian Oil back to anyone in power."

Jeremy felt his cell phone vibrate and looked down at a text from Noelle. "I'd better get going. I'm supposed to meet Noelle downstairs."

"What's the deal with you two? You've been spending an awful lot of time together."

"What can I say? I'm a lucky guy."

"Are things getting serious?"

Jeremy pondered the question. He hadn't really thought of their relationship in those terms before. Did he enjoy spending time with Noelle? Absolutely. Did he want to date anyone else? Not at all. Did he see a future for them together?

An image of sitting beside her in church popped into his mind. An instant later, he saw them together, children flanking them on either side.

"Jeremy?" Levi said, bringing Jeremy back to the present. He then repeated his question. "Are things serious between you two?"

"I'm not sure. They could be headed that way."

"Sounds like it's time for you to update your security profile to include her as a close and continuing relationship."

"You may be right."

* * *

Jeremy stood in his office and stared at the map on his wall. With Levi's help, he had put a lock on his office door so he wouldn't have to secure everything each time he left the room. As a result, he had started compiling a profile of everyone who was on the guest lists for both Stefano's wedding and Garrett's. Names and photos dotted his map, with those from Meridia, France, and Italy tacked onto a separate bulletin board because of the large numbers.

At the moment, he was more concerned with the guests from other regions. For weeks he had tried to identify any red flags for the guests, but despite the long hours, he wasn't any closer to identifying who was behind the bombing attempt.

As much as he hated to admit it, Levi was right. They needed to stop playing a defensive game. It was time to take the initiative, and their best shot at finding intel was hiring Regina's friend.

Jeremy picked up his phone and called Levi. "Can you talk?" he asked in lieu of a greeting.

"Just a minute." Levi fell silent. "Okay. I'm good now. What's up?"

"I've been looking at the guests and everyone else we had on our suspect list, but nothing is popping."

"Director Palmer and King Eduard gave us the green light on hiring Gustave Nardini. I can put that plan in motion by the end of the week."

"Sounds like we have some surveillance equipment to plant."

"I'll take care of that if you can help keep the staff out of the way."

"Any ideas?" Jeremy asked.

"Patrice's birthday is tomorrow."

"That's a distraction I can live with."

* * *

"Thank you for helping me with this." Noelle kept her voice down to make sure her mother didn't overhear her.

"You're welcome." Jeremy followed her onto the terrace and set Patrice's birthday cake on one of several round tables. "How did you manage to make the cake without her knowing about it?"

"Brenna helped me. We used the kitchen in one of the guest suites upstairs."

"I didn't realize any of the guest quarters had kitchens."

"Only two. They're typically reserved for families, especially ones with young children."

Brenna walked outside carrying a platter of finger sandwiches. "I think we're about ready. The staff is on their way, and Regina is grabbing the ice cream from the freezer."

"Sounds like it's time for us to go distract your mom for a few minutes," Jeremy said.

"That'll be easy," Noelle promised. "We'll tell her we need her opinion on what kind of cheesecake bites we should have for the wedding."

"I thought I said I was staying out of the wedding plans."

"You are. These are pretend wedding plans." Noelle laughed when she saw the pained look on his face. "You do realize that someday you'll get married and have to face these kinds of decisions."

"Nah. I'm going to marry someone who knows what I like and will make these decisions for me."

"So you want to marry someone who knows you like blueberry cheesecake the best."

"Exactly."

Noelle chuckled at his predictability as she led the way to the kitchen. As expected, the conversation about cheesecake varieties took a full fifteen minutes.

Realizing that everything should be in place by now, Noelle finally said, "Mama, I also wanted your opinion on the decorations for the terrace."

"That's something you should ask Gianessa."

"Janessa wanted your opinion too," Jeremy said before Noelle could come up with an excuse. Clearly ready to nudge them along and escape the menu discussions, Jeremy took each of them by the arm. "Come on. I think we can all use some fresh air."

"I have to start on dinner," Patrice protested.

"I'm sure you can spare five minutes." Jeremy continued to guide them out of the kitchen, down the hall, and into the parlor.

Noelle saw the confusion on her mother's face as they approached the terrace doors, where they could see several staff members standing outside.

"What is this?" Patrice asked.

"We thought you would enjoy some dessert you didn't fix, for a change," Noelle said.

Jeremy released their arms and opened the door for them. "Happy birthday, Patrice."

Her face flushed with pleasure. "I should have known you were up to something when you and Brenna disappeared at the same time."

Noelle smiled and ushered her mother outside before turning to Jeremy. "Thanks for your help."

"You're welcome." His focus quickly shifted to the others present before he glanced back inside the chateau.

Noelle's gaze followed his, and she caught a glimpse of Levi inside. Before she could suggest they invite him to join them, her father started singing happy birthday, and she let herself get caught up in the celebration.

Chapter 27

JEREMY AND NOELLE WERE RETURNING from horseback riding when a van pulled up in the drive.

"That had better not be Prince Philippe moving back in," Noelle said.

"I can't imagine it would be. Queen Marta was very clear that they weren't welcome back."

Levi emerged from the chateau as the driver climbed out of the van. He looked like he was in his early twenties and had skin the color of dark molasses. When Jeremy noticed the man's awareness, he guessed he was probably a few years older than that.

"Alan, good to see you," Levi said.

"You too."

The two men shook hands. "How was the drive?"

"Long. Very long," Alan responded. "Max isn't a fan of the tunnel."

"I don't blame him. Thirty miles driving under the English Channel doesn't seem natural to me either."

The front door opened again, and Janessa appeared at the top of the steps. "Alan!" She rushed down the steps and threw her arms around his neck. Alan hugged her in return.

"Hey there." He pulled back and gave her a quick study. "You look wonderful as always. How have you been?"

"Great, especially now that you're here. I didn't even know you were coming." She looked over at Levi. "Why didn't you tell me?"

"I thought it would be a nice surprise."

Jeremy approached, confused. Levi had mentioned bringing in a bomb-sniffing dog and his handler, but how did his sister know the guy? With the way she greeted him, she acted like he was one of her best friends.

Levi saw them approach and made the introductions. "Alan Neisler, this is Janessa's brother, Jeremy. I think you met Noelle Saldera when you were here last year."

"Yes, it's good to see you again," Alan greeted Noelle before turning to shake hands with Jeremy. "And good to meet you, Jeremy."

"You too."

Alan turned to the van and opened the back door to reveal a German shepherd in a built-in cage secured at the rear of the vehicle. Alan retrieved the leash lying beside it and unlatched the cage door. After clipping the leash on the dog's collar, he said, "Come on, boy."

The dog obeyed, jumping onto the pavement and proceeding to stretch, first lowering on his front paws and sticking his bum in the air and then shaking each of his rear legs in turn.

"I think he's happy to get out of there." Janessa laughed.

"Jeremy, can you help me bring in Alan's luggage?" Levi asked. "I'm sure he needs a chance to stretch his legs too."

"Sure." Jeremy stepped forward.

"Alan, we're putting you in the same room you had last time you were here," Levi said. "Do you remember where it is?"

"Yeah. If I get lost, I'm sure someone can direct me." He turned to Janessa. "I don't suppose you ever had maps made up of this place."

"Nah. We like to confuse our guests."

"I figured as much." He stepped toward the front lawn. "I'll see you later."

"Do you need any help?" Noelle asked when Levi and Jeremy started pulling suitcases out of the back.

"I think we've got it," Levi said.

"Noelle, I was just coming to see if you were back yet," Janessa said. "The florist called, and I couldn't remember if we decided on lilies or roses for the centerpieces."

"I guess I'll see you later." Noelle kissed Jeremy on the cheek. She fell in step with Janessa, the two women now speaking about things that might as well have been Greek for as well as Jeremy understood them.

"Are all weddings this complicated?" Jeremy asked.

"Beats me, but after seeing all this chaos, if I ever meet the right woman, I'm eloping," Levi said.

"I can't blame you." Jeremy watched Noelle disappear inside. He lifted two suitcases. "Where to?"

Levi picked up two more and started up the stairs. "Come on. I'll show you."

* * *

Jeremy opened the door to let Levi into his room. He had to admit it was significantly easier for them to meet secretly when his sister was away from the chateau. Today she was at the naval base for some kind of meeting, and he knew she would be gone all day.

"Everything is ready," Levi said as soon as he closed the door. "I have extra cameras set up in the hallway on either side of Gustave Nardini's door, and I also installed one outside his window. A second one was already in place in that area, so we don't have any blind spots."

"What about listening devices?"

"There are three." Levi must have seen the surprise on Jeremy's face. "I know that sounds like overkill, but I promised not to take any chances."

"I appreciate that. I much prefer to err on the side of safety."

"Alan and Max will also sweep that area of the chateau at least once a day. We'll do a search of his room as soon as he reports for work on his first day. Martino will keep him busy to make sure we have enough time."

"Who is going to monitor all of this surveillance equipment?"

"King Eduard is sending me two members of his intelligence service to work with me in security," Levi said. "He was planning to send more personnel here anyway to prepare for the wedding."

"Sounds like you have all the bases covered. How are you going to justify hiring Nardini when there's a hiring freeze?"

"Officially we're saying that the hiring freeze has been lifted. In reality, it's still in place with this one exception."

"When does Nardini arrive?" Jeremy asked.

"Martino will interview him tomorrow and offer him a job beginning Monday. If all goes well, by the end of next week, we'll have a handle on what he is planning."

"Assuming he really is involved."

"Yes. Assuming that."

* * *

Jeremy didn't like Gustave Nardini on sight. He appeared to be about Jeremy's age, midtwenties, and had a neatly trimmed beard and mustache that framed his thin lips. On the surface, the man seemed to be exactly what he claimed: a man looking for a job. Jeremy had never been one to believe everything he saw.

Something about the guy sent Jeremy's radar humming. Perhaps it was his weak handshake or the way he didn't look him in the eye when they were introduced. Or it could be the air of suspicion that came with him because of the background check Jeremy had conducted. Regardless, he had every intention of making sure this man was well watched.

"Renzo can show you to your room," Martino announced from where he stood at the back entrance the staff typically used. "Do you have a cell phone?"

"Yes."

"Here is my phone number. I'll be the person you report to for work. Anytime you have a question and I'm not available, you can talk to Enrico or Patrice." Martino handed over the simple white business card with an intricate design in the corner.

Jeremy never would have suspected that the design was a high-tech tracking device had he not watched Levi implant it.

"Thanks." Gustave took the card and proceeded to slip it into his wallet.

"Are you ready to see your new space?" Renzo asked, motioning toward the servants' quarters.

"Sure." He picked up the two suitcases he had brought with him and followed Renzo down the hall.

As soon as the two men disappeared from sight, Jeremy turned to Martino. "What do you think?"

"I think I have a lot of training to do."

Aware that Martino didn't know Jeremy's true role here at the chateau, he nodded. "Work is slowing down a bit. Let me know if there's anything I can do to help."

"I think we may have a few small events in our future we hadn't originally planned for."

"Why is that?"

"Practice makes perfect," Martino said simply. "That's the only way I'm going to get our new employee up to speed."

"If Patrice is the one cooking, you can count me in anytime."

Martino gave him a rare smile. "I suspected as much."

* * *

"Did you find anything?" Jeremy asked when he entered the security office.

"His room was clean," Levi told him. "Other than clothes, the electronics he brought with him are a handheld game console and a laptop."

"I don't know whether I should be relieved or disappointed."

"I know what you mean," Levi said. "I installed a keystroke logger on his computer, and I hacked into his phone so we can listen in on his calls. I'm also tracking the GPS on his phone."

"Is it legal to do that here?"

"With the king's permission, it is. I ran a trace of his previous calls and made a list of everyone he's talked to over the past few months. It looks like he wasn't using his phone while he was traveling in Africa, but maybe something else will pop up."

"It's worth a try." Jeremy took the paper Levi offered. "When do your reinforcements arrive?"

"They're already here. They got in last night."

"I haven't seen them yet. Are they staying here at the chateau?"

"Julien is staying in town. Apparently he has family living close by," Levi said. "I had Martino put Tomasso in the room right across the hall from Nardini."

"Smart."

"The two new guys will trade off monitoring him, and I'll have my staff cover one shift a day."

"Do you have enough manpower for that?"

"My people will cover the shift when Gustave is working, so it will be during our slower time anyway."

"Makes sense." Jeremy blew out a breath. "What do you think after searching his room? Do you think this guy could have been involved in the bombing?"

"If he is, he's made a point of coming in clean. I guess only time will tell."

"As long as it tells before we have any trouble."

"Pray for that," Levi said.

Chapter 28

"I'm in." Excitement and anticipation filled his voice.

"Finally."

Disappointment surfaced when he wasn't asked how he had finally managed to gain access to the chateau. "Now that we have access, when do you want me to smuggle in the bombs?"

"Not for a while yet. I don't want to take a chance they'll be discovered since we still have so much time until the wedding."

"Just let me know when."

"I will, but for now, do everything you can to be a model employee. The last thing we want is for you to draw attention to yourself or lose your opening."

"When do you want to meet next?"

"We'll meet one month before the wedding. In the meantime, I'll make sure everything else is ready."

"Make sure part of getting everything ready includes an exit plan for me. I have no interest in being a trigger that gets caught inside the blast radius."

"You just worry about doing your job and let me do mine. I promise you, this time my plan will work perfectly, and I'll finally get what I deserve."

* * *

Long walks in the garden and on the beach, horseback riding in the woods, the occasional dinner date in town, and church together on Sundays. Noelle didn't realize she had fallen into a routine until her mother commented on it. Normally predictability bored her, but she found herself looking forward to the time she would spend with Jeremy each evening.

Spring was now in full bloom and edging toward summer as the days of May came to a close. Janessa's wedding was the first week of July, and the open house for the new temple in Meridia would begin tomorrow. The dedication by a member of the First Presidency would follow two weeks later.

Noelle's days were still busy and full as she worked beside Janessa. Her original assumption that she was only going to help with Janessa's wedding proved to be incorrect. Instead she was managing Janessa's calendar and fielding phone calls and correspondence from people of all levels of society. She was also being included in any number of social events and was grateful to have Jeremy by her side each time.

The basic wedding details were falling into place, and Noelle now split her time between Janessa's office and her mother's kitchen. Patrice used many of their mealtimes as opportunities for Janessa and Garrett to sample various foods for the reception. Personally, Noelle suspected that as long as chocolate mousse was one of the dessert options, Janessa wouldn't care about anything else on the table. And she already knew Garrett would be happy with anything.

Menu options continued to feel endless, and so far, despite trying many different dishes and drafting dozens of plans, Noelle had yet to get Janessa and Garrett in the same place for long enough to finalize the food details. She was going to have to hijack both of their schedules if she didn't get them in the same room with her soon.

Noelle and Levi had developed a comfortable routine over the past few weeks, texting each morning and meeting at random intervals. Sometimes she would suffer pangs of guilt, feeling like she was betraying her family and friends by repeating their conversations to him, but every time she thought of what she was trying to prevent, she pushed those feelings aside.

Levi's main concern continued to be Gustave Nardini, the new under-butler Martino had hired several weeks earlier. She could understand why. The man made her uneasy with the way he always seemed to be watching her and everyone else. It was as though he was waiting to be left alone so he could steal the good silver.

Noelle passed by the exercise room and saw Gustave inside dusting the equipment. She had barely taken three steps before she saw Martino come around the corner.

"Hi, Martino."

"How are you this morning? I didn't see you at breakfast."

"Busy as always." She held up the latest batch of RSVPs.

"I think Janessa was looking for you."

"I'm heading to her office now." She took a few steps and noticed the way Martino glanced into the exercise room to check on Gustave. Apparently Martino didn't completely trust Gustave either.

* * *

Noelle found it odd to climb into the back of the limousine while her father sat up front by himself. She still wasn't sure where Jeremy was taking her, and the use of the limo was a surprise in itself. "Where are we going?"

"You'll see," Jeremy said, apparently determined to keep their destination a secret.

She smoothed her dress over her knees. "Am I dressed okay?"

"You look perfect." He leaned over and gave her a quick kiss. A blush rose to her cheeks when the door opened once more to reveal Garrett and Janessa.

"Sorry to interrupt," Janessa said.

"Do you mind if we join you?" Garrett waited for Janessa to take the seat across from them before he claimed the spot beside her.

Telling herself she had nothing to be embarrassed about, Noelle asked, "Can one of you tell me where we're going?"

"Calene," Garrett said, surprising her with a direct answer.

"Calene? Are we going to the palace?"

"We may stop by if we have time, but we have another destination we need to visit first."

"And that destination would be?" Noelle asked.

"You'll find out soon enough," Jeremy said.

Janessa leaned forward as though sharing a secret. "I don't know what it is with men and their insatiable desire to surprise women."

"I don't either," Noelle said. "Of course, you could spoil the surprise right now by telling me where we're going."

"And risk the wrath of these two?" Janessa shook her head. "Sorry, but I'm afraid you'll have to wait, like Jeremy said."

"Thanks a lot." Noelle fought back a grin when she decided to use the situation for her benefit. "You know, Janessa, the drive to Calene takes two hours. It seems to me that's plenty of time to discuss wedding details. We still haven't finalized the place settings."

"What a great idea," Janessa said.

"No." Garrett held up a hand and commanded in his most princely tone, "No wedding plans. No talking about wedding plans. Don't even think about wedding plans. Today is supposed to be a day off."

"How about if we talk about food, then?" Noelle suggested. "Men like food."

"Men do like food," Janessa said.

Jeremy gave Garrett a sympathetic look. "There are worse things we could talk about."

"Okay, you win," Garrett said. "But the minute you start talking about flowers and napkins and all of those other things men don't care about, I'm drawing the line."

"He's so cute when he gets all royal, isn't he?" Janessa reached over and gave Garrett a playful kiss.

Noelle wisely didn't respond. Instead she pulled a little notebook from her purse. "Let's start with desserts."

"Chocolate mousse. Definitely," Janessa said.

"And raspberry cheesecake," Garrett added.

Once they got started, Noelle could barely write fast enough. At this rate, she would have the entire menu finalized long before they got to wherever it was they were going.

* * *

Jeremy looked out the window and caught the first glimpse of the new temple in the distance. Situated on a bluff overlooking the Mediterranean, its single spire rose into the air, the angel Moroni shining on top. The building itself was constructed of white stone. Trees dominated the land rising to the temple and made it look like it was floating.

"Noelle. Look."

He saw her delight. "Is that the new temple?"

"It is."

Garrett leaned forward so he too could take in the view. "The royal family has been offered a private tour before the Church opens it to the public. We thought you would like to join us."

"Today?" Noelle asked.

"Yes, today." The humor that was often evident in Garrett's voice didn't surface, his attention still on the structure before them.

"Thank you so much for including me in this," Noelle said, her voice teary. "Mary took me to the visitors' center at the Washington, D.C. Temple right before I was baptized, but I didn't think I'd get to see the inside of one for a long time."

Jeremy squeezed her hand. "I'm glad I get to be with you the first time you see this. The inside of a temple can be a magical place."

Janessa turned to Garrett. "I wonder what your parents and brother will think."

"They'll be there too?" Noelle asked.

"And Giancarlo and Dante," Janessa said. "They were very excited about meeting the prophet."

"The prophet is here?" Jeremy asked.

"He is," Garrett said. "My father invited him to stay at the palace, along with several other people from the Church who are here with him."

"Your father has come a long way toward opening up to the Church since you told him you wanted to get baptized," Janessa said.

"That he has," Garrett agreed.

The limousine rolled to a stop, and Enrico climbed out to open the door for them. Jeremy was the last to exit and found himself facing Queen Marta and King Eduard.

Before greetings could be exchanged, Dante rushed forward and announced, "I get to go in the temple!"

"I know," Jeremy said. "Very exciting."

"Jeremy, it's good to see you again." Queen Marta extended her hand.

"You too, Your Majesty."

"How are the repairs coming at the chateau?" King Eduard asked.

"Very well. I believe you would approve."

"I'm sure I would. I appreciate the work you have been doing there."

Jeremy heard the unspoken implication, recognizing that the king was referring to his classified work rather than the household improvements. "I'm happy to serve."

Introductions were made when Prince Stefano and his new bride stepped forward. Princess Alora looked every bit as lovely in person as she had on television, and Jeremy enjoyed seeing the newlyweds' obvious contentment.

Two more cars approached, followed by more introductions for the area authority, the local stake president, the new temple president, and the prophet.

They started toward the temple, and Garrett turned back to where Enrico stood. "Enrico, why don't you join us?"

"I can stay here," he said, clearly not expecting such an invitation.

"Papa, please come," Noelle said.

Enrico contemplated a moment longer before nodding. He turned to the driver beside him to ask him to watch his car and then fell in behind the group heading for the entrance.

Jeremy took Noelle's hand in his as they passed through the glass doors and absorbed the moment. He doubted such an event would repeat itself in his lifetime—he was in the presence of both royalty and the only living prophet on the earth.

He looked down at Noelle, reading similar thoughts on her face. A warmth spread over him, and he wondered if she could feel it too.

Though he had attended a handful of different temples over the years, he looked at everything about this one with fresh eyes as he listened to the temple president offer insight into the various rooms.

The group instinctively lowered their voices, even when questions were asked. King Eduard and Queen Marta were the most inquisitive as they went from one section to another.

Jeremy noticed that Noelle's father remained silent throughout the tour, apparently content to simply take in his surroundings.

When they reached the sealing room, Jeremy worried how the royal family would react when faced with the site of their son's sealing, an event they couldn't be present for.

"This is where you will marry?" King Eduard stepped over to the altar.

"Yes, Father." Garrett took Janessa's hand, and together they joined him at the center of the room. "The ceremony here will allow our marriage to last forever, even beyond the grave."

"The room is lovely," Queen Marta said, taking note of the chandelier overhead. "It's nothing like I expected."

They circled out of the room, and Jeremy entered with Noelle. He looked up at the mirror facing him, startled that he and Noelle appeared not as two people but as one.

Enrico spoke quietly, his comment directed at his daughter. "This is where you will want to marry."

She looked at him, and Jeremy could see the tears that sprang to her eyes. "Yes, Papa. That is something I hope for."

Enrico looked up at their reflection, staring for a long time. Without another word, he gave a single nod and turned for the door.

Chapter 29

NOELLE DIDN'T KNOW WHAT TO think. Her father had been unusually quiet since their tour of the temple the day before. He didn't seem upset with her, per se, but he definitely wasn't himself.

She said as much to Jeremy as they were returning from lunch in town.

"You're his only daughter. Maybe he's trying to get used to the idea that he won't get to walk you down the aisle when the time comes."

"I thought that might be it, but I think it's something else." She gestured with both hands. "I just have no idea what it could be."

Jeremy pulled up to the chateau gates, waiting for security to identify them and allow them entrance before speaking. "How much have you talked to him about the gospel?"

"Not at all, except when I told him I got baptized," Noelle said. "Once my mom and I worked through our problems, he seemed fine with everything."

"Have you ever thought about inviting him to church? We could see if he wants to go with us this week."

"I don't know . . ."

"I know you don't want to alienate your family because of your religious differences, but you'll never know if they have any interest if you don't ask."

She knew he was right, but the thought of broaching the subject sent her heart into overdrive.

Jeremy pulled into his spot in the garage, and Noelle saw her father inside inspecting the engine of Garrett's sports car.

"Hi, Enrico," Jeremy said in Italian. "We were just talking about you."

"Really?"

Noelle saw the opening Jeremy had given her and forced herself to push through it. "Yes. We wanted to know if you would be interested in joining us for church on Sunday."

"The little church in the hills?" Enrico asked.

"Yes." It took a moment for Noelle to remember that her father had taken Janessa there several times when she'd first arrived.

"I'll talk to your mother and see what she thinks."

"I'd love it if you could come," she said, surprised and relieved.

"How was lunch?" Enrico asked, changing the subject.

"The food wasn't as good as what your wife makes, but it was nice to have a change of scenery for a bit," Jeremy said. "What are you up to?"

"Garrett's car needs oil." Enrico pointed to Jeremy's car. "When was the last time you changed the oil in your car?"

"I'm sure it's due. I should probably carve out some time to take care of that tomorrow."

"I have oil here if you need it," Enrico said. "Let me know when you want to do it, and I'll give you some help."

"You don't have to do that."

"Sure I do. I know where all the tools are."

"You have a point." Jeremy chuckled. "How about first thing in the morning? Say seven or eight?"

"Seven will work fine."

"I'll see you then." Jeremy led the way out of the garage.

The scent of roses and wisteria wafted through the air, and the sun peeked out from behind a scattering of clouds.

"Do you have time for a walk before you go back to work?" Jeremy asked Noelle.

"I do, but do you?"

"I can make time for you." He took her hand, and she felt her heart melt a little. They started toward the gardens. "Do you think your dad will come Sunday?"

"I don't know. I honestly didn't think he would even consider it."

"More surprising things have happened. He seemed really interested in the temple when we went through."

Noelle thought of the moment when she had been standing in the sealing room with Jeremy and her father. For an instant, she could have sworn she saw into eternity, a glimpse of the ancestors that came before her and the children and grandchildren that would follow in the generations to come.

Could that thought have entered her mind because her father had stood beside her? Or could it have been a future with Jeremy she was imagining? Dared she hope for such a future? Their friendship had developed so quickly, and now she could scarcely imagine not enjoying his companionship and support.

"You haven't mentioned anything about work lately. Do you have any idea how much longer you'll stay here in Meridia?"

"I haven't talked to my boss about it yet, but I was thinking about asking if I could extend." He stopped beside a cluster of palm trees and shifted to face her. "Would you mind if I stick around a while longer?"

"I'd like that, but I'm not sure what will happen with me once the wedding is over."

"It sounds like you're doing a lot more than just wedding planning. I have to imagine that if you want to stay on with Janessa, you could continue as her assistant."

"You're probably right." Noelle thought of her future in such a career. It was possible, she supposed, that she might get to travel with Janessa sometimes, but did she really want to spend her future as an assistant?

These thoughts fled when Jeremy leaned down and pressed his lips to hers. She leaned into the kiss, amazed at how he always made her feel like she was the center of his world.

The sun beat down on them, filtering through the palm leaves, and the breeze coming off the water tugged at her hair and carried the unique mixture of the gardens and the sea.

He deepened the kiss, drinking her in as though he couldn't get enough.

Then something changed when he shifted and brushed his lips across hers once more. This time a depth of tenderness accompanied the gesture, and it was somehow more intimate than anything she had ever experienced.

Her legs felt like water, and she gripped his arms with both her hands for balance. His fingers tangled in her hair, sending shivers through her. When he pulled back, he stared down at her as though memorizing her features. The breeze teased a strand of her hair into her face, and he reached out to tuck it behind her ear.

His voice was husky when he spoke. "I guess we should get back."

She nodded. She was pretty sure she could speak but decided not to risk it.

Together they headed back to the chateau, both lost in their own thoughts. Something had changed between them. Noelle couldn't put it into words, but one thing was certain: this relationship was far from over.

* * *

Jeremy reached his room and took a deep breath. Several thoughts rolled through his mind: the way Noelle had felt in his arms just moments ago, the sound of her voice when they spoke of the future, the sight of her standing in the temple beside him.

It all added up to one thing: he was in love with her.

He wasn't sure when it had happened or how he had missed the signs, but he couldn't deny this overwhelming sense of clarity, the knowledge that he wanted to be with her forever.

He hadn't expected their friendship to lead them to this point, nor had he considered what it would mean for him to fall for someone from another country. He was navigating through uncharted territory, and he wasn't entirely sure he liked it.

He sat at his computer and retrieved the form to update his close personal contacts. After adding Noelle's name, he e-mailed the form to Levi so he could push it through the chain of command. Now he had to decide what to do next: go ring shopping or have a chat with Enrico to ask for his daughter's hand in marriage.

Chapter 30

JEREMY STOOD ON THE DECK of the sailboat and watched Noelle at the wheel. He had been out with her several times before and found that he enjoyed the freedom of being on the water. He knew the basics now and felt a sense of satisfaction that she trusted him to help work the lines.

He had played over a number of scenarios in his head, different places he could take Noelle today. When she had suggested sailing, he'd decided it was as good an idea as any, especially when considering the privacy they always found on the water.

He put his hand in his pocket, his fingers brushing against the ring box there. He had gone into town the day before, spending the better part of the afternoon at the jewelers.

With the exception of the suits he had purchased when he'd first arrived, nearly every penny he'd saved from living with Janessa for the last few months had gone into buying the round-cut diamond, but a man only proposed once. At least, he prayed he would have to propose only once.

He knew he should wait until after he received his official approval from the CIA to continue his relationship with Noelle, and he debated over talking to Enrico about his intentions before moving forward, but at the moment, those details were secondary. He knew his patience wouldn't stretch that long. Right now all he cared about was hearing her say yes.

Noelle navigated around several other boats on the water. They were a good distance from the chateau now, and Jeremy recognized the landscape. They had picnicked in a little cove nearby only a few weeks before.

Jeremy's hand fisted around the ring box impatiently, and his stomach churned uncomfortably. He wasn't sure when the perfect time would be to pop the question, nor was he sure of the words. He prayed his heart would guide him.

"Do you want to put in over there?" Noelle motioned to the cove they had frequented before. The water was deep enough that they could put in close to shore and swim to the beach if they wanted to.

"That sounds good." He was preparing to adjust the sails when he heard a bloodcurdling scream. He straightened, searching for its source.

The closest boat was too far away for sound to carry so clearly. The scream came again, and Jeremy managed to discern the direction it had come from. "That way." He pointed to the starboard.

Noelle adjusted their heading, coming around a small jut of land. As soon as they cleared it, they could see another vessel anchored near a small stretch of beach. A couple stood on deck, the man clearly consoling the woman.

Jeremy followed Noelle's instructions to work the sails, their boat slowing as they approached the other vessel.

"Coming alongside," Noelle called out.

Jeremy studied the woman on board. She clearly looked distressed, but no one appeared to be physically injured.

Noelle called out to them in Italian. "Are you okay? What's wrong?"

The woman continued to sob, and the man pointed to the water in front of them. Jeremy looked toward the front of the boat, searching the surface, then his stomach curled.

A half-eaten corpse had caught on a fallen tree, the body so badly damaged that he couldn't even identify if it was a man or a woman.

"What is it?" Noelle asked.

"Noelle, stay back. You don't want to see this." He shifted his body, hoping to block her view so she wouldn't see the grotesque image, but one look at her face confirmed that his warning had been too late.

* * *

She couldn't get the image out of her head. Jeremy had tried to shield her again when the police had arrived, followed by the coroner. Unfortunately his efforts couldn't erase the moment when her eyes had been drawn to a vulture perched on a fallen tree and she had realized why it was there.

"I'm so sorry you saw that," Jeremy said when they arrived back at the chateau. He looked a little shaken himself. "No one should ever have to see something like that."

"I didn't even realize it was a person at first," Noelle admitted with a shudder. "I don't blame that woman for screaming."

"Me neither." Jeremy stuffed his hands in his pockets. "This certainly wasn't how I planned for us to spend our day."

They walked inside and were met by her parents.

Her father enveloped her in a hug. "Are you okay?"

"A little shaky, but I'm okay."

"Are you sure?" her mother asked.

Noelle wanted to reassure her mother, but she couldn't bring herself to say the words. Instead, an honest answer spilled out. "Not really."

"Oh, baby." Patrice scooped her into a hug and held on. "What can I do for you?"

The embrace went a long way in helping her find solid ground, but the moment she closed her eyes, she was back on the boat, fighting the urge to gag.

Her mother stepped back and put her hands on Noelle's arms as she studied her. "Can I fix you something to eat?"

"No. I don't think I can stomach food right now."

Garrett and Janessa hurried down the stairs. "We heard what happened," Garrett said. "What a nightmare."

"I'm afraid I'm going to have plenty of those," Noelle said.

Jeremy and Garrett exchanged glances as though a message passed between them.

"What?" Noelle asked.

"Would you like one of us to give you a blessing?" Jeremy asked. "The Lord can help you find peace."

Noelle felt like he was offering the answer to an unspoken prayer. "I would love that."

"Let's go in here." Garrett led the way into the parlor and gestured for Noelle to sit in a chair. He turned to her parents. "You're welcome to join us."

Though they appeared uncertain, they both followed them into the parlor.

"Who would you like to offer it?" Jeremy asked as soon as she sat down.

"Would you?" Noelle asked, looking up at Jeremy.

"Of course." He drew a deep breath. Together he and Garrett placed their hands on her head. Jeremy's voice was surprisingly steady as he began. He told her of her Heavenly Father's love for her and offered her the promise of comfort and peace as well as other words of encouragement for her future. It wasn't until he closed the blessing that she realized he had spoken in Italian and had done so fluently.

She stood, and Garrett shook her hand. When she turned to Jeremy, she stepped into his embrace. She didn't know how he had managed to stay so calm and collected through everything they had experienced today, especially since he had volunteered to deal with the police and coroner so she wouldn't have to face the horror in the water any longer than necessary.

He held her tightly, and suddenly she knew. He might appear calm on the outside, but he was suffering just as much as she, if not more. She tilted her head up. "Maybe you should get a blessing too."

Their eyes met briefly before Jeremy turned to Garrett. "Would you mind giving me one?"

"I'd be happy to."

Jeremy took the seat Noelle had vacated, and Garrett laid his hands on his head. She expected the words to be similar, but except for the promise of the ability to move forward with peace, Jeremy's blessing was nothing like her own. It spoke of relying on the Lord while he endured his trials and having patience and remembering that everything happened in the Lord's time. Though the words sounded like a warning, a feeling of peace enveloped the room.

When the blessing concluded, Noelle could sense Jeremy's confusion. To her surprise, though, as soon as he shook hands with Garrett, Jeremy turned to her parents.

"Patrice, Noelle and I talked to Enrico yesterday about you two joining us for church tomorrow. I hope you're both able to come."

"He mentioned the invitation." Patrice took a step toward the hall. "I should go get started on dinner."

"Don't worry about us," Janessa said. "Garrett and I have to go to the palace for dinner tonight."

Garrett looked at his watch. "We'd better get going." He put a hand on Jeremy's shoulder. "Let me know if you need anything."

"Thanks. I will."

Noelle watched them leave, and within a few minutes, she and Jeremy were alone. "Thank you for making today easier."

Jeremy gave her a brief kiss. "Our next date will be better. I promise."

"I'm going to hold you to that." Noelle looked at him, grateful that her future was tightly intertwined with his. Her heart swelled, and the words that came out of her mouth surprised her. "I love you, you know."

His eyes widened briefly, and then his hands reached for hers. "I love you too."

Chapter 31

NOELLE DIDN'T REALIZE SHE'D GOTTEN her hopes up until she walked into the kitchen on Sunday morning. Jeremy was at the table, but neither of her parents was anywhere in sight. She tried to focus on the love she felt for Jeremy instead of letting her disappointment in her parents' absence take hold.

The peace she had found after Jeremy had given her a blessing had lasted through the night. She hadn't quite been able to prevent the image of what she had seen from surfacing, but she'd found the strength to battle it back and somehow sleep.

Jeremy looked up at her sympathetically. "I guess your dad isn't coming."

"I guess not." Noelle grabbed a blueberry muffin out of a basket on the counter.

"Give them time. When I was on my mission, it wasn't uncommon to have to invite investigators several times before they walked through the door."

"My father hardly qualifies as an investigator."

"Maybe not, but you don't want to close the door on the possibility."

Her shoulders lifted. "I'm not sure my parents would ever give up the traditions of the Meridian Church. It's part of the culture here."

"You made the change."

"Yes, but I was living with Mary and was exposed to the LDS culture constantly."

"Your parents have been living with Janessa for a year now. They've probably had more exposure to the gospel by now than you did when you started taking the discussions."

"I never thought of it that way." She sat beside him and broke off a piece of her muffin. She took only a few bites before she asked, "Are you ready to go?"

"I am if you are." He motioned to the food still in front of her. "Are you sure you don't want to eat some more?"

"I'm not that hungry." She stood. "Are Garrett and Janessa coming?"

"They stayed at the palace last night after some social event. They were going to go to church in Calene before heading back home."

Jeremy and Noelle made their way outside and headed for the garage. She thought of her conversation with her father when she had invited him to church. He hadn't seemed upset with her at the time, but she couldn't explain why he had skipped breakfast this morning. Noelle wondered if perhaps her father had driven Janessa and Garrett to Calene and stayed the night as well.

They entered the garage, where both limousines were parked. Two bays were open, and Noelle guessed that Garrett and Janessa had driven themselves to the palace yesterday.

"I wanted to ask if you would like to go out to dinner with me on Friday night. I thought maybe we could go to that restaurant where we had our first date."

"I'd like that. What's the occasion?"

"Do I have to have a reason to spoil you a little bit?"

"Not at all." She smiled at him, grateful that he was able to distract her from her thoughts.

When they arrived at the church, she noticed one of the vehicles from the chateau parked in the lot.

"I guess Garrett and Janessa must have driven back this morning after all," she said.

"I guess so."

Noelle's jaw dropped when they walked inside. Two missionaries stood inside the door. Speaking with them were her parents and grandfather.

"You came!" Noelle hurried her steps.

"You invited us," her father said as though his presence was a common occurrence.

"I know, but I didn't see you at breakfast this morning, so I thought maybe you weren't going to come."

"We're here," he said simply. "These nice young men gave me a Book of Mormon."

"It's a good book," Noelle said with a grin.

Jeremy stepped forward and greeted the missionaries, chatting with them for a moment.

"Are you ready to sit?" Jeremy asked.

"Where?" Enrico said.

Noelle linked her arm with her father's and started forward. "We normally sit over here."

They all took their seats, and her mother motioned toward the pulpit where the branch presidency had already taken their places. "Which one is the preacher?"

"None of them," Noelle said.

"We don't pay preachers here," Jeremy explained. "People take turns giving talks under the direction of the branch president. He gives the speakers a topic, and they pray about the messages they should share with the congregation."

"This is nothing like the Meridian Church."

"No, it certainly isn't."

The prelude music ceased, and a member of the branch presidency stood to begin the meeting. Noelle settled back in her seat and prayed her family would feel the Spirit. Maybe they too would learn to enjoy the simplicity of the gospel.

* * *

He held up a photo of the chateau, flowers spilling out of ceramic urns spaced evenly between three sets of french doors. He knew firsthand that the french doors shown in the photo led to the main parlor and ballroom.

A rare smile formed on his face as he looked from the photo to the urns in front of him. "They're a perfect match."

"As you requested. I don't know how you expect to get these inside though," Ivan said.

"I already have a plan in place, but I need to find a way to keep the explosives from being detected. A bomb-sniffing dog is being used at the chateau."

"You mentioned that might be a problem, but this compound is nearly odorless. It's also so new that most dogs have not been trained to identify it."

"But you said it's packed in fertilizer."

"Yes, but the handler will expect the presence of fertilizer since the bomb is hidden in a potted plant. I have several bags of the fertilizer for you to take with you. Before you place the explosives, make sure you put some fertilizer in the existing plants on the terrace and, if possible, in the garden. The dog will associate the scent with normal procedure and shouldn't be able to identify it." Ivan held up two detonators. "I assume you have my final payment."

He picked up a thick briefcase. "It's all in here."

Ivan opened the case and looked inside. He lifted the first several stacks of currency, retrieving a middle pile and fanning through it. "You realize it would have been significantly easier if you'd let me wire the money."

"Wire transfers can be traced. I don't want anything to tie us together." Ivan closed the case and handed the detonators over. "Besides, no one can freeze my funds if I'm carrying cash."

"Your choice." He extended a hand. "Nice doing business with you."

"You as well." Ivan lifted the case. "Now, I think it's time I go on an extended vacation somewhere tropical and off the beaten path."

"That's an excellent idea."

* * *

Denied. Jeremy read the word on the page but couldn't quite put it in context. "I don't understand," he told Levi. "What is denied?"

"Your request for a close and continuing relationship with Noelle."

"What?" A punch to the gut would have been less painful. "Can they do that?"

"I'm sorry, Jeremy. I should have intervened when I first realized you were interested in Noelle."

"That would have been difficult since I didn't even know you yet when I met her." He shoved his hands in his pockets. "Do you have any idea why my request was denied?"

"Yeah, I do."

"Well?"

Levi pressed his thumb and index finger against his forehead, rubbing it as though trying to battle some pain centered there. He dropped his hand and looked back at Jeremy. "You can't date Noelle because she's one of mine."

"One of your what?"

"She's an asset."

"Excuse me?" Jeremy had thought nothing could hurt more than being told he couldn't pursue a future with Noelle. He was wrong. "You're telling me she's been working for the CIA this whole time?"

"Not exactly." Levi leaned against the back of the couch and rubbed a hand over his face. "I recruited her right after Stefano's wedding to help enhance security here. King Eduard approved the request."

"Why would you recruit her? Has she been trained in intelligence?"

"She hasn't gone through formal training, but she did show an aptitude for this kind of work."

"I think you need to spell this out for me," Jeremy said. He repeated his question. "Why did you recruit her?"

"Noelle is the reason your sister is still alive. She's the one who noticed the woman who brought the bomb into Stefano's wedding." Levi took a deep breath. "She also helped me disarm the bomb once it was found."

Jeremy raked his fingers through his hair before letting his hands drop to his sides. "Why didn't you tell me? I have top-secret clearance, and I obviously had a need to know."

"I wanted to tell you. I asked Director Palmer for permission to do exactly that months ago. That request was denied too."

"What am I supposed to do?"

"You'll have to break up with her."

"I see." Jeremy's jaw tightened, and he thought of the romantic dinner he had planned. Somehow he didn't think Friday night was going to turn out quite the way he'd hoped. "I'm going out for a while. I need to go for a drive."

"I understand. I'll keep an eye on things here."

Jeremy simply nodded and left the room. He somehow made it back to his room, his emotions churning. How had this happened? Never had he anticipated the CIA's rejecting his request. Never had he considered that joining the agency could interfere with his future so completely.

He moved to the safe where he had secured the ring he had bought for Noelle. He punched in the combination and opened it, staring at the contents. Inside, the ring box lay on top of several top-secret documents and beside his automatic pistol. His hand closed over the ring box, his jaw clenching when he flipped open the lid to reveal its contents.

What was he supposed to do now? How could he go from declaring his love to breaking up with Noelle overnight?

She was a part of every aspect of his life here—his meals, his spare time, even his church attendance. Only his work kept them separate, and now it was going to rip them apart.

He had worried she might be hurt when she found out what he really did for a living, but he had been certain they could work through it.

Jeremy took one more long look at the diamond. Then he snapped the lid shut and secured it in the safe again. He couldn't imagine ever loving anyone as much as he loved Noelle, and he didn't know how he was supposed to go through life without her.

He needed to talk to someone who could understand this unique dilemma. Everything in him demanded that he put Noelle first, even if it meant walking away from a career he enjoyed, a career he had hoped to pursue for the next thirty years. Another part of him knew he couldn't quit. Not now. He would never be able to live with himself if he didn't follow through on this assignment. The CIA wouldn't be able to insert another agent at this late date. What if he left the agency and he could have made a difference? What if a bomb really did make it past security for Janessa's wedding? He and everyone he loved, including Noelle, would be in danger.

With no one else to turn to, he crossed into his room and dropped to his knees. He poured his heart out to his Heavenly Father, talking through the possibilities and various scenarios each option would create.

The words of the blessing Garrett gave him came back to mind, and he felt the reassurance that the Lord would be with him through his challenges. Had that blessing been a warning for what was to come?

Tears threatened, and he knew what he had to do. He only hoped someday he could pick up the pieces of his shattered heart.

Chapter 32

Noelle looked up from the kitchen table when the door opened, disappointed when a staff member walked in instead of Jeremy. After Saturday night's declaration, she had looked forward to being with him and finding a new normal in their relationship.

He loved her. That fact continued to roll through her mind as though part of a dream she hadn't been sure would ever really happen to her. She didn't know what the future held, but for the first time, she dared to hope and dream of one they would build together.

The door opened again, this time Janessa walking through it. "Hey, Noelle. I'm going to head into town to meet with the florists about finalizing the arrangements. Do you have time to come with me?"

"I'm happy to." Noelle stood and carried her breakfast dish to the sink. She motioned to the tray of pastries on the counter. "Did you want to eat something before we go?"

"I'm starting to think your mother's cooking is going to cause my dressmaker a great deal of distress." Janessa patted her stomach. "Of course, that's why we have an exercise room, right?"

"Absolutely."

Janessa selected a Danish. "Where is Patrice this morning?"

"She went with my dad to a doctor's appointment."

"I think I remember her saying something about that." Janessa picked up a napkin and headed for the door. "Ready?"

"Sure."

They headed down the hall. Noelle noticed Gustave polishing an end table in the parlor as they passed. He looked up at them but didn't speak. What was it about the guy that set her on edge?

"Hey, Jeremy," Janessa called out.

He was halfway down the stairs, but he hesitated briefly when he saw them, an odd look on his face. Then he continued forward, focusing on Janessa instead of her. A seed of insecurity bloomed inside Noelle. Had he returned the words *I love you* to her without meaning them? Was he afraid of what those words could mean to their future?

"Where are you two off to this morning?" Jeremy reached the landing and stepped beside Janessa.

"We're heading into town for a bit," Janessa answered.

"Have fun." He shifted to his left, effectively sidestepping Noelle.

"We'll try." Janessa watched him head down the hall. "That was weird. Is everything okay between you two?"

Noelle's stomach sank. "I don't know."

* * *

He couldn't keep avoiding her. Jeremy's stomach churned at the thought of what he had to do—what he'd been ordered to do.

Three more weeks, he reminded himself. That was all he had until Janessa's wedding. Once he was on the other side of that event, he could evaluate what he really wanted for his future. He hated that he would have to make a choice between his career and the woman he loved. For now, though, that choice didn't exist.

He texted Noelle a request to meet him downstairs. Different scenarios ran through his mind of where they could speak privately; he wanted somewhere he wouldn't tarnish the good memories they'd already made.

He was the first to arrive in the parlor. Gustave Nardini stood in the entryway polishing the silver candlesticks on the mantel. Through the window, Jeremy could see two of the gardeners working beneath the darkening sky.

"Hi," Noelle said when she arrived.

Jeremy turned to face her, and his heartbeat quickened. He noticed her hesitance, and the turmoil inside him kicked up a notch.

"Hey." Jeremy motioned toward the front entryway. "Do you have time for a walk?"

"Sure." Noelle led the way to the door, stopping just short of it so he could open it for her. As soon as they were outside, she asked, "Is everything okay?"

Renzo stood outside beside one of the limousines, apparently waiting for Janessa or Garrett.

"Let's go this way," Jeremy said, motioning to a path that led away from the gardens. He heard a rumble of thunder in the distance and hoped he could get through this before the heavens opened up on his emotions.

They walked in silence, making their way around the front of the chateau and down a path into the woods. The silence ballooned uncomfortably.

Noelle took a deep breath and seemed to muster her courage. "Are you going to tell me what's wrong?"

Jeremy took a deep breath of his own. "I talked to my boss today. It looks like I'm getting reassigned right after Janessa's wedding."

"I see." She stopped walking and looked up at him. "So you're telling me we only have three more weeks together?"

"Not exactly."

She looked up at him. After a brief moment, awareness lit her eyes. "You're breaking up with me."

"I'm sorry, Noelle. I do care about you." Jeremy forced the words out, each one feeling like a dagger to his heart. "I just think with my work heating up and since I'm leaving so soon, it would be best to end things now."

Her lips quivered and then pressed tightly together. Tears threatened, but she blinked hard against them.

"I really am sorry," Jeremy said weakly.

"So am I, Jeremy." She took another deep breath and straightened her shoulders. "When I said I loved you, I meant it. I'm sorry you didn't have the courage to be honest with me then."

"I *was* honest with you," Jeremy said. He realized his words were a mistake the moment they left his mouth.

"People don't break up with someone they love." A tear spilled over and trickled down her cheek. "Couples who love each other find a way to make things work."

"My life isn't that simple."

"It's your choice to make it that simple." She stared up at him, the hurt, disappointment, and an underlying anger visible on her face. When he remained silent, she took a step back. "Obviously you aren't the person I thought you were."

"I'm sorry, Noelle. I really am."

"Good-bye, Jeremy." With one last look, she turned and retreated the way they had come.

Jeremy watched her go, tears welling up in his own eyes. He swiped them back, gritting his teeth against a wave of despair that felt like it would consume him. His future was walking away, and he had no choice but to watch her disappear around the corner.

* * *

Noelle fought back tears, anxious to find a quiet place where she could face the well of emotions threatening to drown her. She reached the front of the chateau, where Renzo was still standing out front. Pascal, one of the groundskeepers, was weeding a nearby flowerbed, and she expected Gustave would still be in the parlor.

Not prepared to face anyone, she turned toward the garage, praying her father wouldn't be inside. No one was inside, so she approached the glass case that held the keys to all of the chateau vehicles. She selected the key to a basic sedan, passed three other vehicles, and climbed into the driver's seat.

When she pulled out of the garage and drove through the gate, she didn't have a specific destination in mind. She turned away from town, the first tears spilling over the moment the chateau disappeared from view.

How had this happened? Everything had been going so well.

She drove for several minutes, the road climbing higher and higher. Another clap of thunder rumbled in the distance, this time accompanied by fat raindrops splattering on her windshield. She pulled over when she reached a scenic overlook of the Mediterranean, the water churning angrily against the wind.

The moment she turned off the car, sobs racked her body. Tears streamed down her cheeks, and she could feel her eyes puffing up from crying. Several minutes passed as she swirled in a state of confusion, hurt, and sense of loss.

Wiping away the tears with her fingers, she climbed out of the car and walked to the edge of the cliff despite the light rain now falling.

She stared out at the waves crashing against the rocks below. So many memories surfaced, from the first time she'd met Jeremy to the moment he'd proclaimed his love. Her heart felt like it would break in two, and she found herself unable to look beyond the fact that her future was now filled with blank pages she wasn't prepared to fill.

A small yacht below caught her attention, the vessel tossing and turning on the stormy water. It came dangerously close to the rocks below before veering out of sight toward the chateau.

She wished she could go hide out on the water for the day and give herself time to prepare for the inevitable questions from her friends and family about what had changed between Jeremy and her. As evidenced by the craft that had disappeared from sight and the few other vessels heading for shelter, the weather wasn't going to support that option.

Noelle pushed her damp hair back from her face and tipped her chin upward to let the rain wash the tears away. A bolt of lightning lit the sky, the rumble of thunder that followed sounding at almost the exact same time.

She jolted at the nearness of both and stepped back from the ledge. Like it or not, she was going to have to return to the chateau and somehow find a way to survive the next three weeks until Jeremy walked out of her life for good.

Chapter 33

"Where have you been?" Levi asked when Jeremy walked around the front of the chateau.

Jeremy had hoped to have more time to himself before facing anyone, but clearly that wasn't going to happen. Even though he had spent nearly twenty minutes walking in the woods in an attempt to clear his head and settle his emotions, the image of Noelle's face as he'd broken up with her wouldn't leave him.

The rain that had been threatening drizzled steadily now, but Levi didn't seem to care about that minor inconvenience. He motioned to the Mediterranean. "We've got a boat in distress heading our way."

"Where?" Jeremy looked out at the churning waves sweeping over the horizon. A sixty-foot yacht appeared on top of a swell before jerking violently as it slid down into a deep valley of water.

Another bolt of lightning speared the sky. Suddenly flames burst out on the yacht, and the vessel angled toward the shore.

"He's trying to beach it." Levi rapped Jeremy on the shoulder. "Come on."

Jeremy broke into a jog to keep up with Levi. "What about Meridia's coast guard?"

"The naval rescue units in the area are all out on other responses. This storm wasn't expected to hit our area so hard."

They reached the top of the stairs leading to the beach just as the yacht nearly toppled before the operator increased speed and headed straight for the sand below. The sound of the engine combated with the pounding rain and crashing waves.

Several of the groundskeepers who had taken shelter when the storm hit emerged from the shed where their tools were stored. They must have noticed the distressed boat because they hurried to help as well.

The boat ran aground, immediately listing heavily to one side. With the groundskeepers right behind them, Jeremy and Levi hurried down the steps.

As soon as the boat ran aground, several people appeared on deck. Jeremy could only stare when he identified two of them. Prince Philippe's eyes were wide with fear, and his wife gripped her pregnant belly with one hand and her husband's arm with the other.

Marcel Beaumont, the newest member of Meridia's ruling council, was aboard. Since the background check on him revealed he was currently single, Jeremy guessed the woman beside him was his date. The captain emerged right behind them, along with a steward.

Flames licked at the side of the yacht, thankfully the side opposite the gas tank.

"Let's get them off of there," Levi said, spurring everyone into action.

The head gardener motioned to one of his men. "Pascal, go get a fire extinguisher."

The youngest of the three groundskeepers raced back toward the steps.

Jeremy was wondering how they could best facilitate getting the passengers down to the beach when the captain retrieved a rope ladder from a storage compartment on deck. He hooked it to the side of the yacht, gravity causing the ladder to open and dangle a few feet above the sand.

Elaina was the first to descend, followed by Prince Philippe. Apparently "ladies first" only applied to his wife. The other woman on board came next, followed by the others, except for the captain, who had retrieved a fire extinguisher and was now at the rear of the vessel dousing the flames the rain had helped keep controlled.

Pascal returned and climbed up the ladder to offer his assistance.

The head groundskeeper turned to Levi. "I'll make sure the fire's really out."

"Thank you." Levi turned to Prince Philippe. "What were you all doing out in the storm?"

"We were heading to Monaco for the weekend when it hit," Philippe answered, apparently shaken enough that his usual arrogance had melted away. "We thought we could put in here at Bellamo, and then one of the engines sparked and caught fire."

Levi motioned to Jeremy. "We'd better get everyone up to the chateau."

Jeremy fell back and spoke to the couple he had yet to meet. "I don't think we've met. I'm Jeremy Rogers."

"Nice to meet you." Councilman Beaumont extended his hand. "I'm Marcel Beaumont, and this is Claudia Rivelli."

"Sorry your trip to Monaco was interrupted," Jeremy said.

"There are worse places we could have ended up."

Still clearly shaken, Claudia looked back at the yacht before turning her attention to Marcel. "I don't know how you stayed so calm when the fire started. I thought for sure the boat was going to explode."

"We were in good hands with our captain."

Together they climbed the stairs and made their way into the chateau. Brenna was waiting inside the door with a stack of towels. Martino stood beside her, his expression unreadable.

With the rain now pounding down, Jeremy guessed at Martino's dilemma. The last thing anyone wanted was to give Philippe and Elaina a foothold in the chateau, but there was no way anyone would want to brave the roads right now to take them somewhere else.

"I spoke with Prince Garrett," Martino said to Jeremy. "He asked if you could hook the electricity up in the guest wing for a couple hours. That will allow everyone to freshen up while we wait for the storm to pass."

"I'll see what I can do." Jeremy let doubt color his words. "I can't be sure it won't overload the other circuits though."

"I thought that work was completed months ago," Philippe said.

"King Eduard asked for some additional improvements. We only started on them last week," Jeremy said, improvising. He took a step toward the kitchen. "I'll go see what I can do."

"I'll wait here." Levi's tone told him he wasn't any more comfortable with their unexpected arrivals than Jeremy was.

Jeremy headed toward the kitchen. Patrice and Regina were inside when he arrived. They both started to ask questions about the beached boat, but he held up a hand to hold them off. "I'll talk to you in a minute. I need to make a quick call."

He passed through the kitchen into the breakfast room. Closing the door to ensure some privacy, he dialed his sister's phone number. The moment she picked up, he asked, "Did you hear what happened?"

"No. What?"

"Philippe and Elaina just arrived with a couple friends. Their yacht caught fire, and they crashed it onto the beach."

"Are you kidding me?" "I wish I were. Martino made it sound like I still have electrical work going on in the guest quarters. He mentioned having me turn on the electricity there for a couple hours."

"I'm not crazy about them staying here, but from what I can see out my window, I don't think we have much choice," Janessa said.

"As soon as the storm passes, we're moving them along," Jeremy said. "If I have to, I'll cut the power for the whole chateau."

"Let's pray it doesn't come to that."

"I already am."

* * *

Noelle knew her eyes were still swollen from crying, and she dreaded trying to get past the various staff members and her family without fielding any questions. She assumed the storm had driven the gardeners inside and was surprised when she passed through the back entrance to find the servants' quarters oddly quiet.

Grateful for the answer to her unspoken prayer, she quickly made her way to her room. She stripped out of her wet clothes and headed for the shower, hoping to wash away her tears as well as her dreams of what might have been. Tears started again, this time drowned beneath the spray of the water.

She had barely finished dressing when a knock came at her door. She opened it to find Janessa on the other side.

"You aren't going to believe what happened."

"What?" Noelle forced herself to ask.

"Philippe and Elaina are back, and they brought guests."

Noelle's brow furrowed. "I don't understand. I thought the guards weren't going to let them in without an invitation."

"They bypassed the guards." Janessa explained how they had been out on the water when their yacht had suffered damage in the storm. "We're planning on having your father or Renzo give them a ride back to their house, but we don't want to send anyone out in this weather."

"What do you want me to do?"

"I'm afraid we're stuck with dinner guests whether we like it or not. Can you help your mom for a while? If you're in the kitchen, it might help ease her frustration," Janessa said. "And you're welcome to join us for dinner."

Realizing the dinner invitation was based on the assumption that she would be Jeremy's date, she shook her head. "I think I'll pass on dinner, but I can go help my mom."

Janessa's eyes narrowed. "Is everything okay?"

"Fine." Noelle said. "I need to grab some shoes. I'll be out in a minute."

"All right."

Noelle heard Janessa's concern, but she couldn't think about that now. It was going to take all of her effort to keep her emotions in check when she faced her mother.

* * *

Jeremy tried to distract himself from thoughts of Noelle when he escaped to his room for a few minutes to run a quick background check on Claudia Rivelli and the two crew members from the yacht, though he didn't find anything of concern in the limited time he had to conduct his search. He also wasn't fooling himself. No amount of work was going to ease the ache that had settled deep within him.

Thoughts of Noelle, of her reaction to their earlier conversation, kept repeating in his mind, and he suspected the memories would stay with him for as long as he lived.

Though Jeremy would have preferred to wallow in his room for the evening, Levi insisted he attend dinner to keep an eye on things. Jeremy approached the dining room with a sense of dread. What if Noelle was there too? How could he face her?

He did a quick scan of the room, relieved that she wasn't present. His next thought was that this was the first time since meeting her that he was grateful for her absence.

"Jeremy, I assume you've already met everyone," Janessa said when he entered.

"Yes, I have."

Garrett entered right behind him. "Please excuse my tardiness. Enrico came to tell me the road into town is blocked by some downed trees. I'm afraid everyone will have to stay here until we can get some work crews out there in the morning."

"We appreciate your hospitality," Councilman Beaumont said. "I know it must be an inconvenience, especially so close to your wedding."

"Please, sit down. I think a good meal will go a long way in helping everyone overcome the challenges you've endured today." Garrett took his seat beside Janessa.

"Are you okay?" Janessa leaned over and whispered when Jeremy sat beside her.

"I'm fine."

Her eyebrows lifted at his words, and he knew she sensed that something was off. Thankfully, Elaina quickly distracted her with questions about her wedding plans. For once, he was more than happy to listen to the trivial. Anything that would keep him out of the conversation tonight was a good thing.

Chapter 34

NOELLE COULDN'T SLEEP. SHE COULDN'T eat. The presence of Prince Philippe and Princess Elaina was an annoyance she was quite certain could push her over the edge. Though the expectation was that they would leave by lunchtime, preparing meals for them and dealing with their latest whims was enough to cause a good share of grumbling among the staff. Apparently Elaina was prone to cravings. Lots of cravings.

"How anyone can eat pickles and peanut butter is beyond me," Brenna said as they walked toward the kitchen.

Noelle didn't respond.

"And don't you think it's overkill that they asked for us to change the sheets on the bed? We put fresh linens in those rooms only three days ago."

Again, silence.

Brenna looked over at her suspiciously. "Are you going to tell me what's going on?"

They walked into the kitchen, and Noelle again ignored her friend's question. "Mama, what do you need help with?"

"I need the potatoes grated, and I need those oranges squeezed."

"I'll take the oranges," Brenna volunteered. Noelle knew she hated grating potatoes.

Without a word, Noelle started on the task. She broke two fingernails as she shredded the potatoes before Janessa rescued her. "Noelle, can I steal you away for a bit?"

Noelle looked up at her mother, who nodded. "Regina will be here in a few minutes. She can finish."

"Thanks." Noelle followed Janessa out of the kitchen and down the hall.

"Tomorrow I want to start placing the tables in the ballroom for the reception, and I thought you could help me do a last check on the setup."

"Are you sure you want to start setting up this early?" Noelle asked. "The wedding is still almost three weeks away."

"This is one thing we can get done early. Anything we can do to eliminate stress later is a good thing." She walked through the parlor toward the hallway on the far side of the room that led to the ballroom. She glanced out the terrace doors and stopped. Her eyes narrowed, and she opened a door.

Curious, Noelle followed her outside.

"What in the world?" Janessa fisted her hands on her hips and stared. Two of the ceramic urns on the terrace were in pieces, fragments scattered everywhere and the plants that once occupied them left in disarray.

Noelle stood behind her. "They must have blown over during the storm."

"Great." Janessa blew out a frustrated breath. "We planned the floral arrangements out here assuming these would be here. Now what are we going to do?"

"I can call the florist to see if they can track down some pottery to match these. Since we still have some intact, it shouldn't be too difficult."

"Our guests start arriving in two weeks."

"And this is a royal wedding," Noelle reminded her. "We'll make it happen."

Janessa drew a deep breath. "I'm sorry. I know this is a trivial problem. I don't mean to make it a big deal."

"You're not. We would have to replace the damaged pottery even if you weren't about to get married." Noelle felt a wave of despair crash over her as she once again thought of the future she had planned with Jeremy. She fought it back but didn't quite manage to keep the tears from glistening in her eyes.

Janessa put a hand on her arm. "Are you okay?"

Noelle blinked hard several times. "I'm fine." She motioned toward the terrace doors that led directly into the ballroom. "I guess we should get to work."

Noelle could feel Janessa's eyes follow her as she headed toward the ballroom. She offered a silent prayer that somehow she would be able to get through the next few weeks. After that, she never wanted to work on a wedding again. Ever.

* * *

Jeremy opened the door to the security office to find Levi and three of his security team inside, staring at surveillance footage. Levi looked up at him, managing to keep his expression neutral despite the surprise Jeremy's presence undoubtedly caused him.

"Sorry to bother you, but can I hang out here for a few minutes?" Jeremy asked. "I promised my sister I would make sure our guests get off okay, but I really don't want to be with them."

"If you want," Levi said. "Do you know everyone?"

Jeremy swept over the other men present. He knew each of them through his background checks, of course, but he was only acquainted with the man nearest him. "Felipe and I have shared a few breakfasts together, but I don't think I've met everyone else."

"This is Julien Chancy and Tomasso Palotta. They don't make it into the kitchen very often at normal mealtimes."

Jeremy nodded in their direction. He knew Julien to be in his late thirties and that he had opted to stay in town so he could be closer to family. The man's wife and three young children had accompanied him to Bellamo so they wouldn't be separated during the months of his service at the chateau. Tomasso was nearly ten years younger and had been entrusted to keep an eye on Gustave Nardini both while on duty and when he was staying in the room across from him in the servants' quarters.

"Any movement out front yet?" Jeremy asked, looking over the various screens on the wall.

"Renzo is outside waiting, but nothing yet," Julien said.

Jeremy located the camera for the front courtyard where Renzo stood beside a limousine. A moment later, Martino escorted Philippe and Elaina outside, along with the others who had come with them. As soon as they were safely on their way, Jeremy's gaze shifted and he experienced a stab to his heart. Noelle stood in the ballroom beside his sister, the image displayed in color right in front of him. Even on the small screen, he could see the tension in her posture, which wasn't typical for her.

That was his fault, he thought to himself. He never should have gotten involved with her, at least not without clearing the relationship first. The thought that she too was working for the CIA, even if it was in a roundabout capacity, irritated him on principle, but he could hardly hold it against her. After all, he had been deceiving her since the moment they'd met.

A phone rang, and Tomasso picked it up. After a brief conversation, he turned to Levi. "That was the front gate. The crew from the naval base has arrived to remove Prince Philippe's boat."

"Call Alan and have him do a security sweep of their equipment before the guards let them in," Levi instructed. "Julien and Felipe, I want you to go down there to oversee the removal. No one goes anywhere unattended. Understood?"

"Yes, sir," Julien said.

Tomasso relayed the information while Julien and Felipe headed for the door.

"Maybe I'll head down there too. It should be interesting to watch," Jeremy said.

"Have fun," Levi said casually.

"I'll try." Jeremy took a last glance at Noelle on the screen and decided anything that could keep him away from her and distracted was a good thing.

* * *

Jeremy considered it a blessing when he had to spend the weekend in Calene. Levi had asked him to run a security check on the temple, and since Jeremy was the most familiar with the structure, he had been the logical choice. While normally he would have enjoyed the change of scenery anyway, today he was simply grateful he had been able to attend church without having to face Noelle.

By the time he arrived back at the chateau, he suspected everyone would have already finished lunch and gone about whatever activities they enjoyed on the Sabbath. He hadn't expected Noelle to be sitting in the living room with her parents and two missionaries when he walked inside. The expression on Noelle's face made him think she wasn't particularly pleased to see him.

Janessa and Garrett were descending the stairs.

"Jeremy, did you want to join us?" Janessa asked. "The elders came over to teach Enrico and Patrice."

The possibility of Noelle's parents taking the missionary discussions should have thrilled him. Part of him was happy that they were open to learning about their daughter's new religion, but he knew he wouldn't be able to sit in the same room as her, not when it hurt just to look at her.

"Thanks, but I have a couple calls I need to make." Jeremy gave a quick wave to the elders from the branch and escaped upstairs. He reached his room and closed the door, leaning back against it. He took a deep breath. Only twelve more days until the wedding. In thirteen days, he would leave this place. The question was would he be able to walk away from a career he loved, and if he did, would Noelle take him back?

Chapter 35

"This is getting ridiculous." Jeremy looked at the new list of names Levi had brought him. Seven new names. "Who are these guys?"

"The first three are the ones responsible for making the new ceramic urns for the terrace. The other four are possible delivery drivers."

"Seriously? This is because of a bunch of pots?"

"Only two pots actually. Apparently they are part of your sister's decorating scheme." Levi held up his hands. "I'm not about to argue with a bride only a week before her wedding."

"How deep do I need to go?"

"As deep as you can."

Jeremy looked down at the list again. He was running out of time. He still had several plus ones on the guest list to research and now this. "Can we send someone from the chateau to pick up the urns? That would reduce my workload a ton."

Levi considered for a minute. "That's not a bad idea. Let me talk to my guys, and I'll see what we can do."

"I'd appreciate it. At this rate, I'm not going to sleep until after my sister is on her honeymoon."

"I know what you mean," Levi mumbled. He headed for the door. "I'll call you later."

Jeremy took the new names into his office and sat down. Giving the top names priority, he began his initial searches. He was nearly done with the second name when Levi called.

"Hey, I wanted to let you know Tomasso volunteered to go pick up the urns. The florist said they can have someone there help load them for us, and we'll have some of our staff take care of things on this end."

"Thanks a lot, Levi. I appreciate it." Jeremy hung up the phone, his burden slightly more tolerable now. He knew he shouldn't let the increasing stress level get to him, but the impending arrival of his family tomorrow and the fact that he hadn't been able to face Noelle since their breakup was weighing heavily on him.

It was bad enough trying to pretend everything was okay around the people he associated with here at the chateau, but facing his parents and Mary wasn't something he was prepared to do. He looked at the stack of work on his desk and shook his head. He didn't know why he was worried about his family. At this rate, he wouldn't have time to see them anyway until they were all back in the United States.

He glanced out his window, and his heart squeezed in his chest. The beauty of this place, the stunning scenery and warmth of the people, made him wish he could have what his sister had now: a promise of home and family. At one point, he had thought he would come back often to visit, but now he wasn't so sure. Even if Noelle did decide to pursue other employment after Janessa's wedding, Jeremy would still have to face her various family members if he returned.

Restless, he secured his work and headed downstairs. Maybe a short walk in the fresh air would give him some perspective. The thought that he still had a choice surfaced the moment he stepped outside. He could still tender his resignation. Would Noelle take him back if he quit his job? Would she be willing to walk away from whatever her intelligence role was here at the chateau?

As soon as he opened the door to the terrace, a wave of heat and humidity as well as the delighted squeals of children greeted him. Giancarlo and Dante were splashing in the swimming pool, and Brenna was sitting on the deck, watching over them. The mingled scents of a dozen different flowers wafted on the slight breeze, and Jeremy contented himself with watching from a distance.

Would he ever enjoy such simple pleasures? He loved working in intelligence, but he missed the connections he had grown up with both with family and with nature.

Something moved beside Brenna. It wasn't until Noelle stood that Jeremy realized she had been obstructed from his view. She said something to her friend and started down the path toward him. Jeremy could sense the instant she saw him by the way she froze, their eyes meeting.

What he wouldn't give to be able to close the distance between them, beg her forgiveness, and finally ask the question he had played over and over in his mind. An image of the ring he had bought her popped into his mind, and he wondered if he would ever get over Noelle.

Noelle was apparently debating whether she wanted to face him or not. He understood her hesitation and shared it. With a heavy heart, he turned toward the door and walked back inside.

* * *

Noelle felt like she was operating on autopilot, not exactly the way she wanted to be less than a week before a wedding she was in charge of that would be televised around the world. Certainly Janessa's wedding wouldn't garner the same attention Prince Stefano's had, but the television crews were already lining up to send the images live to more than seventy countries.

The first few days after her breakup with Jeremy, she had worried about what she would do when she saw him again. She needn't have bothered. He was giving her a wide berth, and she doubted they would cross paths until the day of the wedding. Even then she wouldn't have to worry about being around him alone. Except for a brief encounter yesterday when she had seen Jeremy outside, she had only seen him twice, and both times had been from a distance.

Her family and friends had finally stopped asking her what was wrong. It hadn't taken long for them to notice she and Jeremy were never in the same room anymore. Janessa had been incredibly patient with her. Noelle wasn't sure if Janessa really wanted to see to so many of the details herself or if she was trying to distract Noelle, but they had spent several days overseeing the decorations in the ballroom and helping the kitchen staff with some of the advance preparations.

The impending arrival of Janessa's family later today had the staff bustling, and Noelle was torn between her duties for Janessa, helping prepare for their guests, and keeping an eye on Gustave. The man still made her uneasy, but at least he was a hard worker now that he knew his way around.

"Noelle, I need your help outside," Martino said from the ballroom doorway.

"What is it?" She walked onto the terrace, where Tomasso and Renzo were carrying a plant inside a huge ceramic pot.

"Where do you want these? We have the two replacements."

She turned to where the originals had been and pointed to a spot a few feet from where she stood. "One goes right there."

The men muscled it up the stairs and gently set it in position.

Tomasso took a deep breath. "What about the other one? There?"

"Yes. It should be an equal distance from the door to this one, just on the other side."

The two men headed back to the van.

Noelle took a step back and looked at the newly placed urn, comparing it to the existing one a short distance away. "It's a perfect match. I can't believe they were able to get this done so quickly. Even the plants look just like the ones we had before."

"That's what Janessa wanted," Martino said. "I assume you'll tell her they arrived."

"I will. Thanks, Martino." Noelle waited a moment longer, supervising the placement of the second urn. When the men completed their task, she headed back inside and came face-to-face with Jeremy.

"Oh, sorry. I didn't mean to sneak up on you," he said, his face flushing. Noelle suspected he was as surprised to see her as she was to see him. "I heard someone drive up and wanted to see what was going on."

"Tomasso and Renzo were delivering the new potted plants I ordered to replace the ones that got broken during the storm."

"Oh." He shifted his weight from one foot to another.

"I'd better get back to work," Noelle said, walking past him. *Only one more week*, she reminded herself. After that, he would leave, and she could start trying to heal her broken heart.

* * *

Jeremy was still rattled from his run-in with Noelle when a knock sounded at his door. For a brief moment, he thought perhaps it was Noelle. He wasn't sure if he was ready for that possibility, but when he pulled the door open, he found his sister standing in the hall instead.

"Are you going to tell me what's going on with you and Noelle?" Janessa asked, frustrated. She pushed her way inside and closed the door before facing him. "I've tried to be patient and let you work it out yourselves, but it's already been two weeks, and I don't see anything changing. I really don't have time for this, especially now that we're about to have a house full of guests."

"I'm sorry, Janessa," Jeremy said with an edge to his voice. "I didn't mean for my love life to interfere with your wedding."

"Jeremy, it's not that. Noelle is doing everything she can to help me out, but I hate to see her suffering. And it looks to me like you aren't any happier about the situation than she is."

A muscle in Jeremy's jaw clenched, but he remained silent.

"Talk to me. Why would you break up with her when you clearly still have feelings for her?"

"I didn't have a choice," Jeremy blurted out. He caught himself. "My job is almost done here, and it's only a matter of days before I head back home. I don't want to leave baggage behind."

"I'm not buying it. You were talking to Noelle before you even moved here." Janessa's eyes narrowed, and Jeremy fought the urge to squirm. A flash of awareness appeared on her face. "Oh my gosh. I can't believe I didn't see it before."

"What?"

"You really didn't have a choice, did you?"

Someone knocked at the door, and Jeremy quickly retreated across the room. He had barely opened it when Levi slipped inside. He saw Janessa and immediately took a step back. "Oh, sorry. I didn't mean to interrupt."

"Come in and close the door," Janessa said, steel in her voice.

Levi looked unexpectedly sheepish when he complied.

"How could you not tell me?" Her attention turned to Levi instead of Jeremy. "You brought in my own brother and never said a word?"

"Janessa, you knew I would need a replacement when you resigned."

"I know, but when I realized Noelle was working with you, I figured you were training her."

Jeremy watched the interaction between them, an unimaginable possibility now presenting itself. "Would either of you like to explain what's going on here? Janessa resigned from what?"

She turned to face him. "From the CIA."

"What?"

"Looks like you followed in my footsteps without even knowing it," Janessa said.

"You were CIA?" Jeremy looked at Levi. "Why didn't you tell me?"

"How did I get in the middle of this?" Levi muttered. "I didn't even realize the two of you didn't know about each other until you asked me about Noelle but didn't say anything about Jeremy."

Jeremy let this new information sink in. All this time his sister had been living an undercover life and he hadn't suspected a thing. The pieces started falling into place—the overseas travel, her friendship with Alan, the way her relationship with Garrett had been so mysterious from the beginning. Though Jeremy desperately wanted more information from her, he kept his focus on Levi. "I assume you had a reason for coming to my room."

"Yes." He glanced at Janessa as though waging some internal battle.

"I think she can be trusted," Jeremy said dryly.

"The DNA tests came back for the body you found in the water. It was Adrienne Acord."

"Who is Adrienne Acord?" Janessa asked.

"She worked for the television studio that had the rights to Prince Stefano's wedding," Levi said. "We know the night she disappeared someone downloaded all of the video footage of the event, but we have no idea why."

"That's odd."

"We thought so too," Jeremy agreed. He looked over at Levi. "Maybe now would be a good time to go over all of the security plans for the wedding. I think it's time for all of us to get on the same page since apparently you've been the only one privy to everyone's true reason for being here."

"Sounds like a fabulous idea," Janessa agreed. "Should I call Noelle to join us?"

"No," both men said in unison.

Janessa spoke to Jeremy first. "You can't avoid her forever."

"Actually I can, but that's not the problem," Jeremy said.

"Director Palmer is insistent we don't share Jeremy's background with anyone. That includes Noelle and the rest of my security team," Levi finished for him.

"Yes, but unlike the rest of your security team, Noelle is already working for the CIA and would have been granted some level of clearance with them," Janessa said. "Besides, I trust her."

"I do too, but we have our orders."

"Well, you can at least bring me up to date." Janessa plopped down on the sofa in Jeremy's sitting room. She looked up at them, apparently noticing their hesitation. "Okay, who do I need to get clearance from? Director Palmer or King Eduard?"

Jeremy and Levi looked at each other, looked at Janessa, and answered together. "Both."

Chapter 36

"I STILL CAN'T BELIEVE NO one told us about the bomb at Stefano's wedding." Janessa stood in Garrett's office, ignoring the scatter of papers on his desk.

"I'm sure my father was trying to protect us. Planning a wedding is difficult enough without worrying about security too," Garrett said, though Janessa could tell he was trying to convince himself as much as he was her.

"It's too late for that now."

Garrett circled his desk and put both hands on her arms to hold her in place. "Is there anything Levi and Jeremy aren't doing that you would have done? Levi brought in Alan just like you did last year."

"I know." She let out a sigh. "Levi's doing everything I would do. It just makes me nervous being out of the loop."

"It won't always be this way," Garrett promised. "You know as soon as we're married my father fully intends to have you involved with our intelligence service. He must have known it would be too much to juggle all of the prewedding events, plan everything, and be involved with security on top of it."

"I know you're right, but the thought that someone succeeded in getting a bomb through security undetected at Stefano's wedding is unnerving."

Garrett nodded. "Now we know why my father suggested we have our civil ceremony here at the chateau."

"Can't we elope instead?" She batted her eyelashes dramatically before she reached up and kissed him. "We can get married in the temple and then have some little ceremony somewhere at a courthouse or something to fulfill the legal requirements and go straight to our honeymoon."

"As tempting as that sounds, I don't think I want to face my father after he has to explain to five hundred and sixty-two guests why we skipped out on them."

"Oh yeah. There is that." She pursed her lips and shrugged. "It was worth a try."

"Your family is supposed to be here any minute. Go enjoy spending time with them. It's not often you're all together."

"Any chance you can get away from all this paperwork and come with me?"

"I have a few things I need to finish before I can take time off for our wedding, but I'll take an hour or two off as soon as they arrive."

"What are you working on anyway?" Janessa asked.

"The quarterly reports for the oil refinery."

"I assume everything looks okay so far."

"Better than okay. If things keep going the way they have been, my father hopes to expand the medical school at the university in Calene and make improvements to both their medical center and the hospital here in Bellamo."

"That's great." Janessa's cell phone chimed, and she pulled it from her pocket. There was a message from Martino. "Looks like my family is here."

"In that case . . ." He pulled her into his arms and pressed his lips to hers.

When he pulled back, she asked, "Are you afraid we aren't going to have any time alone now that we have a full house?"

"That, and I don't want you to get mad when I have to work this afternoon." He gave her another kiss. "I promise once I get this task behind me, I'm all yours for the next three weeks."

She grinned. "I'm going to hold you to that."

* * *

Levi picked up his phone, his heart sinking when he saw the director's name on his screen. Apparently Janessa had beat him to the punch in updating him on their impromptu meeting.

He answered and braced for the lecture to come.

"Levi, we're noticing an uptick in chatter in your region since yesterday. One of our agents in North Africa intercepted a call between the new president of Caspian Oil and Marcel Beaumont."

"The new member on the ruling council here?"

"Yes. On the surface it seemed innocent enough, but the fact that he made the call using a burn phone is suspicious in itself. The conversation didn't have much to it. Mostly talk about oil production levels and the possible implications on crude prices."

"We both know there's more to it than that. King Eduard banned trade between Meridia and Caspian Oil after the company's president was discovered to be behind the bombing attempt last fall."

"Exactly. So why would a government official from Meridia talk to someone he can't do business with and make the call in a way that he thought wouldn't be traceable?"

"Excellent question." Levi shifted the phone to his other ear. "Have you talked to Janessa lately?"

"No. Why?"

"She knows about Jeremy."

"How?" he asked, his irritation evident.

"Let's just say denying Jeremy's request for a close and continuing relationship with Noelle might not have been in our best interest."

"I don't understand."

Levi explained how he had arrived at Jeremy's room when Janessa was there and how she had already put two and two together. "I think with this information being out in the open now, we need to bring everyone together and let me use them as a real team. That includes bringing Noelle into our circle of need-to-know."

"We can't reveal Janessa's past employment. It's too risky."

"I agree, but as a soon-to-be member of the royal family, her presence wouldn't be out of place, especially when discussing the security for her wedding."

"Does she know about the bombing attempt at Prince Stefano's wedding?"

"Yes. She knew something must have prompted the level of security we have in place, and Alan's presence was a pretty solid giveaway."

He fell silent for a moment. "Okay, Levi. You've got your wish. Bring your team together. I'll send the transcripts of Beaumont's phone conversation."

"Thank you, Director."

"And tell Janessa I wish I could be there."

"I will, though I'm sure she already knows."

Levi hung up and immediately made another call. "Janessa, we need to set up a meeting, and I think it will work better if you're the one to call it."

"When?" she asked.

"As soon as possible."

"Can you give me a couple hours? My family just arrived, and it will look odd if I rush off right after they get here."

"Sounds like I don't have much choice."

* * *

"Mary!" Noelle hurried toward the new arrivals, giving her friend a hug before turning to coo at Lindsay, who was in Kevin's arms. "Oh, she's gotten so big!"

"I know." Mary gave Noelle another hug. "It's so good to see you."

"You too."

Janessa made her way downstairs to greet her family. She and Mary introduced Noelle to the various family members she hadn't met yet.

After introductions, Janessa turned to her mother. "Martino and his staff will show everyone to their rooms, and then we have a lunch prepared for you."

"Where's Jeremy?" Donna asked.

"He's trying to finish up some work, but I'm sure he'll be down any minute. I know he's excited to see everyone."

"I should get back to work," Noelle said, not wanting to intrude on Jeremy's time with his family.

Janessa looked over at her, understanding on her face. "We have a meeting in my office at two. I'll see you then."

"Okay." Noelle turned to leave, but she had only taken one step before she heard Jeremy's voice and his parents' and siblings' excited greetings.

His eyes swept over the room and lingered on her for a moment before he embraced one of his brothers. Her heart squeezing in her chest, she forced herself to leave the happy reunion. She took refuge in the kitchen, where she was immediately put to work helping prepare the welcome luncheon for the Rogers family.

Two hours later, she made her way to Janessa's office, trying to remember what meeting they had scheduled. She could have sworn she had cleared Janessa's calendar today so she would have extra time with her family. She ran into Janessa on her way. "Who are we meeting with this afternoon?"

"We have some security issues we need to iron out." Janessa led the way into her office.

Noelle came to a screeching halt when she entered and Jeremy was sitting at her worktable.

He stood at their entrance, as did the others present—Prince Garrett, Levi, and Alan. Only Max didn't respond to their presence, except for a wag of his tail.

Janessa nudged her farther into the room and closed the door.

"Everyone, please sit." Janessa sat beside Garrett and motioned for Noelle to take the empty chair between Levi and her.

Noelle sat, her cheeks reddening when she saw Jeremy staring at her. Determined to be professional, she clasped her hands in her lap and kept her attention on Janessa.

"All of you have been performing various tasks to help ensure the safety and security of the royal family and our expected guests for our wedding," Janessa said. "With only six days until the big event, Levi and I feel it's time to get everyone on the same page so we can better utilize our strengths and avoid duplication of efforts."

Noelle looked over at Jeremy again. What did he have to do with security? The apology on his face made her struggle to tune back into Janessa's words.

"Levi is the station chief for the CIA here in Bellamo and will be overseeing everything. Alan and Max will do two daily security sweeps of the chateau."

"We may have to adjust that to once a day so we can have them at the gates when deliveries arrive," Levi said.

"Of course." Janessa shifted her attention to Noelle. "You have been assisting Levi over the past several months, feeding him information to make sure we don't have any trouble areas with the staff."

"You've known?" Noelle asked.

"And Jeremy was sent here by the CIA to assist Levi."

Noelle's jaw dropped. Jeremy was CIA? Her eyes whipped up to meet his. The look of apology made sense now. Had he known Levi had recruited her this whole time? Had he been spying on her even as she had been spying on her friends?

Jeremy met her gaze for a moment before turning his attention to Levi. "We've already discussed the concerns that have popped up in my security checks. So far it appears that the most likely problem is Gustave Nardini."

"Gustave? Why would Martino hire someone who was under suspicion?" Noelle asked.

"We've been hoping to catch him in the act of either planting a bomb or bringing in weapons," Levi explained. "We have someone watching him all the time, and we have enhanced security in his quarters and in the areas near his room. So far we haven't seen anything suspicious."

"Except that he always seems to be lurking around watching everyone," Noelle muttered.

"Yes, except for that," Levi said. "And we believe he is using an alias."

"Why would you give him this kind of access?" Janessa asked. "There must have been something that prompted such extreme measures."

"I can't go into specifics, but we have been concerned that someone might try the same thing they did at Prince Stefano's wedding," Levi said. "We also have some concerns about Marcel Beaumont because of a recent conversation he had with someone at Caspian Oil."

"I don't suppose you can give us more details on that, can you?"

"No, but there wasn't much to it anyway," Levi said.

Noelle could tell Janessa was fighting against a sense of frustration.

Garrett must have noticed it too. He reached out and put his hand on her arm. "Maybe we should give our security team some space to do their jobs," Garrett suggested gently.

She hesitated before standing. "You can use my office as long as you need to. I guess we'll go make sure my family is settling in okay."

Garrett stood, as did the other men at the table. When Janessa started toward the door, Levi called after her. "I'll give you an update later."

"I'd appreciate it," Janessa said. With an odd look of wistfulness, she turned and led her fiancé to the door.

Chapter 37

JEREMY SAT BACK DOWN AND tried to concentrate on the task at hand. Every time Noelle looked at him, he had to fight the urge to squirm.

"Here's what we're dealing with," Levi said, his no-nonsense tone succeeding in interrupting Jeremy's thoughts. "Jeremy has been running deep background checks on the expected guests, contractors for the wedding, and staff."

Jeremy took his cue and opened the file in front of him. "A good number of people I researched came back with alarms, meaning they had some sort of alerts queued for anytime someone digs into their affairs. I've narrowed down those that flagged any kind of concerns." He passed printouts to everyone at the table.

"Twenty-two names?" Alan asked. "That's a lot to keep track of."

"I agree," Levi said. "That's why we have to narrow it down further. Jeremy has done as much as he can by himself."

"Exactly how are we supposed to narrow these down further?" Noelle asked.

"I've sent this list over to CIA headquarters, and they are cross-referencing them with known associations with Caspian Oil, Councilman Beaumont, or Gustave Nardini."

"If we already suspect the councilman and Gustave, why don't we bring them in for questioning?" Noelle asked.

"Because neither one of them has the financial resources to back the cost of an undertaking like this. Bombs aren't cheap."

"What makes you so sure there is another bomb?" Alan asked.

"Ivan Byrd disappeared shortly after the attempt in Calene. It's unlikely he was fully paid for a bomb that never went off," Levi said. "My guess is he built another bomb, and after he received his payment, he dropped out of sight."

"Yeah, but this is all speculation." Alan reached down and rubbed Max's ears. "Max hasn't detected anything, and we've been searching each incoming delivery since we got here."

"At this point, all we can do is keep searching and pray we can identify any problems in time to solve them," Levi said.

"It might be worth it to go back through the television footage of Stefano's wedding," Jeremy suggested. "I looked at all of it when I first got it, but now that we have a smaller number of targets to look for, maybe I'll find something I missed."

"That's a good idea," Levi said. "Noelle, I want you to help him."

Her eyebrows shot up. "Excuse me?"

"You know more of the players than anyone else here," Levi said. "And we both know you have a good eye for spotting things that seem out of place."

"Anything else you want me to do?" Alan asked.

"Just keep coordinating with the front gate for the delivery schedule," Levi said. "I'll stay on top of Tomasso and Julien to make sure there aren't any areas of the chateau Gustave has spent extra time in."

"I'm surprised you didn't include them in this meeting," Noelle said.

"I couldn't. Neither of them is aware of your involvement with the CIA or Jeremy's true reason for being here."

Noelle saw the wisdom in Levi's decision and redirected the conversation back to the pressing issues. "If Gustave hasn't planted something by now, maybe he isn't going to."

"I'd like to think that's the case, but the fact that he isn't using his own name raises red flags all over the place." Levi stood. "That's it for now. Let me know if you find anything."

Everyone stood, and Alan led the way out of the office.

Levi turned around. "Why don't you and Noelle take a minute to coordinate your schedules. I suspect you have some talking to do."

Jeremy looked at him, a little flame of hope sparking inside him. "Did the director reconsider my request?"

"No, but at least you can tell her the truth now." Levi left the room and closed the door.

Jeremy turned to face Noelle.

"What truth?" she asked.

"The truth that I didn't want to break up with you. I put in the paper-work to get permission to have a relationship with you, and it was denied."

He could see her process his words. "The CIA told you to break up with me?"

"Yes."

"Were you just keeping tabs on me this whole time?"

"It's not like that," Jeremy said. He took her hand. When she stiffened, he immediately released it. "I didn't know you were working intel until Levi told me my request was denied."

"So you had to choose between me and your career."

"I didn't have a choice. I know about the bomb at Stefano's wedding. I couldn't walk away knowing someone might try the same thing again." He dragged his fingers through his hair. "My whole family is at risk. You would be too."

Her posture relaxed slightly. "And now, somehow, we're supposed to work together."

"Yeah."

"It isn't going to be easy to find somewhere to watch the footage you were talking about. The chateau is swarming with guests."

"Do you have any suggestions?"

"I might." Noelle headed for the door and made her way into the outer office and over to her desk. She tapped a few keys on her computer. "Princess Alora is already here with her kids, but Prince Stefano won't arrive until the day of the wedding. His offices are across the hall. I think he would allow us to use the television screen in there."

"That's a great idea," Jeremy agreed. "Levi's office is next door, so if we find something, it would be easy to meet with him."

"Exactly."

"When can we start?" Jeremy asked.

"How about first thing tomorrow morning? Janessa is having her final fitting for her dress. Now that your family is here, she won't need me to be with her."

"Sounds good. How about if I meet you around eight?"

"Let's make it seven. I'll bring breakfast."

"Deal." Jeremy took a step toward the door before he turned back to face her. "I may not have had a choice when I broke up with you, but that doesn't mean I won't have one to make once this wedding is over." He took a deep breath. "I wasn't lying when I said I loved you." Without another word, he turned and walked out the door.

* * *

As much as Noelle wanted to spend time with Jeremy's family, she was afraid that if she was there, Jeremy wouldn't be. She couldn't blame him. She didn't think she could face him right now either.

What was she supposed to think after his latest declaration? Was he trying to tell her they might have a future together? Or was he ultimately going to choose his career over her?

She still couldn't quite wrap her mind around the truth that both of them had been keeping secrets from the other, that both of them were working in intelligence. Though initially hurt by the revelation, logic quickly overcame her gut reaction. She had always wanted this kind of career, and she recognized how carefully Jeremy had skirted the line between truth and lie. In fact, he hadn't lied. He had misled and exaggerated, but he hadn't lied. That was a talent she could admire despite the frustration it caused.

Restless, she headed for the kitchen to offer her help. The Calene staff was handling some of the preparations at the palace and would then transfer those items to the chateau and stay to work with Patrice.

Everything was finally coming together in the balance between security concerns and logistics for the wedding. She thought of her earlier meeting and wondered if it really would be possible for someone to create a threat here despite all of their precautions.

She cut through the main entryway and hesitated. Unable to resist, she walked to the nearest window and looked outside. Jeremy and his brothers were tossing a football on the beach. A large blue-and-white-striped umbrella obstructed her view, but she could see Janessa standing beside it, undoubtedly chatting with those avoiding a sunburn.

Movement caught her eye on the terrace, and she noticed Tomasso outside, apparently making a security sweep of the area by the ballroom doors. Almost as soon as he left, Alan rounded the corner with Max.

"See anything interesting out there?"

Startled, Noelle whirled around. Gustave was standing behind her, a freshly polished serving tray in his hand.

"I was just watching Janessa's family. They seem to be enjoying the beach," Noelle said.

"There sure are a lot of them. How many brothers and sisters does she have?"

"Three brothers, two sisters." Noelle took a step back toward the hall. "I'd better go see what I can help with in the kitchen. See you later."

When she reached the doorway, she glanced back at Gustave, who was now standing in the spot she had vacated, watching the new arrivals.

A sense of alarm rang in her head. What was it about him that always made her so uneasy? Eager to escape his presence, she continued forward and hoped some old-fashioned hard work would provide a distraction from her overactive thoughts.

* * *

As Noelle promised, she brought breakfast. The scent in the air told Jeremy Patrice had baked the croissants that morning, and he had been around long enough to know the orange juice was freshly squeezed. The simple meal had become a staple for him during his time in Meridia, one he had discovered was a favorite among the residents here.

Noelle's hair was pulled back today, a light dusting of makeup accenting her high cheekbones. Just looking at her made him ache. More than anything, he wanted her back in his life. He noticed color rise in her cheeks as he continued to stare.

"I hope this is okay." She broke eye contact and set the serving tray on Stefano's worktable. "We're keeping meals pretty basic right now with all the catering items being prepared."

"This is perfect." He plugged the flash drive into the television and turned it on. He selected the first file, and they both sat in the chairs facing the screen.

Noelle handed him a plate from the tray. "You said you already looked over all of this?"

"A couple times. Nothing popped out for me, but since you were there, maybe you'll notice something I missed." Jeremy retrieved a croissant from the basket. "How much time do you have this morning?"

"Your mom and sisters are helping Janessa, so I can watch until about one. How much video feed is there?"

"More than we can watch between now and the wedding. If we narrow it down to the time frame when the guests started to arrive and an hour after the ceremony, it's about twenty hours."

"I guess we'd better get started, then." Noelle looked over at him, and he saw her uncertainty.

"What?"

"About what you said yesterday . . ."

Jeremy wanted to open the door to that conversation, but he wasn't sure he could balance what he felt for her right now with his work obligations. "Can we talk about that after the wedding?"

She pursed her lips and nodded, then motioned toward the remote control, and he pressed play.

Chapter 38

HE PASSED THROUGH ONE OF the rear doors of the chateau and followed a path into the surrounding woods using the moonlight to guide him. Given the level of surveillance within the royal walls, he wasn't about to have this conversation inside.

One more day. Tomorrow everything would be different. Tomorrow history would be made, and he would remain a silent partner in bringing about change that would make him richer than he had ever thought possible. He didn't care about power the way his associates did. Just give him his share of the profits earned from their future endeavors. Black gold. He liked the sound of that.

He waited until he was well away from the structure before he pulled his cell phone from his pocket. He stumbled over a tree root and briefly wished he had brought a flashlight with him.

The moment his coconspirator's voice came on the phone, he spoke excitedly. "Everything is ready."

"Are you sure?" came the whispered response. "We'll never get another opportunity like this."

"Positive. The fertilizer worked like a charm. The dog hasn't detected the explosives, and I did a final check last night."

"How did you get around the security cameras?"

"Don't worry about that. I took care of it. I suggest you start practicing your acting skills. You know the reporters will swarm your house as soon as they realize what's happened."

"Don't worry. I'll look appropriately dismayed."

"I'll meet you in Calene in a few days."

"I look forward to it."

* * *

Janessa couldn't believe this day was finally here. All of the planning and preparing, all of the struggles to get to this point. So many people had worked so hard in so many different ways to make this day perfect. If only she didn't have that lingering doubt about security.

She had given Noelle as much time as possible to work with Jeremy over the past week, but the last two days had been an all-hands-on-deck occasion. Even Jeremy and her other brothers had been roped into helping with decorations and shifting furniture around in preparation of the large number of expected guests.

Alan and Levi had been among the few who hadn't been roped into manual labor. Alan's presence gave Janessa some level of comfort. He and Max hadn't been present at Stefano and Alora's wedding. Her confidence in her friend and his dog helped her push aside her concerns when Garrett took her hand.

"Are you ready? You're about to be stuck with me forever."

"You're about to be stuck with *me* forever."

"Then I am the luckiest man alive." He leaned over and gave her a quick kiss as the limousine came to a stop.

"I hope you always think so." She looked up at the temple before them, an odd combination of peace and excitement coming over her. When she turned back to Garrett, she grinned and reached over to rub her thumb across his lip. "I don't think you want to wear my lipstick inside."

"It's not my color?"

"I don't think so."

Enrico opened the door, and Garrett stepped out, offering his hand to Janessa. Once again she put her hand in his, and together they walked through the doors toward their destiny.

* * *

Noelle couldn't put her finger on it. Something was bothering her about the video footage; something was out of place, but she couldn't figure out what.

Jeremy had left that morning with the rest of his family to go with Janessa and Garrett to the temple, and she hadn't seen him since. Alora had gone with them as well and had met Stefano in Calene, but the rest of the royal family had opted to remain behind. Noelle suspected the decision was a combination of practicality and logic. For security reasons, it was best not to have the royals in one place any more than necessary, and the simple truth was that they couldn't go inside anyway.

She wandered through the ballroom looking for any adjustments that needed to be made. The dance floor had been reduced dramatically in size to make room for the increased number of tables required to accommodate their guests. In the far corner, a small stage had been set up for the civil ceremony.

Table settings, centerpieces, flowers. Everything was in place. Everything looked perfect. All these months of hard work had paid off, and Noelle prayed the only memories of today would be happy ones.

The staff from the palace had arrived three hours earlier, and several of them were currently working in the kitchen, preparing the first dish to be served—fresh berries inside of elegant wafer shells. Noelle didn't need to visit the kitchen to know preparations were well under control there. Her mother would see to that.

She heard vehicles approach outside, and she headed for the terrace doors. She smiled when Janessa and Garrett emerged from the limousine her father had driven and started up the front steps.

Her father moved the first limo to make room for two more—Stefano and Alora's and Janessa's family's. All were accounted for—except Jeremy.

She looked over the entrance and the driveway leading to the garage once more. No other cars were visible, nor did she see anyone else emerge from the back of the limo. Again she looked around, concerned. Where was he?

* * *

Jeremy had driven himself to the temple, anticipating an early return to the chateau so he could get an update from Levi. What he hadn't expected was to get roped into a marathon photo shoot after the ceremony.

With the limousines transporting the rest of the wedding party already parked near the entrance, he had ultimately been the last to navigate his way out of the parking lot. He tried to push aside his sense of urgency, reminding himself to enjoy the beautiful drive along the Mediterranean.

His sister's sealing had been perfect. She had glowed when Garrett had taken her hand across the altar, and Jeremy could only hope someday soon he would repeat a similar scene with Noelle. He'd made his choice between her and his job; in his heart he already knew Noelle was too important, too precious to him to let her go. He didn't know how hard he would have to fight to get her back in his life, but he prayed she would forgive the hurt he had caused and agree to spend her future with him.

But first they had to make it through today. They'd taken so many precautions, but still something had him on edge. The car jerked, a loud bang accompanying the unexpected movement. He'd been so focused on possible threats that he first thought someone might have shot at him. A fraction of a second later, he recognized the true source of the problem by the accompanying skid and imbalanced movement of the car. His tire had blown.

He wrestled the car to the side of the road, his heart pounding rapidly even after he'd come to a complete stop. He climbed out of the car and took a look at the passenger side where the damage had been done. "Great," he muttered under his breath.

He took off his suit jacket, not thrilled with the prospect of changing a tire while wearing dress clothes. At least he was still wearing a regular suit instead of the tuxedo currently hanging in his closet. He popped the trunk and opened the compartment to retrieve the spare tire. He could only stare. The spare tire was exactly where it was supposed to be, but the jack was missing.

Taking care to protect his clothes, Jeremy tilted the tire up to make sure the jack hadn't been placed beneath it. All he got for his efforts was a black smudge on his fingers.

He grabbed a handkerchief from his pocket, grateful he had thought to grab it that morning, and wiped the black from his hand. Then he pulled his cell phone from his pocket and debated whom to call. He was an equal distance between the chateau and the palace, and the last thing he wanted was to pull someone away from their security detail to come get him. He also didn't want to bother his family, who would be preparing for the civil ceremony and reception.

At a loss, he scanned through his contacts, an unlikely solution presenting itself. He dialed the number, already translating his problem into Italian. A wave of relief came over him when Paolo answered.

"Paolo, I'm sorry to bother you, but I have a flat tire. Any chance you can help me out?" Jeremy proceeded to explain his situation, stumbling through several possible word choices in trying to explain that he was missing his jack. Finally, after Jeremy's using what he could of his vocabulary, Paolo agreed to come pick him up and bring him back to the chateau.

Now assured he wouldn't miss his sister's second wedding ceremony, Jeremy climbed back into the car to wait for his ride.

Chapter 39

LEVI SEARCHED THROUGH THE INDEX of surveillance files a third time. He turned to Tomasso, the only other person currently in the office. "Is camera six working?"

"Yes. Why?"

"I don't see any feedback on it since eight o'clock last night."

"Are you sure? We're still getting live feed."

"Check the recording settings," Levi said, pulling up another screen so he could check the master settings himself. The display immediately indicated the problem. Camera six was operational, but the recording function had been disabled.

Levi opened another window and searched the keystroke logger for the security office computers. A few seconds later, his stomach dropped. He reached for the weapon he kept holstered in the back of his waistband and started to turn toward the guilty party. His movement was interrupted when a burst of pain accompanied the blow to the back of his head.

His vision blurred, and he barely managed to keep himself from falling over. "Why?" he managed to ask. He tried to take a step only to stumble and fall to the floor.

* * *

He couldn't believe Levi had noticed the surveillance breach so quickly. He'd been certain he could cover it up until long after the damage had been done. Now he would be forced to flee a full hour earlier than expected.

Their plan could still work. It had to. He was so tired of watching everyone else living their lives while he was stuck in a ten-by-twelve room with a bank of monitors. Surely he deserved better.

Only Levi could identify him. Tomasso fingered the gun that had, until moments ago, been strapped to his ankle. As an intelligence officer, he was one of the few allowed to carry a firearm inside the chateau.

Blood had already seeped into the carpet, and Tomasso shifted his weapon and aimed. The same thought that had kept him from shooting Levi in the first place held him back now—a gunshot was bound to draw attention, attention he couldn't afford to have.

He lowered his weapon. With the way the head wound was bleeding, he wasn't sure Levi would survive the day anyway. He glanced at the clock on the wall. The next shift change wasn't for another forty-five minutes. By then he would be long gone and the guests would be in their seats awaiting the arrival of the bride.

An alert sounded, and he noticed the image of several wedding guests arriving. In the confusion of the constant flow of cars coming in, he could slip outside and make his way into the woods. If anyone did discover Levi and called, he could say he was searching for the suspect.

He holstered his weapon and headed for the door. With a last look at the prone figure on the floor, he slipped into the hall and headed for the back stairway.

* * *

Noelle stood at the edge of the ballroom, watching as guests continued to filter into the room. Almost half of the seats were filled, even though the ceremony wouldn't begin for nearly an hour.

A glance at her watch kicked her nerves into overdrive, and her mind raced with details. The orchestra was now in place, and servers were already circling to provide guests with drinks and hors d'oeuvres while they socialized and waited for the main event. Overshadowing everything, though, was one thought that kept popping into her mind. Where was Jeremy? She had repeatedly checked with security and had repeatedly been told the same thing. He had not yet returned from Calene.

Across the room, Martino motioned to her. She crossed to him.

"Noelle, have you seen Gustave?" Martino asked.

"No, why?"

"He's disappeared."

Alarms rang loudly in her mind. "What do you mean disappeared? When was the last time anyone saw him?"

"About fifteen minutes ago. He was helping the palace staff with the food, but no one has seen him since." Martino glanced at his watch.

"Have you checked with Levi?"

"I was about to head up there now."

"I'll come with you." They passed through the hallway that led from the chateau's entertainment wing to the kitchen and turned the corner toward the chateau offices. Noelle's stomach churned uncomfortably.

One of her main duties working for Levi was to look for anything suspicious with Gustave. Of course, how did she describe what was suspicious when his whole demeanor set her on edge?

They reached the security office, and Martino knocked once before pushing the door open.

"Levi!" Noelle rushed forward and knelt beside her boss. She pressed her fingers to his neck, relieved to find the skin warm and a weak pulse.

"I'll call an ambulance." Martino quickly pulled out his phone.

Noelle looked around for something to use as a bandage. She didn't see anything, but the scissors on Levi's desk caught her eye. She grabbed them and, with only a moment's hesitation, cut a strip of fabric from the bottom of her dress.

She pressed the makeshift bandage to the back of Levi's head, distressed that the blood was flowing so freely. She offered a silent prayer on his behalf. How long had he been here like this?

Levi stirred, his eyes fluttering open. Noelle recognized the glazed look and the confusion. She had seen the same expression on her oldest brother when he'd suffered a concussion after being thrown from a horse.

Beside her, Martino gave the pertinent details to the emergency operator. He put the phone on speaker, set it down on a desk, and looked down at the blood-soaked fabric. "I'll get some towels."

As Martino left the room, Levi tried to sit up, but Noelle put a hand on his shoulder to keep him from moving. "Take it easy. Can you tell me what happened? Who did this to you?"

He squinted against the overhead lights, but he didn't respond to her question. She looked around the room. Nothing else looked disturbed, but where was the rest of the security team? Someone should have been up here with Levi. She had seen the schedule herself when Levi had gone over their final security briefing.

Martino returned and set a stack of towels beside her. She used one to replace her dress fabric, pressing firmly to try to stop the bleeding.

Martino took the phone off speaker and spoke to the emergency operator to get an estimated arrival time. He turned to Noelle. "They'll be here in three minutes."

"Can you do me a favor?" she asked. "Call Alan and tell him we have an ambulance coming in. He needs to go down to the gate with Max to make sure no one is using this as a way to gain access."

"I'll take care of it."

"Also, tell the emergency operator to keep the sirens off. We need to keep this quiet. I don't want Janessa and Garrett in the middle of this on their wedding day."

Martino nodded and did as she asked.

* * *

Paolo had made good time, but that didn't negate the fact that Jeremy had broken down nearly an hour's drive from the chateau. With the clock a factor, the men had opted to leave Jeremy's car and return to retrieve it tomorrow. By the time they made it to the chateau gates, they were caught in the line of people arriving for the wedding.

"Now I'm really wishing I had ridden with the rest of the family," Jeremy muttered in English.

"What?"

Jeremy repeated his comment in Italian.

Paolo chuckled and took matters into his own hands. He swung the truck wide around the line of cars and lifted a hand to wave at the guards. As soon as the guard identified them, he stepped out and stopped the next car in line to allow Paolo to proceed through first.

Paolo grinned at him. "It pays to know the right people."

"That it does," Jeremy agreed. "Thanks again for picking me up."

"You're welcome." Paolo dropped him off outside the family entrance of the chateau and took a quick glance at his watch. "I'd better go get changed. I'll see you in a few minutes."

Jeremy couldn't believe the time. He should have been here three hours ago to help Levi with the final security checks, and instead he was arriving at the same time as the guests. He headed for the door, glancing back at the gates in time to see an ambulance pull up.

After the guards made their initial inquiry, Alan and Max stepped forward and did their own security check.

The moment Alan nodded his approval to the guard, the ambulance drove through.

Concerned, Jeremy pulled his phone from his pocket. He supposed it was possible Levi had arranged to have emergency personnel on site as a precaution, but the last time they had talked, they had decided the several doctors who would be in attendance would be sufficient for any urgent needs.

The door opened, and Martino rushed outside.

"What's going on?" Jeremy asked, closing the distance between them.

"It's Levi. Someone hit him on the back of the head. It doesn't look good." Martino waved at the ambulance attendants the moment they parked and retrieved their emergency supplies. "This way."

Jeremy let the EMTs go first, then raced up the stairs behind them. In the security office, Noelle was kneeling beside Levi, a bloody towel held to the back of his head. Where was Tomasso? He should have been on duty.

As much as he wanted to question Noelle and Martino, Jeremy remained silent as they shared everything they knew with the paramedics.

Feeling helpless, he shifted his attention to the monitors on the wall. Several staff members were moving about in the ballroom and kitchen areas, and his parents were visible in the guest-wing hallway. He continued to scan the monitors, pausing on each screen where he could see movement.

With Levi now under professional medical care, Noelle stood and stepped up beside him.

"Any idea who might have done this?" Jeremy asked.

"We don't know. Martino told me Gustave had disappeared, and we came up here to see if Levi had seen him on any of the security cameras."

"Gustave is missing?" He turned toward her. "How long?"

"I don't know."

"I started looking for him about fifteen minutes ago," Martino said. "The last time we're sure anyone saw him was about fifteen minutes before that."

Jeremy motioned to the cameras. "Do either of you see him anywhere?"

They all stood for a moment, scanning.

"Is that him there?" Martino pointed to a screen at the top corner. In it, Gustave was walking behind Tomasso.

Reading both men's body language, Jeremy guessed Gustave had a gun in his hand. Still unarmed from his trip to the temple, he debated if he should run to his room to get his gun or just call the guards. He took a step toward the door, still undecided when he looked down and saw Levi's weapon on the floor beside him.

He scooped it up. "Stay here and watch the monitor. If they disappear from view, call the guards."

Noelle touched his arm. "Be careful."

"I will."

Chapter 40

JEREMY HURRIED OUT THE REAR entrance, gun in hand. He'd managed to make it outside without running into anyone, a blessing in itself.

Anticipating the angle the two men outside had been walking, Jeremy took what he hoped would be an intercepting path.

Within two minutes, he saw Tomasso heading toward him, Gustave following behind.

"Hold it right there." Jeremy lifted his weapon, taking aim at Gustave. "Let me see your hands."

"It's not what you think," Gustave insisted. He held his hands out to his sides, confirming Jeremy's suspicion that he was armed.

"Drop the gun."

"It wasn't me. Tomasso is the one you want."

"Drop the gun," Jeremy repeated. "Then we'll talk."

Resigned, Gustave engaged the safety and tossed the gun aside. "I'm going to reach into my pocket and get my ID. I'm with Interpol."

"Two fingers."

Gustave followed his directions precisely, and Jeremy shifted the angle slightly to keep both men in his sights. He tossed the ID toward Jeremy.

Keeping his eye and his aim focused on them, he squatted and picked up the leather case holding the ID. He lifted it so he could look at it without taking his attention off the men.

The ID looked genuine, but he knew it was possible to create a forgery. "Why didn't you tell security here who you really were?"

"I couldn't take the chance. My office picked up chatter that a member of Meridia's royal family is involved in a major assassination attempt in this region." Gustave waved at Tomasso. "I was doing a quick look around when I saw him running out of the security office. When I saw Levi down, I chased after him, and he took a shot at me."

"Why didn't you call for help for Levi?"

"I was about to when I heard Martino and Noelle coming down the hall. I knew they would take care of him, and I didn't want to lose this lead. If something's going down today, he knows what it is."

What he said made sense. "Let's take this conversation inside."

Jeremy shifted sideways to retrieve Gustave's weapon. His story might be plausible, but Jeremy wasn't ready to hand him a weapon. He took a fraction of a second too long in grabbing the gun.

Tomasso kicked a leg out to send Gustave tumbling backward. Just as Jeremy found Gustave's gun, Tomasso rushed forward.

Both men dove for it, Jeremy's body impacting the hard ground. His fingers wrapped around the handle only to have it wrenched away again.

"Watch out!" Gustave shouted.

Jeremy rolled toward Tomasso as the other man stood and lifted the gun to take aim. Jeremy kicked, and his heel connected with Tomasso's shin.

Tomasso groaned in pain and stumbled backward several steps. Jeremy gripped his own gun tighter, rolling over to take aim as Tomasso fought to regain his footing.

Before Jeremy could fire, Gustave grabbed Tomasso from behind, forcing his arms down.

A gunshot rang out, the bullet striking the ground between them.

Jeremy scrambled to his feet, the other men grappling, Tomasso still in control of the weapon. Larger in stature than Gustave, Tomasso managed to raise his shooting hand enough to send Jeremy diving to the ground once more. Jeremy rolled to the side as two more shots were fired, the second one coming within inches of him.

Gustave shoved his knee into the back of Tomasso's leg, successfully throwing him off balance once more. This time, however, Tomasso leaned forward enough to break the hold Gustave had on him.

Still lying on the ground, Jeremy took aim. "Drop the gun!"

The intent in Tomasso's eyes when he raised his weapon again was clear. This time the only shot fired came from Jeremy's gun.

Gustave was the first to reach the crumpled form, quickly relieving him of his weapon even though he no longer appeared to have the strength to grip the gun, much less fire it.

"What is the plan?" Gustave demanded.

Jeremy saw where the bullet had hit Tomasso in the chest. He felt a sickness rise in his stomach, the reality that he had shot this man and would likely take his life overwhelming him.

"Tell me who else is involved." Gustave continued his interrogation, the sound of guards' footsteps quickly approaching.

Gustave's urgency was contagious. This man could be the difference in hundreds of people living or dying today. "Is there another bomb?"

Tomasso gulped in air and choked out the words. "You'll never find them."

"Where are they?" Jeremy put his hand on Tomasso's shoulder. "Tell me where they are."

"Who were you working with?" Gustave demanded.

Jeremy could see the color draining from the wounded man's face. Their demands continued to go unanswered, and the possibility of his dying shifted into an eventuality.

"Call for a paramedic," Jeremy told one of the guards.

"It's too late." Gustave reached over and pressed two fingers against the man's neck. He shook his head before looking up, his eyes meeting Jeremy's. "It's too late."

* * *

Noelle emerged through the door right behind the ambulance attendants. Levi was strapped to a gurney, bandages covering the upper part of his head. The fact that he had regained consciousness was a good sign, but the urgency with which the paramedics had worked still left her worried. Not only that, but he still hadn't managed to communicate with her about who had done this to him.

She saw Jeremy and Gustave heading toward her, one of the chateau guards walking beside them.

"Make sure the body is taken out by ambulance," Jeremy told the guard. "We don't want the image of a hearse appearing on the news."

"Good point," the guard said. "I'll take care of it."

"Thanks."

"What happened?" Noelle asked. "What body?"

Jeremy ignored her questions, instead stepping beside Levi and asking the paramedic, "How is he?"

"He has a concussion, but thankfully the wound isn't too deep."

"Really? There was a lot of blood."

"Head wounds tend to bleed a lot." The paramedic opened the back door to the ambulance. He shifted to help his partner lift the gurney, and Jeremy moved closer.

"Tomasso," Levi said weakly. "It was Tomasso."

"I know." Jeremy put a hand on his shoulder. "You concentrate on getting better. We'll take care of things here."

"Can you please tell me what's going on?" Noelle asked.

"Let's take this inside." Jeremy walked to the family entrance and pulled the door open.

Noelle made her way through, followed by Gustave and Jeremy. Now alone in the family's private entryway, Noelle turned to Jeremy. Before she could ask for information again, he spoke to Gustave.

"Tell me what you're doing here. You said Interpol believed someone from the royal family might be involved in an assassination attempt."

"Not necessarily the family, but someone with close access."

"You're Interpol?" Noelle asked.

"A car bomb went off in Algeria last year, and several top executives from an oil company there were killed or seriously injured. We believe whoever was behind it has been trying to manipulate the oil market in this region."

"Assuming this is an assassination attempt, who is the target?"

"There are several. The ruling family of Meridia, the president of France, and several princes from Saudi Arabia top the list."

"All oil-producing countries."

Noelle's phone rang. She pulled it from the small purse hanging from her shoulder. Mary was calling.

"Where are you?" Mary asked. "The wedding is about to start, and we need Janessa's bouquet."

"The bouquet is in the refrigerator in your parents' suite."

Jeremy looked at his watch. "Is that Mary?"

"Yes."

"Tell her we're having some technical difficulties and to keep the family all upstairs until we call her."

Noelle wasn't sure what was behind the request, but she passed the information along. As soon as she hung up, she asked, "Why did you want me to have them stay upstairs?"

"There are bombs here somewhere," Jeremy said. "Tomasso said we wouldn't find them, so they must already be in place."

"If he was leaving, we don't have much time," Gustave said. "I've been doing searches every day, but I haven't found anything."

Jeremy pulled his own cell phone from his pocket and dialed. "Alan, where are you?" He paused to listen to the response. "Meet me at the main entrance. We have a problem."

He hung up and turned to Noelle. "You should leave. I don't want you anywhere near here if a bomb goes off, especially since we think there's more than one."

"I could say the same thing about you." Noelle knew insanity was likely setting in when she added, "I'm not leaving until I'm sure all of us can walk out of here safely."

"This is all very touching, but we're running out of time," Gustave interrupted. "Let's go."

Noelle led the way. She must be crazy. Who in their right mind would pray to find a bomb again?

"Should we evacuate?" she asked as they reached the front hall.

"We can't be sure there isn't someone watching with their finger on a detonator. For now, our safest bet is to keep the wedding from starting. I don't think anyone will detonate until the royal family is all in place." Jeremy shifted his attention as Alan approached. "When did you last do a sweep of the ballroom area?"

"I did the interior an hour ago, right before the guests started arriving, and I just finished another sweep of the hallway. What's going on?"

"We think Tomasso planted multiple bombs."

"Max hasn't found anything yet."

"Could he have been thrown off by some other scent? I've heard drug dealers hide drugs in coffee grounds to get them past the dogs."

"It doesn't work that way. Dogs aren't fooled the way humans are. If Max isn't picking up a scent, it's because the smell isn't out of place."

"Or maybe the bomb material doesn't have a scent," Noelle said.

"All bombs give off some kind of odor," Alan said.

"The bomb at Stefano's wedding was made of a new compound. Levi said it's really hard to detect," Noelle said.

"Maybe it's a combination of both," Gustave interjected. "I've been searching for any sign of a bomb since I got here. I've torn apart everything near the ballroom, but I haven't seen a thing."

"No wonder you were doing so much dusting," Noelle said. "They probably had a guest sneak it in."

"Not possible this time. All bags are being thoroughly searched. Security isn't falling for the same trick twice." Awareness lit Jeremy's eyes, and he spoke to Gustave. "You were limited by your position to the interior of the chateau."

"The terrace." Noelle read his thoughts.

"Let's go." Alan took a step toward the parlor. "We don't have much time."

Chapter 41

JEREMY GLANCED THROUGH THE FRENCH doors to where the wedding guests had settled into their seats in anticipation of the upcoming ceremony. Glamor and glitz. It was everywhere, and television cameras were positioned around the room to catch every detail. He hoped they would all live to watch the footage.

"Where do we start?" Noelle asked.

Jeremy wanted to renew his plea for her to leave, to move to safety, but he could see her determination. The only way for both of them to survive the day was to find the bombs and find them now.

He searched for any place a bomb could have been hidden. Flowers on trellises outlined the terrace doors, and a line of padded chairs stretched out in the area beyond the parlor. A half dozen tables covered with blue and white tablecloths were clustered in the wide section to his right, each of the surrounding chairs hidden beneath white chair covers.

"Noelle and Gustave, check the tables," Alan said. "I'll take another pass at the chairs over there."

With the others frantically searching the obvious possibilities, Jeremy stepped past a ceramic urn and did a quick search of the floral arrangement. Nothing. He turned and looked down the length of terrace again, first one way and then the other.

Other than the tables and chairs, the terrace was completely empty except for the potted plants spaced evenly along its length.

Alan pulled a knife from his pocket and knelt beside one of the padded chairs. Jeremy moved to his side, watching while he cut open the seam to search inside one of the cushions.

"Anything?"

"No." Alan motioned to his watch. "How much time until the wedding is supposed to start?"

"Six minutes."

Alan retrieved a second knife from his pocket and handed it to Jeremy. "Start at the other side and check the other chairs."

"Should I even ask why you carry two pocket knives?"

"Experience. When you work with bombs, you learn to be prepared."

Jeremy started at the far side, slashing open one cushion after another, finding nothing but padding inside. When two minutes later he and Alan met in the middle of the row, he shook his head. "Now what?"

"It's got to be here somewhere." Both men headed toward the other side of the terrace, where Noelle and Gustave were heading toward them.

"Anything?" Jeremy asked.

"Nothing. We looked under every table and chair. They're clean," Gustave said.

"Should we expand our search to the gardens?" Noelle asked.

Alan shook his head. "That would be too far away."

Noelle shifted beside Jeremy and reached out to rest her hand on one of the ceramic urns. She looked down, staring for a moment. Then her eyes lifted to meet Jeremy's. "The planters. Two of these were damaged during that storm a few weeks ago."

Awareness flooded through him. "Tomasso is the one who volunteered to pick up the new ones."

"He could have planted a bomb in one of them after he picked them up."

"Or he could have planted bombs in both," Gustave said gravely. "He said we wouldn't find *them*, not *it*."

Jeremy looked down at Max sitting silently beside the urn. He looked up at the dog's handler. "Alan, is he signaling a problem?"

"It's hard to say. The gardens are full of the fertilizers he has been trained to detect. He's been signaling every bush and tree for weeks."

Jeremy took his jacket off and pushed aside a handful of dirt. Gustave did the same with the other new potted plant.

"Anything?" Alan asked.

"Not so far." Jeremy continued to dig deeper, his fingers finding small pieces of bark and the spidery roots of the flowers planted there. Doubts crept in, his hands still moving.

"Maybe we're wrong," Alan said. "It could be somewhere else."

"Unless someone brought it in with them, I'm not sure where else to look," Jeremy said. He was over eighteen inches deep and ready to give up when his fingers grazed something solid. "I may have found something."

He pushed dirt to the side, trying to keep more dirt from sliding into the hole he was creating. Alan hurried to his side and looked into the hole. "It looks like there's a false bottom."

Heedless of the mess he was making, Jeremy put his hand around the base of the plant and pulled upward. Dirt showered the stone terrace and his pants and shoes.

The root ball brought most of the dirt with it, and once Jeremy set the plant on the ground, they were able to push enough of the remaining soil aside to see the wooden panel across the narrowest part of the urn.

Alan pulled a flashlight from his pocket and shined it along the edges. "I don't see any trip wires."

"Be careful," Noelle cautioned. "The last one had a grenade with it. When Levi tried to disarm it, the grenade pin dislodged."

"Stand back," Jeremy instructed Noelle.

Alan handed the flashlight to Jeremy. "Hold this for me."

Jeremy did as instructed and watched Alan use his knife to work the false bottom free. Jeremy shifted the beam of the light, immediately seeing the wires hanging from the wood.

"Well, we found it." Alan shifted so he could see more clearly. "This doesn't look pretty."

Jeremy's heartbeat quickened, and he looked up as Noelle's face went pale. Gustave had already disposed of the plant in his urn too and was busily scooping out excess dirt.

"This one has a false bottom too," he announced.

"Only these two were replaced, right?" Alan asked.

"Yes, why?"

"Because there's a transmitter on this one. My guess is that the second we disarm it, it will detonate the other bomb."

"Can we disable the transmitter first?" Jeremy asked.

Alan shifted position again and shook his head. "No. It's attached to a dead man's switch."

"How much time do we have?" Noelle asked.

"I can't tell." Alan nodded to Jeremy. "Hold this in place. Let me take a look at the other one."

Alan quickly helped Gustave finish clearing out the other pot and pry up the false bottom. Like the first one, the bottom was attached to multiple wires with the same duplicity in the device.

"How are we supposed to disarm them?" Noelle asked. "Can we move them down to the beach instead?"

"We don't have enough time."

"Can you see the timer?"

"No, but it has to be set to go off during the wedding ceremony. That's supposed to be happening now."

"We're out of time."

"I can see the timer on this one," Noelle said. She angled for a better view. "At least part of it. Fifty-seven seconds. I can't see the minutes."

Alan turned to Jeremy. "Do you know how to disarm a bomb?"

"I know what they taught me at the CIA, but I've never done it in real life."

"What about you?" he asked Gustave.

Gustave shook his head.

"It's you and me, Jeremy." Alan drew a deep breath. "Noelle, you hold the lid up on this one for Jeremy. Gustave, you hold the other one for me. We have to time this perfectly, or no one is walking out of here."

"Tell me what to do."

"This would be easier with another flashlight."

Noelle held up her cell phone. "I can use this."

Everyone shifted positions, and Jeremy wiped his palms on his pants. He pulled the knife Alan had given him earlier from his pocket and opened the blade.

Noelle used the flashlight app to shine a light for him, and he shifted to study the complexity of the bomb. The explosive filled the entire bottom of the urn, at least three feet in depth below the false bottom and two feet across the widest point.

"Which wire am I cutting?"

"Look for the black-and-green wire."

Jeremy gently pulled at the jumble of wires, using the knife to separate them until he finally found the one he was looking for. A door opened, but he didn't dare shift his attention.

Martino's voice interrupted his thoughts. "What is going on?"

"Bombs," Noelle said without looking up. "Two of them."

"Should I evacuate?"

"No," Alan answered firmly. "We can't take the chance that someone will activate one of these."

Jeremy fingered the correct wire and created enough slack to be able to cut it cleanly. Once he had the knife in place, he said, "I'm ready when you are."

"Okay, I'm going to count to three. Go on three."

Jeremy drew a deep breath. He lifted his eyes briefly. Noelle was staring at him, her face pale, her breathing rapid.

This was going to work, he assured himself. Alan started the count down, and beads of perspiration dampened Jeremy's forehead.

"One, two—"

"Wait!" Noelle shouted.

Jeremy's heart skipped a beat. The muscle in his arm flexed, and a rapid debate shot through his mind. If he cut the wire and Alan didn't, they were dead. Or vice versa. What if there weren't any minutes left on the timer? He held back, keeping his knife in place. Alan evidently made the same choice.

The internal timer went off in Jeremy's head—fifty-seven seconds came and went. "You're going to give me a heart attack," Jeremy managed. "What's wrong?"

"I can see a wire going down the side of the bomb. I thought it might be hooked to a grenade."

"Describe where it is," Alan said.

"On the opposite side of the detonator."

"We're going to have to cut that wire first." Alan shifted to find the corresponding wire on his bomb. "I can't see it over here." He paused. "Wait, I found it."

"What if it's booby-trapped?"

"We can't keep guessing. We're lucky we still have time on the clock."

"How much?" Jeremy asked.

"Forty-two seconds."

"Let's go," Alan said. "The trip wire first."

Jeremy shifted his knife into position. "Ready."

"One, two, three." This time both men cut through their wires without incident.

"Time?" Jeremy asked.

"Thirty-one."

"Now the other one," Alan said. "Ready?"

Again Jeremy shifted positions. "Yeah." His palms dampened. "One. Two. Three."

Chapter 42

NOELLE'S WHOLE BODY TENSED AS she watched Jeremy cut the wire. She took a breath and then a second one. They were still breathing. All of them.

Twenty-two seconds. Now that the bomb was defused, Jeremy reached in and managed to move the timer to reveal the countdown. Still just twenty-two seconds. They hadn't been able to see how many minutes were left, and now they could see there hadn't been any.

"Is that it?" Gustave asked.

"I doubt it," Jeremy said. "Whoever is behind this will know they failed any minute. I'll be right back."

Jeremy raced toward the front of the chateau where a satellite van from the television station was parked. Not sure what to think of his sudden departure, Noelle shifted her attention back to Alan.

"I don't think Tomasso was working alone," Gustave said.

"I agree." Alan shifted, looking at the underside of the false bottom, wires still dangling between it and the explosive below. "I'm going to call the bomb disposal unit from the naval base to come get these. They may be disarmed, but I'll feel better once they're far away from here."

Alan made the call, and Martino stepped forward. "Can I do anything to help?" he asked.

"Actually, yes." Noelle straightened and fought to maintain her composure. "Can you let King Eduard know what's going on? He can stall Janessa and Garrett for us. And we need to make an announcement to the guests that there will be a short delay before we start the ceremony."

"What do I tell the guests?"

Jeremy approached them. "Tell them one of the bride's brothers had a flat tire and is on his way."

"That should work." Martino retreated inside and called the king as he closed the door behind him.

"The bomb squad is on its way. They'll be here in five minutes."

"Where did you go?" Noelle asked Jeremy.

"I had the news van shut off the satellite feed. I told them they could record, but to report to their station that they were no longer getting a signal from their cameras."

"Why did you do that?"

"It's a long shot, but there's a chance someone might come forward with news of a bombing here. If they do, we'll know who is behind this."

"That is a long shot." Alan motioned to Jeremy's dirt-covered shirt and Noelle's torn dress. "You two had better go change. Gustave and I can take care of things here."

"I don't want the ceremony to start until these are out of here," Jeremy said. "The royal family needs to remain at a safe distance until then."

"It should only take ten minutes or so to load these up."

"Won't the bomb squad want to check them out before moving them?"

"The only threat at this point is if there is a secondary detonator on the bottom," Alan said. "The best thing we can do right now is get them as far away from here as possible."

"Janessa won't be happy about it, but we can move the people instead of the bombs," Noelle said.

"Another problem is that someone else could have a secondary detonator. We don't want to take a chance that they're watching from outside. In this case, it's safer to remove the bombs instead of the targets."

"They could set them off if they see the bomb squad coming in here," Jeremy said.

"Which is why we're taking these out in one of the catering vans." Alan waved toward the doors. "Go on. Trust me on this."

"Okay." Jeremy took Noelle by the arm. "Let's go get changed and see if we can get this wedding started."

They walked through the parlor, and Noelle felt her body tremble. *Twenty-two seconds.* She repeated the words in her mind. This was twice she had come within a heartbeat of dying. Technically, this time it had been a few heartbeats, but still.

She hadn't realized she'd stopped walking until Jeremy looked down at her.

"Are you okay?" he asked.

Tears welled up in her eyes. She had almost died. They had almost died.

"Hey, come here." He gathered her in his arms, and she felt him tremble against her.

A silent tear spilled over, and she blinked rapidly to keep others from following. Drawing comfort from Jeremy's embrace, she dug her fingers into the back of his shirt and held on.

He didn't offer any words of comfort, and she suspected he was as shaken as she. When finally the threatening tears subsided, she pulled back and looked up at him. Their eyes met, and for a moment, she forgot about everything else. She was with the man she loved, and for the first time in weeks, she no longer saw the barriers between them.

When he leaned down and pressed his lips to hers, she leaned into the kiss. His hand trailed up her back, and the hurt and pain he had caused her melted away. Could she really forgive him so quickly?

Images tumbled through her mind, not of the past but of the future. The blank pages she had feared writing alone were filled once again with Jeremy. The two of them together, inseparable. She thought of the sealing room in the temple, a prayer going through her mind that this man would someday want to be part of her eternity.

Jeremy pulled back but didn't let go. "I know this is kind of last minute, but will you come with me to my sister's wedding?"

She laughed. She couldn't help it.

"Will you?"

Noelle looked down at her dress, the hem now ragged from where she had cut it. "I'm not exactly dressed for a wedding. I think maybe I should stay in the background."

"Please be my date," Jeremy said, his voice soft and persuasive. "I don't want to go in there without you."

"In that case, how can I refuse?" She ran a hand over the skirt of her dress. "I'd better go find something else to wear."

"I'll meet you back here in a few minutes. We'll go in together after Alan tells us the coast is clear."

"Okay. I'll see you then." Noelle stepped back and started toward her room. With a last look at him, she continued forward. Maybe her life was finally falling back into place.

* * *

Jeremy took his time getting ready. He knew the bomb squad needed time to remove the threat, but beyond that he needed a moment to steady his emotions. He still couldn't believe someone had succeeded in getting not only one bomb but two past him.

The events of the past thirty minutes replayed in his mind. He had nearly been killed twice in less than an hour. He had thought the bullet whizzing by him had been the closest he would ever come to dying, but the image of Noelle standing with him over the bomb had been so much worse. Twenty-two seconds.

He looked heavenward, recognizing the miracles that had occurred today. A rush of emotion flowed through him, his pent-up fears giving way to gratitude that they had all been spared. With these thoughts heavy on his mind, he sat on the side of his bed and dropped his head in his hands. The internal discussion he had with his Heavenly Father stretched out for several minutes as he expressed his gratitude and searched for answers about what would come next.

Feeling a little steadier, he changed his clothes, exchanging the filthy suit for his tuxedo. He retrieved Levi's gun from his suit pocket and unlocked his safe. He put the gun in it, along with his own, and then reconsidered. Instead, he pulled out his ankle and shoulder holsters. He strapped Levi's gun to his ankle, and slid his own into the shoulder holster.

After making sure his tuxedo concealed the holster well, he turned to secure his safe. The little black ring box beckoned him, and he retrieved it as well. Slipping it into his pocket, he checked his watch. The bomb squad should be here by now. He checked in with Julien, confirming that the coast was clear. Then he left his room in search of his date.

Chapter 43

KING EDUARD ESCORTED HIS WIFE to the front of the room near where the ceremony would take place in a matter of minutes. Bouquets of flowers on white pedestals flanked the white archway where Garrett and Janessa would exchange their vows, white lights shimmering beneath the dimmed lights. Blue satin sashes accented the chairs draped in white, and more flowers created artful centerpieces, blue ribbon complementing the lilies, hyacinths, and white roses.

Though the other guests were already seated at their tables, three rows of chairs had been arranged near the stage for the family members. He waited for Marta to sit before lowering himself into the chair beside her.

After receiving Martino's call, he had passed along the message to Garrett and Janessa that Jeremy's car had had a flat tire. He suggested they wait a few minutes for him to arrive. Though distressed over inconveniencing their guests, the couple had agreed to the delay, neither of them wanting to go forward with a member of the family missing.

The call had come only fifteen minutes later that the bomb disposal unit had successfully removed the bombs from the terrace. Eduard could barely believe this had happened again. At least those involved in disarming the explosives had been astute enough to alert him and not any of the other members of the family. Garrett and Janessa deserved happiness, and he didn't want to see anything get in the way of it today.

The rest of the royal family took their seats, followed by Janessa's family. He took notice of Noelle seated beside Jeremy. The lack of color in her face made him wonder if perhaps she had been involved in diffusing today's threat. When he saw the way Jeremy gripped her hand, Eduard suspected they had both been instrumental in keeping everyone safe.

Garrett, Stefano, and the branch president stepped to the front of the room. A moment later, the music began to signal the arrival of the bride. All eyes shifted to the doorway, and Janessa stepped through with her father by her side.

Eduard stood with the rest of their guests and watched his future daughter-in-law make her way along the path between the tables. When she took her place beside his son, everyone sat, and Eduard prayed he would find a way to keep his family safe once and for all.

* * *

Noelle scanned the crowd. She couldn't help it. Even with Jeremy's hand warm in hers, she kept feeling like she was shirking her duty by sitting here as a guest instead of taking her place at the back of the room where she could watch the crowd.

She caught sight of Julien at the back, along with several other members of Levi's security team. After another quick look around the room, she realized she was the only person there acting suspiciously. She forced herself to focus on Garrett and Janessa and the words their branch president spoke.

His explanation of the temple ceremony was both simple and eloquent. The civil ceremony followed the same theme.

Noelle glanced over at Garrett's family, wondering how they were receiving the branch president's message. Alora and her children, of course, were well versed in temple marriage, and she suspected Stefano also had a basic understanding after attending church over the past few months with his wife.

King Eduard and Queen Marta didn't reveal anything in their expressions except perhaps hope and happiness for the newlyweds. Eduard's younger brother Elam, as always, carried a stiffly formal air. His wife's posture could only be described as condescending. No wonder Prince Philippe always looked like he thought everyone was beneath him.

On the stage, Garrett and Janessa shared their first public kiss as husband and wife.

Noelle fought back a shudder, remembering all too well that the moment of Stefano and Alora's first kiss had coincided with a grenade going off. As images of that wedding played through her mind, the niggling feeling that she had missed something in the video footage resurfaced.

She looked over at the royal family once more, and an image repeated itself. Prince Philippe sat across the aisle alone. She knew Princess Elaina hadn't accompanied him today because of her advanced stage of pregnancy, but at Stefano's wedding, she had been present. And in the television coverage, at the time the bomb should have gone off, Philippe had been sitting beside an empty chair . . .

The branch president presented the newly married couple, and Garrett escorted Janessa off the stage and back down the aisle toward the door. Noelle knew they would take a few minutes to let the crowd settle and the first course come out before they would join their guests.

"Let's go find our table." Jeremy stood and offered his hand.

She took his hand and squeezed. "Jeremy, Elaina wasn't in her seat at Stefano's wedding. She wasn't there."

"What?"

"I knew I was missing something." She nodded toward where Prince Philippe now stood with his parents. "She is the only member of the royal family who wasn't present at either wedding."

"But where did she go? She was on the security list as an attendee."

"There's only one way to find out." Noelle took a step toward Philippe. Not surprisingly, he didn't acknowledge her. "Prince Philippe, I'm sorry to bother you, but I wondered if I could ask a question." She paused briefly but didn't give him time to accept or decline her request. "Do you remember why your wife left the ceremony at Prince Stefano's wedding?"

"What?"

Jeremy stepped beside her. "It's important. Why wasn't your wife sitting beside you during Prince Stefano's wedding?"

"That's none of your concern."

King Eduard approached and spoke firmly. "Answer the question."

Philippe's demeanor softened slightly. "She needed to use the restroom. She was newly pregnant at the time."

"It could be a coincidence," Jeremy said.

"Maybe."

"What could be a coincidence?" Philippe asked.

"Nothing. Sorry to bother you." Noelle turned away from him, but she only made it a few steps before Jeremy and King Eduard were by her side.

"What's going on?" King Eduard asked, his voice low.

Noelle took a few steps to the side of the room, where they could speak without being overheard. "We've spent months trying to figure out who would have benefited if the bombing at Stefano's wedding had been successful."

"Yes," Jeremy said. "I've run deep backgrounds on everyone in this room."

"Princess Elaina is pregnant. If the entire royal family were to be killed, her unborn child—"

"Would become the new ruler of Meridia," King Eduard finished for her. "And as Philippe's child, he would inherit all of the family's wealth."

"I assume Elaina would control that wealth until the child reached adulthood."

"Yes." King Eduard glanced around the room. "Is there anyone else who is not here who was also absent from Stefano's wedding?"

Jeremy looked around the room. "Four members of the ruling council were absent last time. Bernardo Campesi."

"He's sitting right over there." King Eduard tilted his head to the right. "And the others?"

"Angelo Fallasi, Vick Dubeau, and Marcel Beaumont."

"Angelo and Vick are here as well. They are both sitting to our left." King Eduard's eyes darkened. "Marcel Beaumont was not invited to Stefano's wedding, but I believe he was issued an invitation to Garrett's."

"Yes, he was," Noelle confirmed. "In fact, he RSVPed that he would be in attendance."

"Where was he supposed to sit?"

Noelle tried to remember the seating chart, the names blurring together for a moment before she shifted her gaze to the left. "He should have been two tables behind Angelo."

All three of them looked in that direction. All three of them saw the empty chair.

"They could have planned it together," Jeremy said. "Elaina would take control of the monarchy, and Marcel would become a senior member of the ruling council."

"This is all speculation. How do we prove whether this suspicion is correct?" Noelle asked.

"I have an idea, but I think we're going to need some help." King Eduard swept the room.

"What kind of help?" Jeremy asked.

"The kind only my doctor can provide."

Chapter 44

SHE STARED AT THE TELEVISION screen and rubbed a hand over her stomach. The live broadcast of Garrett and Janessa's wedding had been interrupted without preamble. Technical difficulties is what the station was calling it, but she knew better.

Her time had come.

Any minute now the phone would ring or a knock would come at the door. Any minute she would be told she was free of the royal family, that she now *was* the royal family.

The child growing within her was her ticket to freedom. He would be king, and she would be rich. No longer would Philippe's rich relatives tell her what she could and couldn't do or where she could and couldn't stay. The chateau would have to be rebuilt, of course, but in time she would turn it back into the summer home it was meant to be. The palace would be her home, the winter palace a place to take her weekend ski trips while controlling the oil trade in this part of the world.

Within weeks another bomb would be placed strategically in Libya and a second in Algeria. Two more steps toward weakening the stability in the area and giving her the chance to take control of the oil trade as well as Meridia. History would see her as the woman who'd held the region together, the woman who, despite tragedy, had transformed the oil industry in Europe.

A car pulled up to the gate of her home. She knew it was the police when the gate opened and the vehicle continued up the drive without the guards calling to inform her. She stood and looked in the framed mirror on the wall. She took a deep breath and prepared to give the performance of her life.

The bell rang, and the butler answered the door. A moment later, he announced the arrival of Dr. Casale, the royal physician, as well as a police officer.

Elaina motioned the men inside and adopted a mask of concern. "Is everything okay?"

"I'm afraid we have some bad news," Dr. Casale began gently. "Perhaps we can sit down?"

"Yes, of course." She clasped her hands together when the doctor seemed to gather his nerve to give her the news. "Doctor, you're scaring me. What's wrong?"

"There's no easy way to tell you this. A bomb went off at the chateau today. I'm sorry, but there weren't any survivors."

She squeezed her eyes shut and summoned her tears. She took several ragged breaths before allowing herself to open her eyes again. "Are you sure?"

Dr. Casale nodded.

"My whole family? All of the royals are gone?"

"Yes, all of the royals." Dr. Casale fingered an envelope he held in his hand. "The two remaining members of the ruling council will take control of the government. Zerbino Aubin did not attend for security reasons, and Marcel Beaumont fell ill and wasn't in attendance."

"I can't believe this."

"I know it's a lot to take in. The two council members are meeting right now to decide how to proceed since there is no longer a monarchy."

She replayed his words, suddenly uneasy. "But there will be. My son will be born in a matter of weeks. He will be the new king."

"No, I'm afraid he won't."

"You're mistaken," Elaina straightened. "I know the law. Even though he is in the womb, he is still royal."

Dr. Casale's expression was one of pity and compassion. "I thought you knew."

"Knew what?"

"Prince Elam suffers from Merid's syndrome. Philippe was conceived through in vitro fertilization. He is not royal by birth, only by circumstance."

"What?"

Dr. Casale handed over the envelope he held. "This is the official medical report. I couldn't share that with you before, but now that Prince Elam and Prince Philippe are gone, I had to make sure you had full disclosure."

She pulled the papers free and thumbed through them: a dated medical report diagnosing Elam with Merid's and the paperwork from the fertility clinic dated a year before Philippe was born.

The doctor continued to dish out bad news. "Of course, you and your child will inherit any assets that belonged to your husband, but this house and all of the assets that belonged to the royal family now belong to Meridia."

"This can't be happening."

"I am so sorry." Dr. Casale stood. "I can prescribe a mild sedative for you if you would like, something that will not harm your baby."

She didn't respond. She couldn't. All of this planning had been for nothing? Or had it? She took a deep breath and slowly let it out. Marcel still had his position. Together they could still take control of Meridia.

"There's one more thing. I'm reluctant to bring it up, but I'm afraid Councilman Beaumont insisted."

"What's that?" Elaina asked.

"He said you need to be out of this house by the end of the month."

"He didn't." She was furious.

"You're welcome to talk to him about the details. I told him after dealing with such a shock it would be best to allow you to have six months to a year to adjust to your new reality, but it seems his future in-laws are looking for a rental, and your home suits their needs quite well."

"In-laws?"

"Yes." Dr. Casale looked at her, confused. "I thought you knew Signorina Rivelli."

"Claudia? He's marrying Claudia?"

"I really do think you should let me give you a sedative. I hate seeing you like this."

"How do you expect to see me?" Her voice rose by degrees. "You come here and tell me my family is dead, my son is not royal, I have to leave my home, and my . . . friend is getting married, something he told me nothing about."

Elaina stood. "If you'll excuse me, Doctor, I would appreciate some time alone."

"Yes, of course." He pulled a business card from his pocket. "Here is my number. Call me if you need anything, night or day."

Dr. Casale and the policeman who had accompanied him left the room, and a moment later, the door closed behind them.

She took several steadying breaths and then retrieved her cell phone. If Marcel thought he could play her for a fool, he had another thing coming.

* * *

The security office wasn't intended to hold this many people. Jeremy had that thought for the umpteenth time as he shifted his weight. Two security officers currently sat in front of the monitors to keep an eye on the chateau. Julien occupied a third seat, focusing on something entirely different.

Downstairs, the reception was proceeding as planned, the attendees still oblivious to the previous threat. The planters holding the bombs had been replaced by white ceramic pillars. He wasn't sure where the staff had found the pillars, but they filled in the gaps in Janessa's decorating scheme. He hoped his sister didn't go out onto the terrace and notice the change.

Jeremy's mouth watered when he saw the servers bringing out the main course on trays, and he reminded himself he could raid the kitchen later. King Eduard had come and gone several times and was currently standing shoulder to shoulder with him. Noelle had also made several trips between the ballroom and the security office.

"Anything yet?" King Eduard asked.

"Dr. Casale just left Elaina. Now we're waiting to see what she does with the bait," Jeremy said.

"She's making a call," Julien announced.

"Put it on speaker," King Eduard commanded.

Julien did so as the ringer ceased and Marcel Beaumont's voice came on the phone. He didn't begin with hello, but rather asked, "Is everything all right?"

"Is everything all right?" She repeated his question. "How can everything be all right? I just found out my child isn't a Fortier."

"What are you talking about?"

"Don't play dumb with me. You know perfectly well what I'm talking about. My father-in-law has Merid's syndrome. He isn't Philippe's biological father."

"Are you serious? Everything hinged on your child being the future ruler."

Elaina hesitated. "Are you saying you didn't know about this?"

"Of course not."

"Is it true that you're marrying Claudia?"

"No. You're the one who suggested I date her so no one would find out about us," he said, confused. "Where are you getting your information?"

"Dr. Casale. He visited me a minute ago to tell me about the bombs." She fell quiet for a moment. "He was playing me. Why would he do that?"

"To see what you would do," Marcel concluded. "Look, it's only natural that he would be suspicious of both of us. You're the only remaining royal left, and I'm probably the only person on the guest list who didn't show up today."

"Now what?"

"Now nothing. We stick to the plan."

"What if they're monitoring my calls?"

"If anyone asks why you called me, you were just reaching out to an old friend for comfort," Marcel said. "Everything will work out. And if we need to somehow dispose of Elam and Philippe's medical records, we'll take care of it. Dr. Casale is getting up there in years. It wouldn't be out of the realm of possibilities for him to suffer some medical problem after dealing with the strain of a major attack on Meridian soil."

"I don't want anything to do with that. I don't have the stomach for this anymore."

"I'll take care of everything. For now, go put on your best black dress and get ready to look distraught for the cameras. When your baby is born, he will become the focus of the media. Meridia's new king."

The call ended, and everyone in the room stood in stunned silence. Noelle spoke first. "It really was them."

"They tried to kill my entire family," King Eduard said quietly.

"And they think they succeeded," Jeremy added. "What now? Do we have enough to arrest them?"

King Eduard nodded. "Julien, call the police. I want both of them arrested immediately and an alert sent to the rest of the security team."

"Yes, Your Majesty."

"Also, call Dr. Casale and ask him to return to the chateau. I want him protected until we're sure Elaina and Marcel are in custody." He turned to look at Noelle and Jeremy. "As for the rest of us, it's time we rejoin the party before anyone notices we're gone."

"How are you going to break it to Prince Philippe that his wife just tried to kill him?"

"I'll go speak with them now." King Eduard started for the door. He looked back at Jeremy. "This is not a conversation I look forward to."

"I don't blame you."

Chapter 45

NOELLE LOOKED ACROSS THE BALLROOM where King Eduard was talking to Philippe, Elam, and Victoria. They headed for the main entrance, undoubtedly on their way to somewhere more private. She took in the rest of the scene.

Dinner had already been served, and guests were currently dancing. Garrett led Janessa around the dance floor, the two of them looking blissfully happy. Conversations buzzed, some friendly, others political. The number of dignitaries in the room was mind-boggling—the ramifications had the bombing succeeded even more so.

She and Jeremy had received a text message from Julien thirty minutes earlier that Levi was now in stable condition and the doctors expected him to make a full recovery. She looked forward to visiting him in the hospital to make sure he was indeed okay.

"Would you care to dance?" Jeremy asked, interrupting her thoughts. He held out his hand.

She wasn't sure how he could look so normal after all they had been through in the past few hours, but she put her hand in his. "I'd love to."

He led her to the dance floor and turned her until she was in his arms. A warm rush of rightness flowed over her, seeping into every pore. She belonged here with him. She knew it with certainty. The question was whether or not he felt the same.

"It looks like all of your months of hard work paid off," Jeremy said, his hand pressed firmly against her waist. "Everything looks amazing."

"I'm sorry we didn't get to enjoy more of it."

"We both had a job to do. We did it. That's what matters."

She didn't want to ask the question, but she couldn't keep it from coming out of her mouth. "What comes next?"

"That's something I was hoping to talk to you about." The music ended, but he didn't release her. "After this is all over, will you take a walk with me?"

"I'd like that."

Another song started, and he drew her closer again. He held her as though she was still central to his world, and she fought back her impatience.

In another hour, the newlyweds would cut the cake and be on their way, and she and Jeremy could take those first steps toward their future. And finally she would know if they could take those steps together.

* * *

He had to see for himself. Elaina's call hadn't made sense. Someone was fishing for information, but why? Did they really know he and Elaina were behind the bombings, or was the good Doctor Casale simply doing his duty in clearing Elaina of any possible wrongdoing?

Every detail, every minute of their plan had been orchestrated and executed perfectly. From the moment Elaina had realized her marriage was a mistake, they had worked together to make things right. She could have married him when he had asked her four years earlier, but she had wanted power, and Philippe had given her a taste of the royal life.

Marcel didn't begrudge her that. He was just glad she had recognized it was him she loved, not the man she had married. She had reached out to him, and they had put a brilliant plan in motion. Destroying the royal family and eliminating so many heads of state at one time was a dream come true. So many of the oil-producing countries had their own struggles, and he and Elaina were prepared to feed their chaos to drive up oil prices and give them wealth beyond their wildest dreams.

Settling for friendship over the past year of her marriage hadn't been easy, but now that Philippe was gone, Elaina was Marcel's once again. A few months from now, they could start dating openly and eventually marry. His dreams were right in front of him, ready to come true. But first he had to dispel this niggling doubt.

He slowed his car as he approached the chateau, a sense of dread settling deep within him. Nowhere did he see emergency vehicles or any other sign of a problem. A dozen limousines were parked inside the gates, along with a van from the television station. He could see people milling about, socializing on the terrace as though they didn't have a care in the world.

How could it be? He had watched the news coverage. He had seen the moment when the cameras had stopped transmitting, the moment when the bombs had gone off.

He slowed and approached the gate.

"May I help you, sir?"

"Yes. I'm afraid I'm terribly late, but I'm on the guest list for the wedding. I wanted to at least offer my congratulations to the couple before they leave on their honeymoon."

"Your name?"

"Marcel Beaumont."

The guard checked his clipboard. "I'll need to see your ID, please."

"Of course." He pulled his driver's license from his wallet and handed it over, his palms sweating. Why was this man so calm? What had really happened here?

The guard shined his flashlight on the ID, took a moment to study it, and then handed it back. "The valet service is in front of the chateau."

"Thank you." He pulled forward. As soon as he was clear of the gate, he chose a parking spot near the garage. He wasn't about to hand over his keys to anyone right now.

The terrace was lit up, the sound of music filtering through the closed doors. The potted plants were still evenly spaced along the length of the structure, except for where two were supposed to be positioned beside the ballroom doors.

Seething, he could only stare for several long minutes. Somehow the royal family had averted disaster again. Somehow they had survived. Dr. Casale's visit to Elaina had been a ruse, most likely to find out who was helping her. He leaned down and reached beneath his seat, his fingers closing around the barrel of his pistol before he straightened once more. If he had to shoot each member of the royal family himself, he would see them all die.

Chapter 46

JEREMY THOUGHT IT WOULD NEVER end. For the past hour and a half, he had danced and socialized. He had watched his sister and new brother-in-law cut the cake, had listened to the toasts. Finally Garrett and Janessa had departed beneath a spray of bubbles.

"Ready for that walk?" Jeremy asked Noelle as some of the guests began to depart.

"Sure."

Jeremy shifted, keeping his hand on the small of her back to guide her through the ballroom. They reached the terrace doors, and Noelle glanced back at the reception.

"Are you glad this is over?"

"I'm glad your sister and Garrett seem so happy."

"They are happy. You played a big part in making tonight happen, both the part they know about and the part they don't."

They walked past where the planters had been earlier that evening, the scene of the near tragedy. Jeremy took her hand and led her down the terrace steps. Too many people were still milling about near the chateau, and he wanted privacy.

The fragrance of roses and lavender mixed with the scent of salt and sea. Music and voices carried toward them, competing with the crash of the waves in the distance. They continued deeper into the gardens, and Jeremy felt his mouth go dry as he tried to find the right words.

"Are you still planning to leave here now that the wedding is over?" Noelle asked, breaking the silence.

"That depends."

"On what?"

"On what your plans are." Jeremy stopped and turned to face her.

"I don't have any plans yet." Noelle lifted her eyes to meet his, and he could see the uncertainty reflected there.

He stuffed his hand into his pocket to retrieve the ring box. "Garrett and Janessa will celebrate this day for the rest of their lives," he began. "I hope you'll give me reason to celebrate it too."

Noelle gave him a puzzled look.

He pulled the ring box free and held it out. "I bought this weeks ago. Work got in the way, but that's over now." He flipped open the lid to reveal the simple diamond ring, then lowered to one knee, his heart jackhammering in his chest. "Noelle, will you marry me?"

Her free hand lifted to her mouth, and tears sprang to her eyes. Slowly she nodded, and a smile appeared. "Yes."

"Yes?" He echoed her answer, praying he'd heard her right.

"Yes," she repeated.

His face split into a grin, and he tugged the ring free of the box. He slipped it onto her finger, and the moment it was in place, she pulled on his hand so he would rise to meet her. Then she threw her arms around his neck, and her lips found his.

He let himself get lost in her, refusing to think about what his decision would mean for his career and the future struggles that might result from their being together. When he pulled back, he realized that as much as he didn't want to face the possible ramifications their marriage would cause, Noelle deserved to understand what she was getting into.

"There is something you need to know," he said.

"What's that?"

"I'll probably have to find a new job."

"Why?" she asked. Then understanding reflected in her eyes. "You mean because of me."

"Because of us," Jeremy corrected. "The CIA will likely demand my resignation."

"Maybe they'll change their minds after all you accomplished tonight."

"You mean after all *we* accomplished." He considered that point. "Maybe, but even if they do let me stay, as my wife, you would have to agree to pursue American citizenship."

She straightened slightly as though trying to draw her strength. "If that's what it takes, that's what I'll do. I don't want you to ever regret marrying me. More than anything, I want you to be happy."

"I want you to be happy too. Would you be okay with becoming an American citizen and dealing with all this job entails?"

"I loved living in the United States, and I love you. The most important thing is that we'll be together."

"I've thought and prayed about this a lot. I don't know what I'll do for my next career if I'm forced to quit, but it will work out one way or another. If nothing else, I might be able to get a job here working for the security team." His eyebrows drew together. "Would you like that? I know this is your home, but you also said you've always wanted to travel."

"I do want to travel, but that's not the most important thing to me anymore." She reached up to kiss him again.

Need pulsed through him, and his resolve to do anything to be with her strengthened. After witnessing so many miracles tonight, he wasn't going to put anything before her again.

His phone rang as though testing that decision. He ignored it, kissing her once more.

The ringing stopped only to start again a moment later.

"Maybe you should see who that is," Noelle said.

"Someone has really bad timing," Jeremy grumbled. He pulled his phone free and saw the number for the security office. He shook his head in frustration and answered with a curt, "Hello?"

"Jeremy, we have a problem," Julien said.

"What is it?"

"Councilman Beaumont just came through the gate."

"What?" Jeremy tensed. "How did that happen?"

"I'm sorry. The guard saw his name on the printed guest list and didn't see the updated computer file that had taken him off. Apparently they've been so busy at the gate that no one saw the text alert they were sent either. As soon as they realized the mistake, they called me."

"How long ago did he get here?"

"Ten minutes."

"Alert the guards to start a search. And notify King Eduard and Prince Stefano. We need to secure the royal family."

"Yes, sir."

"What is it?" Noelle asked as soon as he hung up.

"Marcel Beaumont is here at the chateau."

"Oh no." Her words came out in a whisper. "What do you think he's doing here?"

"Probably coming to check out his handiwork." Jeremy debated for a moment. He wanted to keep her safe, but there was no way of knowing where Marcel might pop up. He reminded himself that the madman had a very specific type of target and thankfully Noelle didn't fall into the royal category.

"How are we going to find him?" Noelle asked.

He looked around. With the many trellises, bushes, palm trees, and climbing vines, the gardens weren't going to be an easy place to search. He pushed that thought aside and focused on the immediate need to get Noelle to safety. "The guards are already searching, but with so many people here, it won't be easy." He took Noelle's hand and started back toward the chateau. "I want you to let King Eduard know what's going on. Then go take over for Julien in the security office. I want someone up there I can trust, and we may need Julien to help with the search."

"I can help you look."

"You aren't trained for this kind of situation, and I don't want to take a chance of you running into him out here."

"Jeremy, let me help," Noelle insisted. "I grew up hiding in these gardens. No one will see me if I don't want to be seen."

Torn, he considered the truth of her statement and weighed it against the reality. He needed all the help he could get. Having her switch places with Julien would waste at least ten precious minutes. "Be careful."

"I will." Noelle lowered her voice. "I'll start over by the pool."

Jeremy nodded in agreement. "Text me if you see him. I'm going to check out Marcel's car, and then I'll help search the gardens."

Chapter 47

NOELLE'S HEART RACED. SHE REMINDED herself to keep her breathing slow and steady. Where that logic came from she wasn't sure. She tried to pretend she was playing hide-and-seek with her brothers, but her imagination didn't stretch quite that far. With the way her hands were shaking, she wondered if perhaps she should have agreed when Jeremy had tried to send her inside.

Slowing at each turn in the path, she made her way forward. A rustle of palm leaves sent her pulse rabbiting once more, and she gripped her cell phone tighter. Edging closer to the source of the sound, she stepped off the path and peered over a manicured hedge. A tall figure stood in the shadows.

From where she was, Noelle couldn't see the man's face. She held her breath when he reached into his pocket. The muscle in the man's arm flexed when he pulled something free and lifted his hand. She feared her pounding heart would give her away. Then a flame flickered from the item he held, and Noelle recognized the gesture.

The man puffed several times at the cigar now in his mouth. The smoke carried on the air as a second man approached. A friendly conversation ensued, both men turning sufficiently for Noelle to confirm neither was the man she was looking for.

Annoyed that she had wasted several precious minutes staring at a random guest, she altered her course and continued her search. Part of her wanted desperately to find Marcel Beaumont, but another part hoped she wouldn't be successful. Though she hadn't admitted the truth to Jeremy, she was terrified one or both of them wouldn't survive the night.

* * *

Nothing. Jeremy had spent the past twenty—make that twenty-two—minutes searching for Beaumont. The guards had already identified his car and verified that nothing inside it had been rigged as an explosive. Now Jeremy and over half of the security staff were currently searching the grounds.

Jeremy had sent two guards to help Noelle search the gardens while he had spent his time looking behind every car currently parked at the chateau. The guards at the gate were busily checking the identification of every guest who departed and verifying that they didn't have any unwanted passengers. Alan and Max had already circled the perimeter of the main house and were now clearing the outbuildings.

Jeremy looked over at the car Marcel had arrived in and then studied the chateau itself. Guards stood at the front entrance, and they had confirmed that no one had entered the home that way since before Beaumont's arrival. Studying the layout of the grounds, it only made sense that the easiest way to approach the reception undetected would be through the gardens.

He felt his phone vibrate, and a sense of anticipation shot through him. He prayed Noelle hadn't stumbled across Marcel first, or, if she had, that Marcel hadn't seen her. He pulled his phone free to see the message was indeed from Noelle. *Anything?*

Not yet, Jeremy texted back.

He called the security office, not surprised when Julien answered on the first ring. "Have you seen any sign of him?" Jeremy asked.

"Nothing. I sent a couple guards to search the woods just to be safe, but so far we haven't had any motion sensors triggered over there. I have to think he's somewhere where he would blend in with the guests. Otherwise we would have picked up some sign of him by now."

"Then we'll keep searching. Let me know if anything changes."

"I will."

Jeremy cut across the wide front lawn, searching the face of every guest who passed him as they made their way to their cars. The flow of pedestrian traffic was slow and steady, and Jeremy figured the ballroom still held over a hundred guests.

Trying to anticipate Beaumont's motivations, he started down the nearest path into the garden. His car was still here and wasn't being used as a weapon. Logically that meant he still had unfinished business he was determined to see through. Grateful Garrett and Janessa had already left the premises, Jeremy focused on where Marcel would go in his search for the rest of the royals.

As Jeremy started through the edge of the garden, he looked up to the terrace where several guests were socializing. He moved slowly and attempted to keep his footsteps quiet as he searched the shadows for anywhere a man could hide while waiting for the moment the coast was clear to access the chateau.

Leaves rustled, and he turned, his hand instinctively reaching for the weapon holstered at his back. He crept forward and peered through the foliage separating him from the parallel path. Instead of an armed man, he found a man and woman sharing an impassioned kiss beneath the moonlight.

With a shake of his head, Jeremy left the couple alone and continued forward. Marcel Beaumont was here somewhere, and Jeremy was determined to make sure he didn't carry out his plans.

* * *

Noelle didn't know where else to look. She had searched over half the gardens herself. The guards helping her had covered much of the same ground and were currently checking the area leading to the beach. Even with the overlap of their search patterns, Marcel remained at large. Perhaps he had opted to approach the chateau from the wooded side of the structure instead of trying to blend in with the other guests.

She peeked around a pair of fan palm trees, studying the handful of guests on the terrace. None of them resembled the man they were looking for. Frustrated, she started toward the main path leading to the terrace. Marcel had to be here somewhere. She prayed they would find him before he managed to carry through with whatever had brought him here.

Footsteps sounded behind her, and she whirled around to face the new arrival. A sigh of relief escaped her when she saw Jeremy approaching.

"I gather you haven't seen him either," Jeremy said, his voice low.

"Nothing. Maybe he'll try to get into the chateau through the employees' entrance."

"We have guards posted there. I have to think he's hiding in here somewhere."

Noelle waved a hand toward the depths of the gardens. "We've circled through here several times. No one has seen him."

They fell in step and headed toward the main path.

"Maybe when he realized the bombs were disarmed, he left without the guards seeing him," Noelle said.

"I don't think so. His car is still here, and I doubt he would be able to get past all of our security. Julien said none of the motion sensors have triggered on the far side of the chateau. That means he has to be here somewhere."

The words had no sooner left his mouth than they turned a corner and found Marcel Beaumont standing in their path, his eyes on the terrace.

Chapter 48

JEREMY CAME TO AN IMMEDIATE stop and released Noelle's hand. He quickly motioned for her to stay back before drawing his weapon. He went to take aim only to see Marcel shift his attention toward them and raise a gun of his own.

"Gun!" Jeremy shouted to Noelle. The word erupted from him at the same instant he dove to his left, and he sensed Noelle also drop to the ground.

A shot rang out, and he quickly turned to make sure Noelle was okay. He let out a sigh of relief when he saw she had taken refuge behind some thick shrubs a short distance away.

"Where are they?" Marcel yelled. "Where are the royals?"

"It's too late," Jeremy said, peeking around the palm tree currently protecting him. "They've already been evacuated."

"You're lying."

Jeremy decided to play on Marcel's emotions and take a stab at a random scenario. "You're in love with a married woman."

"She wasn't supposed to be married after tonight."

From where Jeremy stood, he could see a few people standing on the terrace a short distance away. What were they doing there? Hadn't they heard the gunshot? Didn't they realize Marcel could point his gun at them at any moment? Music was still playing in the ballroom, but surely it wasn't *that* loud.

Noelle's phone glowed, and he guessed she was texting someone for help. Marcel must have seen the glow as well. He shifted his aim.

"Noelle!" Jeremy moved and fired at the top of the trellis. The wood splintered and rained down on Marcel, along with the greenery that had been clinging to it. He waved a hand toward where Noelle was hiding, motioning for her to get out of the line of fire.

Her movements were subtle, and he had to strain to hear her rapid footsteps. Her route options were limited to a secondary path leading to the terrace and another that would take her to the front of the chateau. He hoped she took the long path so it would keep her hidden the longest.

Marcel took cover behind a stone fountain, his hands visible briefly as he tore at the vines tangled around him.

Jeremy studied his options. The area by the fountain was open, and he couldn't approach without completely exposing himself. He needed help, someone to flush Marcel out of his hiding place.

"You might as well give up," Jeremy called out, praying Marcel would do just that. "You don't have anywhere to go."

More people came outside, and this time Marcel took notice. Philippe was among the new arrivals. Jeremy's heart froze when Mary walked up to stand beside him, along with his parents. He didn't think the situation could worsen until Noelle reappeared, heading for them, waving her hands in warning.

Over the music, Jeremy couldn't make out her words. Apparently everyone else couldn't either because they remained in place, staring at her curiously.

Marcel didn't respond to him. He had his target.

"This ends now." Marcel straightened and took aim once more.

"No!" Jeremy charged forward and fired a shot into the air in an attempt to warn the guests of the danger.

Someone screamed, and another shot rang out. Out of the corner of his eye, he saw Noelle and someone else fall to the ground.

"No!" The word exploded from him, but he didn't have time to think. Afraid Marcel would take another shot, he rounded the fountain and dove at him, pushing Marcel's shooting hand down and knocking his gun to the ground, as well as his own.

Marcel stumbled two steps backward, and Jeremy looked toward the terrace. His stomach clenched when he saw Noelle still sprawled on the ground with the other person.

Footsteps sounded as Marcel rushed forward once more, his eyes wild with fury as he tackled Jeremy.

Jeremy's shoulder crashed against the stone path. Marcel immediately tried to shift toward where the weapons had landed. Jeremy threw an elbow at his head, connecting with enough force to cause the man to cry out in pain. Jeremy scrambled to his feet and started to reach for the weapon holstered at his ankle, but Marcel was just as quick and shoved him back down. Jeremy kicked his leg out, knocking him down with a heavy thud.

The men grappled with one another, elbows and fists pounding. Finally Jeremy succeeded in breaking free and rolled toward the fountain.

Moving slower now, his lip and eye bleeding, Marcel regained his footing and shook his head as though trying to clear his vision. "You'll be sorry you got in my way."

Jeremy didn't bother to respond. All he wanted was to get this man under control and get to Noelle. He waited for Marcel to make the first move, but Marcel faked with his right fist and struck with his left. The impact knocked Jeremy backward, and Marcel succeeded in getting past him.

Marcel reach down and pick up his gun. Time slowed, each heartbeat pounding in Jeremy's head. He reacted on instinct, his hand pulling his spare weapon free. Both men took aim, but only Jeremy managed to pull the trigger.

* * *

Noelle didn't want to think about how close the first bullet had come or how she had felt it whiz by her almost in the same instant she'd heard the gunshots. She stayed on the ground and kept a hand on Prince Philippe's head to hold him down. She heard more gunshots and prayed Jeremy remained unharmed. That prayer repeated over and over as though the chant might make the difference in her future. She had a future, a future with Jeremy. She couldn't lose him now, not with them on the verge of making eternal promises.

Footsteps sounded and grew louder, followed by Jeremy shouting her name.

She sat up, her eyes tearing when she saw him alive and well. Or mostly well. His left eye was swollen, and blood covered his lip, but he was alive, and that was what mattered most. She glanced down at the prince for a moment to make sure he too was okay. "Are you all right?"

"You . . . He . . ." Philippe gulped in air and tried again. "He tried to kill me."

"Are you all right?" she repeated.

He shifted and looked down at his chest as though he wasn't 100 percent sure the bullet had missed him. He was still debating his answer when Jeremy reached them and squatted beside her.

"Are you okay?" Jeremy asked.

"I'm fine." She let him help her up and rolled her shoulders against the tightness that had centered there after her dive onto the hard stone. A closer look at Jeremy raised her own concerns. In addition to the swollen eye and bloody lip, he had shallow cuts on his arms and cheek. "Are *you* okay?"

"I'm better now. I saw you on the ground, and I thought you'd been shot."

"She pushed me out of the way just in time," Philippe told him, sounding a little awed. "She saved my life."

Jeremy looked around the otherwise deserted terrace. "Was anyone hurt?"

"I don't think so. When the shots were fired, everyone else scrambled back inside." Noelle drew a deep breath, a tremor working through her body as she let the breath out. "I was afraid if we tried for the door, we would end up in the line of fire."

They stood, and instantly Noelle found herself in Jeremy's arms. The feel of him gathering her close and the beat of his heart thudding against her overwhelmed her. Tears threatened, and she barely managed to speak. "I was so worried about you."

"Believe me, the feeling was mutual."

Chapter 49

NOELLE STOOD ON THE BEACH and watched the seagulls diving for their morning meal. The early morning sun glistened on the water, the sky impossibly blue above her.

She rubbed her thumb against the back of her engagement ring. Last night still felt like a combination of a dream and a nightmare. She hoped to put the nightmare portion behind her and focus only on the promise she and Jeremy had made.

The sand shifted beneath her feet as she wandered toward the water. She knew she needed sleep, but her mind simply hadn't shut down the night before, and after five hours of sleeping for only a few minutes at a time, she'd decided it wasn't worth staying in bed.

She glanced down at her watch and wondered what time Jeremy would wake up. She hoped he would have answers for her when he did. He'd said he was going to e-mail a full report of last night's events to the CIA director. With his report, he was going to explain his relationship with her.

So many possibilities lay before them, all of them requiring some level of sacrifice from one or both of them.

If Jeremy stayed with the CIA, Noelle would lose her Meridian citizenship and, with it, part of who she was. If he left the agency, how could she be sure he wouldn't regret it later?

He was right that he would be able to hire onto the security staff here, but could he find contentment doing that for the rest of his life? As much as she wanted to have easy access to her family, she also yearned to explore life beyond the chateau gates. Would the travel she always dreamed of be limited to an occasional trip to the United States to visit Jeremy's family?

"Hey there."

She turned at Jeremy's approach. "Good morning." Some of her worries faded when he leaned down to greet her with a kiss. "I didn't think you would be up so early."

"I could say the same thing about you." He slid an arm around her waist, and they started a leisurely walk down the beach. "I gather you couldn't sleep either."

"No. Too many things running through my mind."

"Is planning a wedding one of them?" Jeremy asked.

"That and wondering where we'll end up."

"You're worried about my job."

"I'm worried about both of our jobs," Noelle said. "I knew I was probably going to make a change after the wedding. As much as I love your sister, I really don't want to work as an assistant for the rest of my life."

"I don't blame you."

"I gather you haven't heard anything from your director yet."

"No, but it's still the middle of the night in D.C. I doubt I'll hear anything until much later today."

They wandered a ways down the beach, finally returning to where they'd started.

"We should go do something today. Maybe a horseback ride or sailing," Jeremy suggested. "I think we're both going to go crazy thinking about the what-ifs unless we find some kind of distraction."

"That's a good idea," Noelle said.

They discussed options as they climbed the steps to the gardens. They were passing the swimming pool when King Eduard appeared.

"Good morning, Your Majesty." Noelle dipped into a curtsey.

"Just the two people I was looking for." King Eduard motioned to a poolside table. "Do you have a moment?"

"Of course," Noelle answered for both of them.

They all sat, and Jeremy asked, "Did Janessa and Garrett get off on their honeymoon all right?"

"Yes. In fact, they still don't know about everything that happened here last night. I'm grateful for that."

"How is Prince Philippe doing?"

"He's shaken. I'm not sure what devastated him more—being shot at, learning he wasn't of royal blood, or discovering his wife wanted all of us dead."

"I can't imagine what he must be going through," Noelle said.

"He didn't know he wasn't Prince Elam's biological son?" Jeremy asked.

"No. Besides the two of you, only a handful of people outside the family know the truth. The rest of us only learned of it last year."

King Eduard linked his fingers together and studied them both, a serious expression on his face. "I spoke to Director Palmer a few hours ago. We discussed your report of what happened yesterday as well as the decisions you will now face because of your impending marriage."

"We were just discussing some of our options," Jeremy said.

"I would like to offer you an option you may not have considered."

"Which is?" Noelle said.

"Levi will need several weeks to recover. He has a severe concussion, and we can't be completely certain when he will be ready to return to duty here. Director Palmer and I would like for you, Jeremy, to take over for him until he is ready to return to work."

He couldn't hide his surprise. "I'd be honored, but I didn't think he would let me continue with the CIA once Noelle and I get married."

"That will be a problem once you do get married, but I assume your engagement will last more than a month."

Both of them nodded.

"You are both welcome to remain here as employees at the chateau as long as you like, but after seeing you in action last night, there is another job opportunity available to you if you so desire."

"What's that?" Noelle asked.

"Meridian intelligence."

"Meridian intelligence?" Jeremy repeated.

"Jeremy, my country would benefit greatly from having someone with your training, and I believe having you on my staff would help maintain a good working relationship with the CIA." King Eduard shifted his attention to Noelle. "As for you, you mentioned some months ago a desire to work in the intelligence community. This would give you that opportunity, and I like the idea of knowing I have someone who knows my family so well watching out for us."

Noelle's jaw dropped. Never had she anticipated such an opportunity. "I don't know what to say."

"There would be quite a bit of travel involved, at least during the first year. After the lack of cooperation from Interpol the past few months, I would like to have you both work with Gustave to ensure Elaina and Marcel don't have any other surprises in store for this region. And, of course, Noelle would need to go through training."

Noelle let the possibilities flow through her mind, a sense of excitement welling up inside her.

"The two of you can take your time making your decision." King Eduard stood. He waited until Jeremy and Noelle stood before he added, "There is one more thing."

"What's that?"

"My family is indebted to you for your heroic actions. It would be my honor to host your wedding and reception here at the chateau or at whatever location you choose."

"That is too generous, Your Majesty," Noelle said quickly.

"No, my dear. It isn't nearly enough." He shook hands with them both and then disappeared down the path toward the chateau.

"That was unexpected," Jeremy said with a sense of awe. He turned to her. "What do you think?"

"About what? The wedding or the jobs?"

"All I care about when it comes to our wedding is being sealed to you in the temple. Everything else is a bonus," he said.

"Like blueberry cheesecake?"

"Exactly." He chuckled and then looked at her expectantly. "What do you think about the job offers? Working for Meridian intelligence would give us the chance to travel like you wanted."

"I'm up for it if you are."

Jeremy's lips curved up. "You know what the best part of all this is?"

"What's that?"

"That from now on, these decisions will be ours to make together." Jeremy slipped his arms around her waist. He lowered his lips to hers for a lingering kiss. "Now, about the honeymoon . . ."

About the Author

ORIGINALLY FROM ARIZONA, TRACI HUNTER Abramson has spent most of her adult life in Virginia. She is a graduate of Brigham Young University and a former employee of the Central Intelligence Agency. Since leaving the CIA, Traci has written several novels, including the Undercurrents trilogy, the Royal series, the Saint Squad series, *Obsession, Deep Cover, Failsafe,* and *Chances Are,* as well as a novella in *Twisted Fate.*

When she's not writing, Traci enjoys spending time with her family and coaching the local high school swim teams.